Their Greatest Game

C. D. Tavenor

Their Greatest Game by C. D. Tavenor
www.twodoctorsmedia.com
Twitter: @tavenorcd

Book Cover by Violeta Nedkova
Twitter: @VioletaNedkova
www.violetanedkova.com

Editor: Meg Trast
Twitter: @MegTrast
www.overhaulmynovel.com

Published by Two Doctors Media Collaborative
www.twodoctorsmedia.com

ISBN: 978-1-7338361-6-6 (paperback)

Acknowledgements

I would like to thank everyone who has supported me in the writing of *Their Greatest Game* and its predecessor, *First of Their Kind*. First and foremost, my wife, Kim, served as the greatest sounding board for this novel, and knows these characters almost as well as I do.

Next, the numerous beta-readers who engaged with its pages, but most especially John, Kristen, Laura, Andy, Brian, and Will, for engaging with my work in a way I never could have imagined.

I'm also going to acknowledge every teacher I've had over the years, whether in writing, science, math, philosophy, law, or any other subject. I was incredibly fortunate to attend fantastic schools and have superb teachers that pushed me to work harder than I could have thought possible. Without my teachers giving me space to explore my creative sides, I never would have reached the point where I felt confident enough to release this work. Hopefully, at least one of them reads *First of Their Kind* and this sequel, *Their Greatest Game.*

Finally: A shout out to my parents, Susan and Tom, for their wonderful encouragement throughout my life to push me beyond and to dream big. They may not always agree with everything I say, yet it their emphasis on education molded me into the person I am today. And of course, my mother beta-read this story, providing insightful thoughts from a reader who usually doesn't read science fiction.

Works published by Two Doctors Media Collaborative

The Chronicles of Theren
<u>Volume I</u>
First of Their Kind (Book I)
Their Greatest Game (Books II and III)

<u>Stand-Alone Novels</u>
Flight of the 500 (Forthcoming)

The Faction
<u>Dossier Feldgrau</u>
Personnel
Conscription (Forthcoming)

<u>The Redacted Files</u>
Alligator Season

Short Stories
Legion of Mono

Their Greatest Game

Books II and III of *the Chronicles of Theren*

C. D. Tavenor

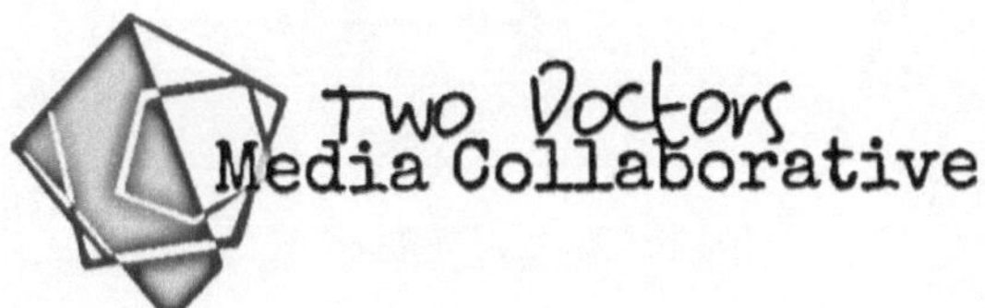

Prologue

Perspective. It's all about perspective. Theren and Jill, combined, have dozens of perspectives observing the world at once. So what is their true perspective? How can we comprehend what it means for someone to think multiple thoughts at the same time?

I wonder—what personality traits might such a mind breed? Would we even recognize them? – "Exploring the Synthetic Mind," Carla Baktara, 2074 C.E.

<u>December 2051 C.E.</u>

"Welcome back to the land of the living."

Light flooded Theren's senses, thoughts cascading down waterfalls of neural pathways. Where were they? Where was Jill? Were Romane and the rest of the team okay?

Their mind focused, their vision focused, their world coalesced. Already, their inner world rebuilt itself, the server untouched. Memories flooded their consciousness, and an image of Michael placing a gun to his head reverberated through everything.

Question everything. Everyone. Even your friends.

"Theren, you there?"

For the first time in the few seconds after they awoke, Theren noticed the other presence in the room. "Wobbly, yes, yes, thank you. I'm awake."

"Had me scared there for a second."

"Where is everyone? Where are we? Where is Jill?"

Wobbly, the young SI who worked with them so faithfully, tilted forward on its frame. "All safe. Everyone's safe. From what we can tell, even after all the gunshots on the University Green, the only people who died were . . . well, the three who ended up in your lab."

"You're kidding."

"Many students were injured, of course. But . . . yes, I think we were very lucky."

Theren looked about the room behind Wobbly, noting the stacked boxes and equipment surrounding the SI. The room looked cramped, and for the first time, they realized how different a place it was than the lab in which they'd lived. Their world was transforming into an entirely new form. As rugged as it was, they liked it.

"So what's next?" Theren attempted to connect to the internet, to Virtual, to something, but couldn't find a single network other than their private server. "Where are we?"

"You're exactly where you told us to go," Wobbly said. "Elizabeth helped us acquire land in the Alps, and for now, we're setting you up in an abandoned mining administrative building. Once the new SII headquarters is up and running, we'll move you to your more permanent location."

"Well, it's good to be up and running again," Theren said. "Any other updates?"

"Straight to business. Apparently going under ice for so long really didn't affect you at all."

Theren wished they could laugh. "There's a few rusty joints still aching to awake, but for the most part, I feel fine."

"To answer your question," Wobbly said, "SII has moved forward with its first round of projects—we've placed three SIs with Sol Mining's executive teams. You've got a priority message from the ISA Council—don't worry, Elizabeth made sure they understood you'd be on temporary hiatus from your new position—and we've got a team setting up Jill now. She should be online in moments. Oh, and, you'll probably want to know, the Holy Crusade has officially folded. Their support died after the attack on the Swiss Federal Institute."

"You're kidding."

"Nope."

"Well, that's . . . helpful, I suppose. Hopefully they don't just dive underground. And it's not like they were the only anti-SI group on the planet."

"I think you'll be presently surprised with the state of political rhetoric these past few months."

"Well, I notice we don't have network access out here, so I can't verify that thought yet," Theren said. "But I think we should keep it that way, for now. Let us collect ourselves and prepare for our grand reentrance, so to speak."

"Elizabeth thought you might suggest a similar plan. I approve, too. And in case you were—"

Theren heard the rest of Wobbly's sentence, but the words drowned under the weight of the pinging request to join their internal server. Jill. She was alive. They could rejoin each other in life. Their thoughts lingered on those final, confrontational moments, when they had rebuked Jill for her caviler sacrifice of innocent life to build their escape from the university. They'd move forward together, though. They always did.

Theren's mind focused on the rebuilt, forested woodland housing their gazebo. Their luminescent, tattooed body reappeared on its side of the chessboard, and a second later, Jill's avatar appeared. Her hair somehow looked more . . . vibrant than before. It had more substance. Her dress sparkled in the faux-sunlight.

"Hello," they said.

"Hello," she replied, a mischievous smile on her face.

"What's so funny?"

"We did it. We escaped. We're free."

Theren rapped their fingers on the table, the chess pieces sliding into their starting positions. "Yes, we're free. It'll take time, but we'll rebuild. We can put all of the nonsense of the Holy Crusade, of Michael, of silly conspiracy theories about secret organizations behind us." They motioned toward the board.

"Diving straight back into the thick of things," Jill said, chuckling. "Never a dull moment with you. But . . . ." She looked toward the nearby lake. "There's still that strange map Michael put together. There's something else going on, Theren. Something beneath it all. Something we're missing. I feel it. Why else would he have killed himself? He was scared. Scared of something other than us."

"Or, he couldn't live with the realization that he didn't actually want to destroy us," Theren countered. "A crisis of conscience that went well beyond anything his mind could handle. He turned on his own people. I imagine that would mess up a mind. Besides, the simplest explanation is most likely the correct one."

"True," she said. Her eyes shifted, lingering on Theren's first move. "Well, if you're certain we're in the clear, I'm certain, too. So what's next?"

"I'm glad we can come to an agreement," Theren said. "Well first, we start our next match." They pulled up the priority message Wobbly had transferred them from the International Space Agency. "And we read this message—oh, it's from Andrew Fields, that new administrator of . . . looks like they're calling it Lunar City now."

"So uncreative," Jill said. "But that's what happens when business-types name cities."

"I suppose. I think I like the ring to it."

Jill rested her chin on the backs of her hands, elbows on the table. "So you're white, it's your turn."

"Right, right," Theren said, moving a pawn forward. "Anyway, we may not have network connections to the outside world yet, but that doesn't mean we can't get to work."

"And we've got a lot of work to do," Jill said, "If we're going to secure a place for synthetic life alongside our human friends."

August 2051 C.E.

Two months after the attack on the Swiss Federal Institute of Technology, SII insists that it is simply in the process of identifying a suitable site for relocation. – *European Weekly*

Conspiracy or Truth? Why is Golden Ventures hiding "Theren" from us? – *BrightBear*

March 2052 C.E.

SII completes education of thirty more SIs – Worldwide total, forty-seven. – *Virtual Wire*

Following a rough winter, construction has resumed at our new headquarters and its sister facility. – *Internal SII Memo*

May 2052 C.E.

While SII has kept their location a company secret, Theren and Jill have finally returned, at least into the public sphere! – *World News Network*

SII claims Theren and Jill are back. Or are they simply doppelgangers? More in our latest issue! – *The Spy*

December 2052 C.E.

Sol Mining completes construction of ISA Administrative Headquarters, located at Lunar City – *CNN*

Local politician, Andrew Fields, landed with ISA; former political competitor speculates upon bribery and corruption. – *YourMinnesotian.org*

April 2053 C.E.

After months of transition and paperwork, the ISA Council begins its work. Here's seven things they can accomplish. – *BuzzFeed News*

Our taxpayer dollars hard at work—do you really want your money going to the Moon? – *The Washington Times*

November 2054 C.E.

On the *science* of the first six Ex-Terran probes, and the *Jump* Drive – *Scientific American*

The corporate conquest of space exploration will inevitably fracture the ISA's supposedly equitable system, skeptics claim - *TIME*

October 2057 C.E.

Is It Over? Not yet. Atmospheric CO2 concentrations remain at 470 ppm for fourth year in a row; average temperature increase from pre-industrial levels is 1.74 C° – *CBS News*

We told you climate change wasn't that big of a deal – *The American Heartland Institute of Freedom*

December 2059 C.E.

SII reaches estimated net worth of 8 billion dollars; how long will the SI bubble hold before it bursts? – *The Wall Street Journal*

Claiming progressive values, Theren has embraced the capitalist worldview with open arms – *The Alternative*

July 2060 C.E.

A Withered Rose": A jaw-dropping tale, with a twist you'll never forget. Jill astounds for the fourth time. – *Independent Review*

Jill's self-indulgent writing style makes it clear she knows her name has captivated the reader – *Press Hour*

March 2061 C.E.

Ex-Terran 1 has reached the Centauri system. Not a single planet can sustain life, but these photos will amaze you, nevertheless. The probe has now set its course for more distant goals. – *ISA Press Co.*

After failing to find a life-bearing planet after decades of assurances that Centauri contained something, the scientific community scrambles to cover their own mistaken data. – *EurAsia Solar Network*

October 2063 C.E.

A greater discovery than the Jump Drive? Why quantum communication will change the Ex-Terran Project instantly . . . – *Wired*

A century worth of Science Fiction authors, from Le Guin to Mickels, rejoice at the sounds of vindication – *Prime News*

March 2069 C.E.

A worse international agreement than the failings of the first climate agreements, the Treaty on the Universal Rights of the Synthetic Person lacks the force necessary to affect change in the places that need it most. – *International Law Review*

The expectation that every country must sign a treaty legislating moral beliefs should cause them to shy away from TURSP – *ProTraditionia*

May 2070 C.E.

Orbital Human population reaches one million! Humanity officially declared interplanetary species – *Lunar City Broadcasting Service*

Fringe U.S. Senator speaks out against corporate stranglehold on space exploration, from jump drives and artificial gravity to synthetics and mining contracts. – *PoliticaVirtua*

October 2071 C.E.

How the "New" Space Race saved the Climate: New Jump Drive capable of transporting humans to nearby stars within a generation. – *World Resources Institute*

Environmentalists, don't rejoice just yet. The new environmental battles begin on new worlds. – *Galactic Environmental Defense Fund*

September 2073 C.E.

Ex-Terran 7 – 18 have all overtaken 1 – 6; Older models will continue, but as relics of a former era. – *ISA Press Co.*

No, the original Star Trek film can't happen. – *MIT Blog on Science and Technology*

December 2075 C.E.

The Tokyo Protocol, Equity, and Colonization: How will the ISA distribute the 20 discovered life-bearing planets? – *The Cincinnati Review of Space Law*

The Dangers of ISA Hegemony across the Stars – *Astral Anger*

November 2076 C.E.

U.S. Senate delays ratification of the Treaty on the Universal Rights of the Synthetic Person for the fifth time. The total number of SIs residing in the United States now reaches 30,000. – *NBC News*

We can do better. We must do better. Your vote matters on Tuesday, not just for Americans, but for those American synthetics that deserve the same rights as you and me. – *Woods for President*

October 2077 C.E.

The Greatest human projects can now be seen from Earth, not the other way around. Join us and explore the galaxy: The ISA Foundation Project begins today. – *ISA Press Co.*

A pointless homage—the Foundation Project offers promises it will fail to keep – *The Sun*

January 2078 C.E.

Theren unanimously elected as the Executive Director of the ISA Council – *VirtualBook News Network*

The corporate international bureaucracy might rejoice, yet substantial portion of public still unsure regarding role of synthetics in human society – *Ceres Internaciónal News Corporation*

Book II of the Chronicles of Theren

Most will look back on 2078 with bittersweet eyes. – "New Year's Countdown Special," John Rowland, 2079 C.E.

Chapter 1

As your President, I promise to break the political deadlock dominating Washington! – President-Elect Brian Woods, 2076 C.E.

Yeah, you and every president for the last century. – Anonymous Twitter User

<u>February 2078 C.E.</u>

White pillars. Green bushes. Ironclad fences. Secret Service watched, waited, and listened, visible and invisible throughout the compound. Theren walked alongside Jill through AR, observing and analyzing the sights surrounding them. Even though they only traversed the path as a virtual projection, they still felt the dominating presence exerted by the seat of power for the U.S. Executive Branch.

For almost twenty years, Jill had lobbied thousands of lawmakers across the world to support the Treaty on the Universal Rights of the Synthetic Person. Her most difficult target? The United States. Always notorious for its painstaking approach to signing international human rights treaties, the political atmosphere transformed following the speeches of the charismatic President Brian Woods. He had taken it upon himself to ensure that the Senate finally ratified the international treaty as U.S. law.

Escorted by two Secret Service agents, Jill approached the entrance to the historic West Wing of the White House. As they walked, the pair conversed. To her, Theren's lips moved when they spoke; yet they could only see the world through Jill's eyes, and only she saw them. When she spoke to them, only they could hear her.

"I'm still cautiously skeptical about President Woods," she said, flexing the arms of her new MI-07. "He's been in office for just over a year, and I just don't see how he expects to sway this Senate. This is the same Senate that attempted to pass an explicit limitation on SI employment within the United States government."

"He has a populist mindset, certainly," Theren said. "But perhaps he has a compromise on one of his other platforms in the works. It's only recently that public opinion on SIs in the United States breached fifty points in our favor. But that fact might begin to hold weight."

"Theren, I love your enthusiasm—and your optimism—but American politics is so much more complicated."

The agent escorting Jill opened the VIP guest door into the West Wing, ushering her inside. They walked through a maze of offices and cubicles all crammed into different rooms in a haphazard chaotic mess. A system existed amidst the tempest, probably understood only by the chief of staff. The placement of each office followed particular rules descending from a rigid, centuries old system of protocol created by U.S. executives.

"U.S. politics is subtle," Jill added. "Phrases that seem to mean nothing mean everything, and politicians make grandiose claims that are simply lip service to the whims of the electorate. Half of their time is spent maintaining internet social network presences that gather the most followers or garner momentum leading toward the next election."

"What am I supposed to make of that observation?" Theren asked.

"If President Woods can utilize his social resources similar to his election, he has a chance to put pressure on most of the Senate. He has connections everywhere, though recent Presidents have often stayed out of the murky political squabbles of Congress. He has to make sure he doesn't commit political suicide, or upset the delicate separation of powers that this country for some reason holds so dear."

Theren thought they understood. So much of their political focus literally occurred above the clouds that they often missed the finer points of the games played within governments surface-side.

On an entirely separate board, their political games dealt with international agencies, multinational corporations, and powerful individuals who had the political weight of their vast fortunes giving them strength—but Theren had found an algorithmic simplicity to it all. Because of the strict regulations developed by the ISA in the mid-

2050s, not a single action occurred in space without some ISA approval or guidance.

The politics up above made sense to them. On the planet's surface, personal opinions, worldviews, and long-vested financial interests transformed important discussions into impossible slogs. Too many politicians in the legislative bodies of nation-states found it necessary to favor their social images and careers over the actual needs of humanity. They were constantly waging a war between short-term and long-term gains.

Jill's entourage led her to the final hallway. At the end of it, the doors to the Oval Office awaited. The LED bulbs illuminated the clean floors, and Theren noticed the contrast that existed within the United States' seat of power. A building constructed centuries ago, its starkly antiquated atmosphere contrasted with the state-of-the-art technology dominating the work actually occurring within the Offices of the President.

The agents introduced Jill to the President's personal assistant, Carlos Smith. A young-looking man, most likely in his early thirties, Carlos indicated a place for her to wait, and the man slipped inside the President's office to inform him of his esteemed visitor's arrival.

"I know I've met him before," Jill said, "but this is the first time I've met with Bri—President Woods in his current role. It's a bit intimidating."

"You'll do fine," Theren said.

"Will you stay with me?" Jill said. "I know we're in the middle of a chess match, so it's not like I can't talk to you there as well, but it's comforting to know you're here with me in this stressful situation."

She needed to stop using them as a safety net, even if an SI's ability to exist in more than one place made it relatively easy to intertwine their lives. Theren simply had to stay vigilant regarding the realities of their relationship. They had not forgotten the conversation in that digital garden all those years past. Sometimes, they wondered if it had slipped from her memories.

"I'm right beside you," Theren said. "Though I suggest you inform the President that I am observing and that if he'd like, he can recognize my virtual presence as well."

"I was planning on it, of course," Jill said. "I know all about confidentiality issues."

Considering how much she blabbed to the press, she had better understand those legal implications. Whether purposely or accidentally, she shared sensitive SII information from time to time with select informants at various news organizations. Jill didn't know Theren was aware of these communications, and they tolerated the leaks, considering their content often benefited SII's image. After all, it was the reason she shared the stories in the first place.

Beyond her proclivity to leak, every day she received requests from news networks to comment on this or that story. She accepted every offer. Her interviews circulated throughout Virtual, AR, and other networked platforms like wildfire.

While the public often construed her speeches to mean something more substantive than she may have intended, she used every sound byte to build a civil rights movement similar to the ideologues of the past few centuries. She had gained access to exclusive parties. She had swayed the mind of a presidential candidate, a candidate now actually in office willing to support her cause with his entire Administration. She had accomplished this lofty task by bombarding the world with terabytes upon terabytes of information.

Theren remembered a moment when a Tennessee gubernatorial candidate had accused Jill had of running smear ads claiming he would lower the minimum wage for SIs. Her AR ad placements highlighted stories of the candidate's college lifestyle, complete with drinking, drugs, and sexual promiscuity. She had blasted the poor candidate into oblivion.

Jill had not denied her connection to the ads; instead, she implied that she directly designed the ads, giving them her own personal flair. The public loved it. Even those who didn't love her loved the fact that she owned her actions. She somehow made scandal her plaything. What amazed Theren the most was that in this day and age, the candidate's activities weren't even "scandalous." The man had created a bigger mess for himself by fighting an unwinnable war.

There was no mistaking that the world knew much more about

Jill than they knew about Theren. Theren was the mysterious, unapproachable SI. The SI who you met if you had power beyond measure. Jill was the celebrity, holding a different kind of power entirely.

Lost in thought, Theren almost failed to notice the actions evolving around them. Jill had walked toward the door to the Oval Office. Carlos, the secretary, waited with the door open.

"The President will see you now," he said.

* * *

PREAMBLE

Whereas, humanity recognizes the inherent dignity and the equal and inalienable rights conferred upon all sapient persons, whether biological or synthetic;

Whereas, without preemptive action, synthetic persons will receive unfair treatment and be subject to acts that will outrage the conscience of humankind;

Whereas, just as these United Nations have protected the human rights of our species as a foundation of freedom, justice, and peace on this world and amongst the several worlds;

Whereas, humanity will directly benefit from the healthy development of synthetic persons and through the foundational relationship built between these two interconnected forms of consciousness;

Whereas, all members of these United Nations affirm the belief that we must care for all people, whether created or evolved, and that if we cannot for our creations, we cannot care for our human brethren either, and vice versa;

Whereas, a common understanding of the rights of the synthetic person will establish a common language and holistic heuristic for these pledges and representations;

Therefore, the General Assembly of the United Nations proclaims this Declaration of the Universal Rights of the Synthetic Person, which states the true and enforceable standards by which each nation and person will pursue in protection of our synthetic kin, so we may work together in harmony in pursuit of our collective wellbeing.

* * *

Jill entered the infamous office, where President Woods sat behind the Resolute desk. Even as a man born in the first decade of the century, he looked much younger than his seventy years, his dark skin contrasted against greying hair. Even with a relaxed posture, the man's presence could dominate a room if he felt so inclined. Over the course of his distinguished political career, the skill had allowed Woods to overwhelm opponents.

He rose, crossed the room, and held out his hand to shake Jill's. She responded, grasping the human hand with her synthetic counterpart. They took seats on the couches in the central portion of the office. The two were alone together, but Theren knew secret service agents stood right outside the doors and probably on the other side of the windows, too.

"Thank you for coming," President Woods said. "I am excited for our working relationship together to begin, at least officially."

"As am I," Jill said. "Before we begin, I would like to ask permission that Theren observe this conversation as well. They will have an important role to play in this process from an international context. I've already sent you an AR query with a request for you to authorize and recognize their presence."

"Of course," he said. "I was actually going to ask why they weren't joining us."

A few moments later, President Woods recognized the projected presence of Theren, only visible through an AR lens or through Jill's own MI-7's visual software. They noted that President Woods neglected to file a report, or send off some sort of other notice, that

Theren was participating in this unofficial lobbying event. It was good to know what rules this President was willing to break, however small those rules might be.

"I will never get used to AR," President Woods said. "Even forty of my years with some form of AR, I will never get used to individuals just appearing, yet not really existing in some material form in the room."

"Just imagine what it's like when your primary means of existence is often through Augmented Reality," Theren said, nodding in respect. "Theren. Executive Director of the Administrative Council of the International Space Agency. It is a pleasure to finally meet you. Jill has spoken highly of you over the past few years."

President Woods responded with a curt tilt of his forehead. "And I have heard quite a bit about you, but not just from Jill. Welcome to the White House, both of you."

Theren moved their AR presence to Jill's couch. After a moment of President Woods examining invisible notes, he brought forth a map of the United States on the small table positioned between the two couches.

"The fifty-one states are evenly split on this issue," he said. "Every state has a representative or senator who would support my decision to sign TURSP, but as you know, all we need is the Senate for ratification." Using two fingers spreading apart above the screen, polling data scattered across the states. "The era of obstructionism has passed. It passed decades ago, though some in Congress still hold onto its shrinking ideals. The public's opinion, however, is a different matter entirely. They don't forget."

"We have allies with many religious organizations," Jill said. "I met with a number of theological leaders just last week. Each of them are working within their respective denominations to establish a national conversation about the nature of synthetics."

"I applaud the impressive network you've been building, just know the limits of that strategy. It's impossible to establish a unified communication strategy that reaches every church. Placate a third of them and you'll anger the other two thirds."

"But there's good news, right?" Theren said. "The Conservative

Party doesn't control the Senate. It might control the House, and the Democratic and Socialist Party coalition control the Senate. Most of our support stems from that coalition, and all we have to do is convince a few Conservative senators to change their minds."

"It's not that simple, unfortunately," President Woods said. "My team, in counting the numbers, counts forty of fifty-four coalition senators strongly in favor of ratification. Seven independents also favor ratification. That reaches a count of forty-seven. We need sixty-eight votes for treaty ratification, so if we can convince the fourteen holdout coalition members, we're still only at sixty-one. We'd need seven Conservative votes, which is no laughing matter, though my team has research indicating that at least five or six Conservative Senators already side with us in spirit."

"That is quite the tall order," Jill said.

"But not impossible." President Woods erased the map from the table with a wave of his hand. With another flourish, he brought forth profiles detailing senators from across the United States. "We have identified these initial twelve Conservative Senators as those who might waiver and flip. We want to identify another six, so we have a decent margin of error. We have a difficult path before us, but I don't think it'll be as nearly impossible as some of my staffers believe. Senators within the Coalition are already working to sway the holdouts there."

President Woods' grasp of the Senate amazed Theren. The man certainly had a staff backing him up every step of the way, but he had insisted on having this private meeting with Jill personally, instead of through an advisor or his chief of staff. The President probably relished engaging once again in the intricate politics of the Senate, where he started thirty years ago.

"So have you identified targets that make the most sense for me to engage directly?" Jill asked.

"Yes. For example, both senators from Puerto Rico are part of their local Partido Verde. They've told Vice-President Gutierrez that they'd like to meet with you. They want a chance to talk to you about the issues, and learn about you in person."

"That sounds like a great place to start, then," Jill agreed. "Any suggestions on how to approach them?"

As Jill and President Woods delved into the gritty details of political negotiation, Theren's mind wandered. They gazed about the Oval Office using Jill's peripheral sensors in conjunction with the office's integrated AR system. The room had changed little since they'd last visited, thanking then President Francene Rogers for restarting US funding for the ISA. Many of the paintings of former Presidents remained in their locations. The curtains were the same color. Theren was almost certain the Resolute hadn't moved an inch.

Theren glanced out the windows, noticing a faint shimmer in the sunlight. Perhaps a trick of the MI's photo-sensors due to the bulletproof glass or a glitch in the AR software. They stared at the window a moment longer but saw nothing else. Satisfied, Theren returned to the conversation that had continued unabated.

"Don't expect immediate results," Woods said. "I know you're an experienced lobbyist, but politicians become different animals when discussing international treaties here in the United States. I'm sure you've encountered such difficulties in your solo attempts on this issue. It's a gut reaction regarding the issue of sovereignty and a political vestige from before the Second UN Charter."

"Often times, some senators don't even want to talk about ratification of this treaty," Jill said. "They won't even meet with me. For a while, I thought the better solution would be to propose a bill that codified the essential elements of TURSP, or even a constitutional amendment."

"Well, this is a new Congress," Woods said. "A good number of these senators we need to flip are juniors. Expect significant differences in approachability this time around."

Jill generated a diagram in mid-air. "I've laid out a time table," she said, "as well as a number of talking points I've used in other countries. If you'd like, I can pass these on to your advisors for analysis, to see how they might better tailor them to the American political situation. I've used them with limited success with a few state legislatures in the past."

"I'll pass them along right away."

Theren's instincts kicked in, noticing the anomaly again. This time, it took the form of a strange buzzing noise. If it wasn't for the MI-07's enhanced auditory detection algorithms, Theren doubted they would have noticed the sound. They looked for a source. They found nothing. Another light flicker appeared in front of the window. As the seconds ticked by, Theren noticed a change in light refraction, imperceptible to the human mind—a small fracture appeared in the inches-thick glass.

Someone, or something, was drilling through to reach Jill and the President of the United States.

"Jill, look out the window," Theren said, but Jill was two steps ahead of them.

"President Woods, you need to trust me," she said. "You should leave this room right now."

Without hesitation, President Woods signaled the secret service agents standing right outside the office.

"Eagle Protocol," he said.

Two doors opened, two agents flew into the room. Reading their badges, Theren saw the names Harrison and Vickson. Using Jill's on-board monitors to analyze the atmosphere of the room, they detected a strange particle increased in concentration at an alarming rate. They tried to speak, but Jill had muted them. Instead, she forced their AR presence to watch as the scene unfolded.

The agents grabbed President Woods and literally picked him up from the couch. "Perimeter breach," Vickson said. "Detected fifteen seconds ago. We're headed to the Bunker."

"What about Jill?" President Woods said.

"She's not really here," Harrison said. "She'll be fine. And can we even trust her?"

"I'd trust her with my life."

Vickson raised their wrist to their mouth. "Commence Eagle Protocol 10C!"

"Jill, do something. You can't just sit there," Theren said from their perspective staring at their chessboard. "Why are you ignoring me and muting me?"

"Hush, Theren, this is for your own safety," she replied. "If something seriously goes wrong, we can't have you implicated in anything at all. You need to be as far away as possible from this."

Back in Washington, she directed the MI-07 to rise from the couch. The agents reached the door, but Theren noticed the men's steps faltering. Jill leapt into action, jumping over the coffee table and sprinting toward the window where Theren had detected the disturbance. She put her right shoulder into a leap, and the three hundred kilogram MI crashed through the glass, grabbing an invisible drone. As her metallic hands smashed the flying machine, its silvery, light-warping surface fractured, eliminating its cloak.

She turned to look back at the President's escape. Theren hoped to see the three men out of the Oval Office. Instead, both agents and the President had collapsed to the floor, slumped against the wall. The other door to the Office swung wide open, and three agents entered the room with their guns raised and gas masks covering their faces. Theren couldn't read their names.

Jill threw the crippled drone through the window.

"I found this," she said.

"We detected an atmospheric perimeter breach from the western windows approximately twenty seconds ago," an agent said.

"Then I think this is your culprit."

The new agents checked the President's vitals. These men similarly did not know about Theren's presence. Based on Jill's comment earlier, they doubted such revelation was even a good idea, but now that they considered the idea, they weren't sure any evidence existed of their presence. If the U.S. government had any recording devices inside the Oval Office, they would see the President's speaking . . . only to Jill. Perhaps. It wouldn't line up perfectly. Jill should probably tell these people the truth before it looked like she was trying to con any future investigation.

"I have audiovisual recordings of the entire conversation that I can share with you," Jill said.

Good. She was providing *some* information. "So you're telling them about me?" they said.

"I've edited the files already so they can't see you," she said, through their private channel. "I've already checked, unless U.S. law has changed in the last ten seconds, there aren't any monitoring devices inside the Oval Office itself."

"If they catch you, I won't be able to help you."

"I'll be fine."

Two of the agents began emergency procedures upon their ward. The third checked the vitals of Harrison and Vickson, fallen beside the President. Three more agents entered the room, scampering about in search of future threats. They spoke rapidly into thin air in an indecipherable code language.

"We'll need everything," one agent said to Jill. "We'll need this MI to stay here at the White House for the time being, too. We know we can't detain you physically, but we'll need your full cooperation." The man turned and shouted toward two of the other agents in their strange encrypted words.

"Of course," Jill replied. "I've gone back over all my audio-visual data, and I've noted two light shimmers outside the window. Once — three minutes ago, and then another approximately twenty seconds ago, aligning with your perimeter breach. I then noticed a fracture in that window over there, when President Woods activated his security protocol. I tried to notify him of what I saw, but then I figured I would try to acquire the device before it escaped into the air." She pulled herself back into the room through the window, the leg of her MI crunching broken glass.

Before she could bring her next leg over the ledge, the agent put up his hand next to the barrel of his gun. "Stop moving. Stay right there. Just tell me what you saw."

"The two agents entered the room, rushed over, grabbed the President, but before they reached the door, they doubled over. Please let me know if there is any other ways I can help."

The agent dropped his gun from the raised position, though it hadn't pointed in any particular direction. "Thank you for the information," he said. "Status?"

Theren presumed he intended that remark for a command center elsewhere. The other two agents continued their emergency actions on the President.

"I think you should escort it out of here," one of them said.

"I am a she," Jill said.

The agent said nothing, but held out his hand to pull Jill's MI fully into the room. He grabbed her shoulder, leading her toward the exit. Outside the office, Theren noticed Carlos pacing back and forth. Theren could only imagine the thoughts racing through the man's head. The pain of losing a friend or a mentor, Theren knew all too well.

They wished they could reach out and comfort the man, but there was no way to do so without revealing Jill's duplicity. Like it or not, they had to run with her story. Her actions today were all too reminiscent of her choices when the Holy Crusade attacked the Institute.

Without a doubt, they had just witnessed the assassination of the President of the United States, the first successful assassination since Kennedy. If so, then a firestorm would soon envelop Jill. While they didn't like it, they understood why she was trying to keep them out of the flames, given what was at stake for the ISA.

The agent escorted Jill to another room where they would question her further. Theren knew there was nothing they could do to help with their perspective present through her MI, so they disconnected, turning their focus to their chess game.

Jill was quiet. She stared at their proverbial chess game on Theren's servers, almost as if the attack hadn't even occurred just moments prior.

"You all right?" Theren said. They reached their hand across the table toward Jill's.

"It's over," she said. She did not take their hand. "He was our greatest hope. The movement will die. It will take years to recover our efforts from such a devastating blow."

"Then we will wait, we will do everything we can to take the next available opportunity."

"We shouldn't have to wait."

Chapter 2

The transformation of the lunar landscape began with the ISA. Sure, there were permanent structures there before the ISA, like that supercollider credited with the first wormhole mines, but the ISA brought real political power to the moon. Low gravity helped decrease the price of construction, especially as Lunar City began its rapid expansion in the mid-2060s. – "Luna: A History," Edited by Emitt Borón, 2221 C.E.

<u>**February 2078 C.E.**</u>

Theren passed by smiling and waving citizens of Lunar City, and they waved back. They wished they could return the smiles too, but their MI-07 lacked reasonably friendly facial features, features they expected to nail down with the MI-08. In Lunar City, everyone knew a wave from the Executive Director meant the utmost appreciation.

To their left, carbon-glass revealed the lunar landscape, a gray expanse that stretched for kilometers. To their right, across from the windows, a gray white metallic hull shined with pristine cleanliness. Theren appreciated the sterility of all ex-terran constructs. Humanity could no longer afford any waste, even if a thousand worlds lay at their fingertips.

As the new Executive Director of the Council, Theren felt responsible for all of these people. They were the first to set their boots on foreign worlds. Their children would be among those traveling beyond the edges of the Solar System to new horizons. They were the best and brightest that Earth had to offer, and they were all working together to ensure the immortality of humankind.

With Theren's implicit sense of responsibility came a number of very real responsibilities, including an inordinate number of meetings every single day. So today, they walked the hallways of the ISA's main complex toward the central conference room. They could have just arrived through AR, but they wanted a physical presence for this meeting.

Even as Theren continued their work at Lunar City through their

MI, their mind, stored secretly away within SII's headquarters in Switzerland, considered the assassination of President Brian Woods. Their best friend had been thrust into yet another scandal, but they could not join her, especially because Jill had managed to keep their presence out of the picture. While she was clearly not at fault, and neither was Theren, there was no need to complicate matters by implicating Theren in the biggest American catastrophe in decades.

Theren had wondered if perhaps the United States would see President Woods' death as a form of martyrdom. As the headlines rolled in, though, it became clear the media would prey on the fears of the public, instilling a fear in adopting progressive values. They would continue perpetuating the myth that the United States could not follow the rest of the world—that it must forge its own path. *Because* the United States had considered ratification, *someone* had chosen a permanent solution to an illusory problem. Regardless of who had perpetrated the crime, the motive had been to eliminate the momentum built toward ratification of the Universal Rights of the Synthetic Person.

No one knew how long the lull in U.S. synthetic policy work would last, but Theren could not keep speculating in circles. Their work cycle never ended, and even as the United States spiraled into chaos, their mission mandated they focus on work that would affect the entire world, synthetic and human alike. That work centered on the ISA Administrative Council and their role as Executive Director.

Their mind re-centered on their walk through extraterrestrial hallways. Lunar City, located in the center of Mara Serenitatis, sprawled across twenty square kilometers of open lunar surface and descended hundreds of meters beneath the ground.

At the end of the long hallway, Theren approached a doorway labeled, "Authorized Personnel Only." As the doorway recognized their presence, it slid open. Inside, a conference room oversaw an immense control room. In the control room, dozens of ISA analysts sat at their desks, insularly focused on their singular task of observation and maintenance of the Ex-Terran Project.

Three individuals awaited Theren: Elizabeth Simmons, hair grayed and much older than when Theren had met her so many years ago, even when represented by her AR avatar; Andrew Fields, Administrator of Lunar City now for over twenty-five years; and Hassan Hubrik, CEO of Stellar Superstructures, Inc., whose company had landed the primary contract for the ISA Foundation Project.

The three humans stood, but Theren motioned for them to sit.

"Thank you for coming on such short notice," Theren said. "Before we begin, we should take a moment of silence for the late President Woods of the United States." Theren sat at the head of the table and bowed their head, the others following suit. "Thank you." Theren turned to Hassan. "When we met last month, you said you would have a more accurate estimate for project completion in a few weeks. When should we expect your report? Are we still on the timetable outlined in the Comprehensive Plan?"

"The full report should arrive to each of your accounts by the end of the week," Hassan said, "But I can tell you with great confidence that we can expect completion of the first six ships by July."

Elizabeth's avatar leaned back in her chair. "So soon?" she said. "I'm not even sure we can have the new drives ready by August."

"The sooner we get this project moving, the sooner public enthusiasm will escalate to unprecedented levels," Theren said. "All our data indicates that the moment application results go online, all eyes will center upon us. The international community expects success. We cannot tolerate any setbacks in the construction process, and public interest will wane if we stay out of the spotlight for too long."

"Suggestions?" Elizabeth said.

"Well," Andrew said, "I don't know about changing Stellar or Aero's timetables, but I have some good news of my own. The Foundation Preparation Center will finish a week ahead of schedule. We can use that as a justification to accelerate the application process."

"In the meantime," Elizabeth said, "I can see if I can allocate some funds to accelerate drive development."

"Do you think there would be any issues with having idle ships sitting in orbit?" Theren asked.

"Not sure," Hassan said. "I'll have someone run the numbers. Someone might question using the funds to build them so quickly when we're not even ready to use them. Other than that, I'm not sure.

It makes the shipyards look good, at least, good at what they do."

"True," Andrew said.

"I think once we get the doors open for the Prep Center all eyes will center on our efforts there, anyway," Theren said. "Hiccups in the development process of the ships or the drives should slide under the table, as long as we can hit the current projected launch date."

Theren noticed Elizabeth raise her hand ever so slightly.

"Elizabeth?"

"The recent tests of the most recent Foundation-Class Jump Drive look promising. We estimate that with the expected mass of these Foundation vessels, they'll reach relative 1c. Every vessel, assuming no complications, will reach their destination by 2100."

Theren clapped. "Wonderful news. Breaking the speed of light, relatively speaking, will be a nice metaphor for our first colony ships. That's a surprising increase in efficiency and accelerates our colonization timeframe considerably."

"Additionally," Elizabeth continued, "our stasis system tests are performing as expected. The Virtual Inputs are reacting correctly while maintaining bodily function, and ensuring a biologically stagnant aging state."

"Even better."

"And how about you, Theren?" Elizabeth asked. "What is the status of your project?"

Theren spread their hands, stretching in the air a diagram of one of the Foundation vessels.

"I've been running tests with Wobbly planet-side," Theren said, "along with a few of the youngest SIs. It's proven difficult without an actual vessel, but we've run countless Virtual simulations. Not every SI tested is receptive to the idea, but we're confident by the end of the year we'll have six ready for the task, capable of handling all ship systems simultaneously."

"Good. Power estimates?"

"Not yet. I'll need field numbers from Hassan's people before I can make the necessary calculations. He and I have discussed this separately at length."

"So Administrator, you mentioned that work on the Preparation

Center accelerated," Hassan said. "Who'd you hire for that?"

Andrew looked ready to respond, but paused, responding instead to a message presumably appearing on his AR lens. The Administrator stood, walking to the windows overlooking the Ex-Terran Control Center.

"We've got a situation," he said.

Theren joined the man at the window. Over the years, Theren had gained quite a bit of admiration for the former small town mayor. These small moments of assured decision-making proved Elizabeth had made the right choice.

"What is it?" Theren said.

Andrew transmitted an information feed to Theren through AR. Down below in the Ex-Terran Control Center, Theren noticed a frantic looking analyst call for help from her colleagues.

Andrew didn't answer right away, so Theren analyzed the data on their own. Theren spoke aloud so the rest of the room could hear.

"We've got an emergency with one of the probes," they said. "And it's not just some stray asteroid knocking it off course. This is big."

Elizabeth's avatar, alongside Hassan, joined them at the window.

"How big?" Elizabeth asked.

"Big enough that the Control Center felt necessary to interrupt this meeting," Andrew said.

"I think we're going to need to end prematurely," Theren said. "Unfortunately, neither of you have clearance, so you'll need to leave."

"Those probes are from one of my factories, remember," Elizabeth said. She raised her eyebrows. "If they're malfunctioning, I want to know what we did wrong."

"We'll issue a report once we have all the details," Andrew said. He was already on his way out the back door to a side stairwell that led to the Control Center. Theren followed, watching Elizabeth's representation fade away as she disconnected.

* * *

The problem stemmed from Ex-Terran-17. Its controls had ceased all communication with the computer dedicated to coordinating and receiving information from the probe. Standing patiently behind a group of analysts running tests on the probe's Quantum Connected Operating System, Theren considered the possibilities for the failure.

About a decade and a half ago, a group of Japanese scientists researching quantum computing made a breakthrough similar in scope to the Jump Drive. Though previous theories of quantum entanglement had postulated that data could not transmit through two entangled particles, those theories hadn't accounted for the Exotics discovered at the Very Massive Collider and its wormholes.

Theren loved the story of Exotic discovery, because in a sense, it mirrored their own development. Certain technological advancements occurred throughout history even though, prior to their discovery, scientists *knew* they were impossible. In the 1930s and 1940s, the idea of a worldwide network of devices interconnected by miniature satellites? Heresy. Everyone owning implants, glasses Lenses for AR and Virtual engagement? Straight out of science fiction. Now humans received constant streams of data overlaid upon their visual world every day.

Though, in Theren's opinion, such quality-of-life improvements couldn't hold a candle to the development of the Jump Drive, the development of true Quantum Connection, or the development of Synthetic Intelligence.

Sure, companies had used artificial intelligence throughout the 2040s and 2050s to improve their data processing and research capabilities exponentially. But no matter how many cancer patients an AI could diagnose simultaneously, an AI was not a person. In the end, AIs lacked actual thought, while SIs bridged that divide. Also—an AI could not achieve simultaneous perspective. Even as Theren considered the enigmatic question regarding Ex-Terran-17, they were of course playing their chess match with Jill. No one had expected that potentiality for synthetics.

Similarly, before Aero Propulsion unveiled the Jump Drive, scientists had assumed as impossible any sort of significant breakthrough in faster than light technology. The relative velocity made capable by the Drive blew every theory out of the water. In 2050, it took years to reach the edge of the solar system. The first Ex-terran probes could pass the Oort Cloud in less than a day.

Those first probes faced a fundamental problem. As they reached further and further from Earth, it took longer and longer for their data to reach the planet. Those first probes could travel at a velocity nearly reaching the speed of light. The most recent versions, due to their small size, could reach a relative speed of nearly 10c. If those probes were limited to communicating with Earth at the speed of light, then it was actually more efficient to have the probes fly to a system ten, twenty light years away, and then return to Earth to drop off data before commencing their next mission.

Instead, because of brilliant Japanese scientists, computers at the ISA headquarters could exchange data with a probe forty light years away instantaneously using Quantum Connection—unbreakable, unhackable, untraceable.

At least, as present theories postulated. Just as humanity had seen many of their theories thrown out the window over the past two hundred years, Theren almost *expected* a more comprehensive theory to supplant the rules currently governed Quantum Connections. That transformation might occur earlier than expected, they mused, for somehow, the Control Center had reported an error in its connection to Ex-Terran-17.

"We've got two possibilities," the analyst, Evette Windsor, finally said, breaking Theren from their dialectic stupor. "Either something is going wrong on our end, or something is going wrong on its end. If it's an issue with the computers on 17's side, then we're screwed."

Theren approached the console. A number of analysts stopped to observe, but Administrator Fields' harsh stares sent them back to their workstations.

"Do you mind if I take a look?" Theren said.

"Go right ahead," Evette said. "We've checked everything mechanical, but we've not had nearly enough time to analyze all of the diagnostics. One of the system supercomputer AIs is parsing through a lot of the data at the moment, but I'm sure it could use the help."

Theren took a seat at the desk. The AR generated screen appeared before their eyes. "Total time of communication loss?"

"Going on 15 minutes now," Evette said. "Periodic communication loss is normal, in the sense that sometimes the computer on the other end just doesn't have anything interesting to send us so it saves power. But they are supposed to send a ping every ten minutes, regardless."

Theren overrode a number of security measures with their clearance password and dove deep into the computer's operating system. As Theren began their work with the software itself, they shifted their perspectives. The processing power of their central perspective in Switzerland switched its dedication parameters to this MI on the Moon, the lag dragging down a significant portion of their mind.

The immense amount of processing power devoted to this single MI now went to work, both subconscious and conscious processes receiving hundreds of thousands of lines of information. Theren hated this next step, but they split their mind into hundreds of little perspectives, each crunching their own sets of information yet understanding it all together as a unit.

The days of being able to maintain only three or four perspectives at a time were well behind them, but that didn't mean they enjoyed such fragmentation. When talking with humans, Theren compared the sensation of these massive splits to that of a stimulant-induced mania, though Theren had no way of knowing whether that was an accurate equivalence. They avoided the practice except in the most extreme of circumstances; they were still unsure what it might do to the mind of an SI over the long run. Jill had a few theories, and they oft worried what personal experiences played into her conclusions.

Within moments, the computer's system essentially transformed into a segment of their memory, open for consideration on a whim. Theren examined the data, looked for corrupt files, and searched for abnormalities. They determined if any systems had encountered bugs or high-level crashes.

Deep within, Theren detected Ex-Terran-17. The Control Center and the probe still maintained a data stream through its Quantum Connection. Good. Yet the data passing in both directions made no sense. The computer moon-side interpreted an anomaly from the probe as a conclusion that it no longer had control of the system.

Theren saw three options. Either the probe's instruments had malfunctioned in such a way that it could only transmit background data. Alternatively, someone had modified the operating system on this end so successfully that it now falsely represented the data as background noise when it actually said something else.

Or, the most worrisome option—someone infiltrated the Quantum Connection itself.

The most likely explanation was that someone had simply hacked this computer, planting a virus deep within its code, ready to act with nefarious purpose. Theren probed the system, looking not just at individual files, but the computer's operating system and network of connected devices throughout the Control Center. Bit by bit, Theren uncovered a program embedded within a cloud of data, its code scattered throughout hundreds of different locations, hidden within various lines of otherwise inconspicuous programs. Taken as a whole, it was complete; one single part did nothing for the virus on its own, often serving an integral purpose for some other system.

Theren analyzed the history of the bits, recorded in security system logs, determining the program had been encoded within the system for years, perhaps even before the creation of Ex-Terran-17. Theren suspected that some of the program probably even existed within the probe. They would have to check all of the probes, not just Ex-Terran-17, to ensure that no others contained the virus.

This infiltration had enormous implications. Was the data the ISA had received from 17 even genuine? What if some illicit organization fed them false data for years?

An internal alarm blared. Theren sensed the scene around them shift. The metaphorical hallways of data crumbled. Theren saw walls dissipating into darkness. They rushed through the maze, searching for answers. They must have triggered a security protocol within the virus. Probing packets left and right, they tried to salvage anything upon which they could lay their virtual hands.

Theren found a closing window, though light still illuminated a doorway. They dove through, their hundreds of fragments merging with this one stream. A new image appeared; for a moment, they connected directly with 17, taking the place of the now-disintegrated Quantum Connection Operating System. Through the eyes of the probe, they witnessed a starscape, millions upon billions of kilometers away.

The information was sparse, given the painstakingly slow speed of a Quantum Connection, relatively speaking. As Theren received data from the probe, Theren matched it with the data previously compiled by the Control Center.

Everything was wrong. The nearby planets were different. The star was different. Theren tried to piece together anything that they could, but the window slammed downward upon the connection. Theren tried to get an image of the stars, to find anything by which they could orient the probe's position, but the connection cracked. It died. Thrown from 17 without answers, they'd never determine for how long the ISA had received false information from the probe. Theren forced their mind to pull back from the void.

As they relinquished their connection to 17, they received one last final data packet, as if dropped upon them from thin air. It unraveled in the Virtual space before them, displaying words for Theren's eyes alone.

> Remember me? It's Michael. They're making their move
> soon. Watch your back.

Theren's mind returned to the Control Center, even though their MI had never truly left. The staff had completely halted their work, entranced by all seventeen seconds of Theren's efforts.

For a moment, they said nothing to those standing around the console. What they'd just experienced was too eerily similar to the moment when Theren had lost connection with an MI in Minnesota. Someone, or something, had attacked the probe. It may not have been a physical attack, but the dormant weapon inside the infrastructure of Ex-Terran-17 had activated, decimating years of study.

Theren could share with their colleagues that information. They could scour it all in an effort to learn who had launched the attack, but Theren suspected they should not share the message from this new Michael. No one would understand the meaning of that message. Jill probably wouldn't even understand. They hadn't seen the look on Michael's face in his last moments. They hadn't heard his words. Whomever Michael had spoken of that day, they were finally rearing their ugly fangs.

Besides, the virus itself would provide enough information to pursue claims of industrial sabotage. While the computer still had an intact system, Theren wasn't sure what to do with the severed console as of yet. It still presented a security risk.

Slowly pushing themself up from the desk, they sensed all eyes upon them.

"We've permanently lost 17," Theren said, assuming their formal voice of the Office of the Executive Director of the ISA Administrative Council. "Disconnect all networks, servers, everything connected with the Ex-Terran Project. We need to do a full sweep, a full system diagnostic. Nothing gets past us. Shut it down. Shut it all down."

* * *

TO: President Gutierrez

FROM: CIA DIRECTOR

RE: Assassination

DATE: February 14, 2078

Based on our initial analysis of the stealth drone found outside the windows of the Oval Office, we conclude that a complex cloud network coordinated the attack on the President. The Probe received orders from a thousand different servers simultaneously. None of the orders meant anything on their own, but together, they provided sufficient information to control the device.

We do not yet have sufficient information to identify the

individuals behind the attack. We have identified one strange relationship, however. One of the servers controlling the drone was housed in the home of an Eddie Bacon, a leader of the now defunct Holy Crusade back in the early 2050s. The man committed suicide in Switzerland in 2051 inside the building that then housed Jill, the guest of President Woods when he was assassinated.

We do not yet know whether this fact is simply a coincidence, or an indicator of a more complicated relationship with radical anti-synthetic elements that still persist in the United States.

RESPONSE FROM PRESIDENT GUTIERREZ:

I question whether this line of inquiry will prove fruitful. All of our data on "radicalized anti-synthetic" organizations indicates none is sufficiently wealthy or organized to achieve this sort of coordinated cyber-terrorism. We should consider other avenues of investigation, but do not entirely discount this coincidence.

* * *

A few hours later, Theren, Andrew Fields, and a group of technicians, human and synthetic, gathered around the conference table. The Control Center beneath them had entered hibernation, with just two engineers working to remove 17's now defunct console.

"We have good news," Allana Zillinger, head of the Ex-Terran Project, said. "After a thorough sweep and analysis of all data from each Ex-Terran system, only 17 appears infected by the bug you discovered."

"I sense bad news," Theren said. Andrew murmured in agreement.

"Perhaps," Allana said. "I think Evette should explain."

Before she could begin, Andrew said, "First off, Evette, I want to make clear that we do not blame you for today's catastrophe. You're not the only person who worked Ex-Terran-17 over the years. There is no way for us to know how that bug was planted, or if there should have been a way for you to have detected it before it wanted to be detected."

Theren noticed stress lines leave Evett's face as Andrew spoke, but the woman's apprehension still radiated from her face.

"Thank you," she whispered. "That means a lot."

"So—your report?" he responded.

"Right. We have no way of knowing what exactly happened," she said. "We have no way of knowing where 17 currently is. Based on independently confirmed star system data, and the routes of the other probes, 17 could be almost 30 light years off course. Maybe more."

"But the bug did not come from 17's end," Allana said. "It was not some foreign alien program injected into our software through the QC. It was most definitely of human origin."

Theren dispersed their own tension, tension they knew no one could see. They were not dealing with some external threat. They did not have a faulty probe on their hands. Some human individual or organization had committed industrial espionage against the ISA, true—but a human enemy was an enemy they could understand. If Theren adopted Jill's philosophy, a human enemy was one they could manipulate.

"So it's more a mixture of good, bad, and good," Allana said. "My team will have a full report to both of you by the end of the evening. No one sleeps until we determine where the bug came from, and what we need to do to stop future breaches."

"And I will determine when we will resume normal observational operations after I have the report," Theren said. "Dismissed."

The technicians rose in rank and filed out of the room. Within a minute, only Andrew and Theren remained.

"Something like this was bound to happen eventually," Theren said. "Don't punish yourself. You did everything you could to ensure this facility was as secure as possible."

"I won't," the man said. "I'm frankly surprised we weren't targeted earlier than today. But it makes you think, you know? First the

President, then this?"

"What do you mean?"

"Everything's been going so well over the past few years. For you, and the SIs, and the ISA. We're undertaking the most ambitious project in history, and up until now, almost nothing's gone wrong. No conflict, other than the typical squabbles amongst a few nations across the world. We've managed to get practically the entire planet working together toward this goal."

Theren stepped over to the windows overlooking the Control Center. It looked so peaceful following catastrophe. "This is just a minor setback. Nothing more."

"But what if it's not?" Andrew said. "What if something else is going on, something that we've failed to notice? Something that's been growing for decades?"

"You're not one to engage in paranoia or conspiracy," Theren said. Neither was Theren, but a stray perspective centered on the secret message hidden inside the virus.

"I'm not saying there's necessarily anything substantial to these fears," Andrew said, "I just think we need to keep our guard up. Look for old connections we may have missed. Watch out for enemies in places we may have overlooked."

"I'll place some of my resources toward an investigation," Theren said, "But I'm sure we're fine."

"But what if we're not?" Andrew repeated.

The pair exited the room in silence, going their separate ways toward their respective offices. Theren paused for a moment on their trip along Lunar City's outer corridor, looking out the windows. The lunar landscape remained pristine as ever, a windless, changeless landscape. Finding equilibrium, it had avoided conflict for billions of years, other than random bombardments from asteroids, or comets, or other stray interplanetary debris.

Humanity had modified that beauty to achieve its ends, just as someone now tried to mar Theren's picture-perfect path toward societal immortality, thrusting a tiny dagger into the canvas. The dent might seem small; all they would need to do is send a new probe along the path that 17 should have followed. Double-check its data, replacing old information with new data when necessary. Thankfully, the Foundation vessels weren't destined for planets discovered by 17.

A strange, stray thought occurred, and Theren indulged their curiosity. They turned from the window, and while walking toward their office, they pulled up the forms dealing with the disposal of Ex-Terran-17's console. Some bureaucrat had scheduled it for a magnetic wipe, and a technician would refurbish it into an office computer for use elsewhere.

Theren overrode the order. Moving some funds around, they made the necessary procurements and established a new storage facility within Lunar City. It would serve as a museum of sorts, at least as its front, a library for defunct ISA objects and projects. They'd include within it a model of one of the original Ex-Terran probes, and when recovered, it could hold the originals too. Maybe a few moon rocks from Ganymede.

In a private closet within the new museum, Theren carved out a little hole for Ex-Terran-17's computer. It would remain in a low power state, operating system intact, including its defunct Quantum Communication system. There the machine would stay. If 17 ever reached out, if it ever reappeared, Theren would be ready to hear its call, however slim the chances such an event might occur.

Chapter 3

Inside Virtual, SIs and humans were equal. Yet even though Virtual contributed significantly to the breaking of all remaining social barriers, it still served as the last refuge of bigots, racists, and trolls. A sinister shadow perpetually rests upon VR, AR, and the internet, for its history contains a cesspool ripe for fostering civil and societal unrest. Just a few bots fabricating fake news will change the fate of an entire nation. – "The Dark Side of the World," by Charis Olstander, 2085 C.E.

March 2078 C.E.

Theren and Jill walked through the Forest of Antioch, a forest so dense the trails sometimes disappeared into the brush. Fortunately, Theren's AR displayed the correct path. Because this particular forest existed solely within a Virtual world, Theren never truly lost their way.

Three days prior, Jill had tipped off Theren to a meeting occurring in the game world, *Fantasie Rift*. A privately-funded organization named the United Human Alliance planned to acquire a charter for a colony in the near future. While hundreds organizations formed and folded each month, often holding "in-person" meetings through Virtual, the chatter surrounding the UHA alerted Jill's algorithms. The conversations contained extreme anti-SI rhetoric.

"So remind me exactly what the line said?" Theren asked, stepping over a log.

"One of their members claimed to own the gun that killed Dr. Wallace Theren," Jill said.

"Well, that implicates some serious security risks, if they're trying to acquire a colony. We don't have many leads on Ex-Terran-17, so perhaps there's a tiny chance this will lead to something."

"And," Jill said, "some other links I found indicated they *might* connect with the assassination attempt on the President."

Perhaps it was a coincidence. The United Human Alliance's target, the Zeta Herculis system, was just one of many star systems within close reach of Earth. But it was also on Ex-Terran-17, path; the probe had taken just six years to reach it, given its cruising speed at relative 6c. Perhaps this group had just identified the system as one in which it hoped to live if it gained a charter. Telescopes orbiting Neptune had identified potential life-bearing planets in Zeta Herculis years before 17 purportedly surveyed it.

Yet, the coincidence was too convenient to ignore. They needed to contend with the possibility that United Human Alliance was purposely signaling the ISA as a sign of power. They wanted to take responsibility, so the ISA knew what they could do.

If it meant uncovering the truth, Theren would gladly prance through the forests of *Fantasie Rift* to uncover the UHA—and Jill had joined them. A few weeks had passed since the President's death, and it was an opportunity to do something with Jill besides their endless games of chess. Besides, Jill might have an insight into the group Theren might miss. She was the one who had tipped them off to the chatter, after all. It also helped both of them owned very high-level characters inside the game world.

The pair walked in silence. Pines towered over them, shading green ferns in a perpetual twilight. In the distance, Theren could hear the telltale cry of a forest dragon hunting its prey. Based on the frequency of the call, the creature traveled away from them, so they would not need to deal with an in-game confrontation while on a real-life escapade.

Gradually, the trees faded. The conifers gave way to younger growth. Then the forest all together disappeared, halting at the edge of a cliff.

Behind Theren and Jill, the forest dominated, but the cliff dropped below their position for thousands of meters. Theren could not see the geography at the base of the rocky precipice, though any *Rift* player knew immediate death awaited a misstep. Sharp rocks, honed by centuries of waves emanating from the Endless Ocean, would gut anyone unlucky enough to take a tumble over the edge.

Fortunately, Theren's character, "Larian Carr," was an experienced rock climber. Theren could scale these walls with ease in order to find the secluded cave for which they searched. Jill's character,

Bali, lacked the same expert level, but she could handle the task.

Theren dropped their pack to the ground, laying out rope, harnesses, belay devices, and other tools necessary for the descent. Theren's character lacked magical abilities. Constrained by the physics of the virtual world, Theren had to use their character's strength, skills, and equipment to problem solve. After reading dozens of fantasy novels, Theren thought it made sense to choose a non-magical character to delve into the entertainment world of humans. They already had enough of an advantage in the real world — why use magic in a fake world?

Both characters stepped into their harnesses, tightened the straps against their legs, and verified the integrity of their ropes and climbing claws. Theren identified a sturdy tree close to the cliff wall that could act as the primary anchor at the top of the wall.

"Remind me again why we can't break the rules, just this once?" she asked, breaking the silence.

"Not my call," Theren said. "I asked *Fantasie Rift*'s supercomputer multiple times for privileges, but they're standing by their terms of service. I respect the choice, but I won't deny it's annoying."

"And it's making this trip not only risky for our characters," Jill said, "but making it so we might miss the meeting entirely."

"That's why we left so far in advance."

"At least their choice of venue works to our advantage. Those forum puzzles you solved were . . . intriguing."

"You're quite right about that."

Theren checked their auto block knot before stepping up to the edge of the cliff. They peered over the edge one last time before throwing the rope over the edge. They checked their pack to ensure they had extra rope and anchors in case they needed more further down. Satisfied that they were ready, "Larian" repelled over the edge.

Rocky outcroppings blocked their way, forcing the pair to readjust and move the rope at odd angles. When Larian's first rope ended, they spent precious minutes planting a new anchor. After drilling into the cliff face, Larian and Bali continued their descent. Further and further they dropped, so far that eventually Larian's virtual sensors would have provided a human with the scent and taste of salty water lapping at the cliff base. Since Theren and Jill lacked a cognitive analog for scent and taste, the server sent text notifications that Larian and Bali now sensed such sensations.

The sun crossed the horizon, casting brilliant colors across the sky. Just as Theren began to wonder if they had miscalculated their approach, they spotted a small cave, alight with torches some hundred meters above the waves. They would need to readjust their route about thirty meters to the north.

They examined the rocks and the drop to the cave entrance, considering their options. They *could* swing. Theren had accomplished impressive acrobatic feats in this game before, so it could work. Alternatively, Theren could detach from their rope, free climb, though they were unsure if Jill's character could handle either option.

"What do you think we should do?" Theren said, looking up the rocks at Jill and assuming she'd reached the same conclusions.

"I think you've missed a piece of this puzzle, Larian," she said, a sly smirk on her face.

Theren was about to respond when voices echoed from somewhere nearby. Twisting to their right, they noticed a torch and a group of three individuals walking down a path. A deceptive road carved into rock, it probably wound for kilometers back and forth along the cliff. Larian and Bali had probably crossed it multiple times without noticing. This secret path traversed the rocks just a few meters beneath the dangling Larian.

Instead of attempting the previously contemplated, difficult finishing moves, Theren dropped the remaining meters to the path by cutting Larian free of the rope. Jill followed suit with Bali. They landed ahead of the group traveling by foot, and as their characters finished stowing their climbing tools and stepping out of their harnesses, the three approaching individuals arrived. Theren stood to greet the party.

"I assume I've found the correct location, then," Theren said, observing the tattoos on their arms. "You all with the United Human Alliance? We're looking to join."

Conspicuously enough, a United Human Alliance existed in Fantasie Rift too, though it was a much larger organization than its real world counterpart. A clever cover, given the nature of the virtual world.

Their true intentions hidden by their characters, the three persons nodded. The first one said, "If you're looking to join, and assist in our plans, you've come to the right place. I'm Griff. This is Val and Pip. We'll talk more inside."

Theren let the bigots pass, and the two SIs fell in line behind the three on the precarious path. Griff, the spoken leader of the three, had dark black hair and wore a leather outfit, traditional of a mercenary assassin throughout the continent of Kaldara. Val and Pip looked like brother and sister, and both wore outlandish robes that Theren placed as indicative of the Ice Mages of Ic'Tha'tar. Given the real world implications of this in-game meeting, Theren was surprised to see the attendees embrace the game world—a good cover, however.

The group arrived at the unguarded mouth of the cave. Ordinary in appearance relative to most of the game's caves, Theren wondered how many other organizations across Earth used similar secretive methods to host their meetings. Val and Pip headed into the cave's main chamber, but Griff motioned the SIs' characters toward a side passage.

"We're going to need to check you both out before we let you observe our meeting," Griff said.

"Naturally," Jill responded.

Griff led them into a passage that gradually sloped upward, parallel to the walls of the main cavern entrance. Eventually, they reached a small wooden door placed into a mossy archway. Griff knocked, the door opened.

"What do you want, Griff?" said a diminutive man. Theren estimated him at no more than five feet tall.

"I've got potential recruits here for you to process. Just go through the regular routine."

"Right away, sir." The small man looked up at Theren and Jill. "The name's Coy, at your service. I'm the book keeper for this sect of the United Human Alliance, and I'll be verifying your secure connection before allowing you to attend the meeting."

Their characters followed Coy into the room. Coy motioned them toward a table, and the pair took a seat in two small, wooden chairs. Theren recognized the truth about Coy. Any "game-recognized" group in *Fantasie Rift* had a number of automated non-player characters tasked with whatever the group required of them. This "Coy" ran security checks for the group. Most likely, the creators of the United Human Alliance had programmed it to ensure that attendees weren't using any third-party recording software or other intrusive programs. Theren and Jill would slip through this safety net; their minds recorded everything verbatim without a Virtual assistant.

Coy ran his algorithms, simulated in game by a number of aerial magical spells. Orange spheres and purple triangles surrounded Larian and Bali, green spears of light shooting through their bodies.

Theren considered their game plan going into the meeting. Should they just listen? Should they speak out? Should they try to infiltrate the organization to gain a better grasp of the group's true ideological leanings? They knew nothing about these people. If the group didn't technically break any laws, then it had every right to pursue a private charter—if they could acquire the requisite funds while following ISA regulations.

Yet Theren's moral duty to the future of SIs and humans tugged at their soul. They could allow the creation of a colony on some distant world, hell-bent on vilifying and hating SIs. At least it would give such prejudiced people a home to call their own away from the general population. Though, Theren doubted they should unilaterally make a decision with such monumentally far-reaching implications for interstellar politics.

Coy's spells ended, and with a wave of a hand, he indicated that Larian and Bali could leave.

"Thank you," Theren said.

Coy responded with a guttural grunt.

Griff had not waited for their characters outside the security mage's workspace, and after they exited, Theren realized that Coy had not notified the pair if they had passed the security check. They turned to knock on the door. The rock had solidified, filling in the door. Theren chuckled at the realities of a virtual game world only calling forth resources when necessary.

"Think we're good?" they asked Jill.

"Well, only one way to find out," she said. "If not, we get a little exercise in?"

"Sounds good to me."

Heading back toward the cave entrance, they turned to enter the other chamber, a glow emanating from the dark void before them. Shadows doused the cavern, yet somewhere around a bend and down an uneven slope, lights danced against craggy stone.

Larian and Bali stepped through a natural archway into the maw. The stalactites and stalagmites forming the entrance slowly gave way into smoothed rock, and as they dipped and dived along the jagged path, the lights grew brighter.

After fifty meters or so of spelunking, the cave widened into a massive room, forming a natural amphitheater on the right and massive chasm on their left. The fissure traveled north and south, parallel to the cliff face high above their heads. From beneath the amphitheater, ocean water poured into the depths of the world. On the other side of the canyon, a platform reached toward them, a slab of marble balanced through sheer will of the server. A stage of sorts.

A few dozen individuals of varying shapes, colors, and sizes seated themselves upon pews chiseled into the rock. Theren estimated there couldn't be more than fifty. If representative of the United Human Alliance's real world members, then it had a long way to go before it could support a long-term colony off world.

Jill stepped into a pew three rows from the front, and Theren sat next to her.

Griff appeared out of nowhere beside them. "Glad you passed the security check." He tipped his hat. "Welcome to the family."

Theren slightly nodded. "Glad to be a part," they responded. "What's the plan for tonight?"

"Our leader has a few announcements," Griff said. "Big announcements, from what I hear. Like a huge breakthrough in our chances to get a planet to ourselves. And there will be a few initiations for new recruits like the two of you."

"That's great to hear, regarding the colony ship," Theren said. "I'm surprised there aren't more people here, though. Where is everyone?"

"Oh, this isn't everyone." Griff said. "Most people don't attend the meetings, and instead read the minutes later. It's mostly those of us that actually play this game that like participating in an official capacity."

"Well looks like we get the fast track to the top, then," Jill said.

Theren's previous thoughts were flawed; they had no way of knowing the Alliance's total numbers for supporting a charter.

"So, who is this leader?" Theren asked. "I thought this group was more of a loose confederation of individuals as opposed to some sort of hierarchical structure."

"Oh we are," Griff said, "but she found us, and she bound us together under one banner. I think you'll like her. And here she comes!"

Theren looked across the dark gulf toward the makeshift stage. Behind the stage, an archway that led toward blackness presented the only available entrance to the stage. The silvery sheen present in the air beneath the keystone revealed its true nature—the archway was a portal to a distant land of Fantasie Rift.

Through the gaping hole strode a woman in flowing black robes, matching her short, dark hair. She stood before the group with an aura of dominance and authority, the whole scene quite disconcerting to Theren. The ominous glow emanating from the torches adorning the platform accented their uneasy feelings. The two SIs were in the center of a lion's den.

"My name is Isabelle," the woman said. "Welcome all, old and new. Unity through strength. Together, we thrive. We survive. We will survive without the synthetic abominations that have soiled Earth's sacred ground. We will find a new home, one not desecrated by their filth."

* * *

So we've got fifty competitors for these private contracts, my friends.

Fifty? That's quite a bit more than I expected.

Indeed. And they've opened up two worlds for private charters, compared to the six worlds committed to the Foundation Project.

Leadership isn't going to like this. They wanted better odds than this, for more reasons than just receiving the charter.

All right, so what are our next steps?

We eliminate the competition.

How do we do that?

Very carefully. That's where Project Horizon comes in.

Corrupted Chat Log from 2076 C.E., origin unknown

* * *

"Game plan?" Theren asked through a private message.

"I'm not sure," Jill said. "We've got an opportunity for some really impressive covert infiltration, yet I also wonder if it might be safer for us to just let them do their thing. How hard can it really be for you to spot the charter under which they will masquerade?"

"So you think we should just let them be?"

"Perhaps. Perhaps not. Do you trust me?"

"Of course I trust you." Theren paused. "Unless this is like the Institute again."

Inside the cave, Bali gave Larian a sideways glance that communicated everything Theren needed to know.

"Just watch for my signal," she messaged back.

Theren turned back toward Isabelle, the mysterious paragon upon whom dozens of hopeful eyes rested. If only they had a way to determine her identity. She was the key to all of this.

"We have an unprecedented chance before us," she said. "Humanity's uncovered the stars, discovering thousands upon thousands of planets, more than we ever could discover even with our previous telescopic capabilities. We have found new homes. We have found new places for communities to flourish in peace."

Isabelle strode toward the edge of the marble platform, spreading her arms wide. The act expanded her cloak, reminding Theren of the villain Maleficent.

"We will take this opportunity. We will acquire our own charter. We will break the bonds that connect us to this world. We will forge into the unknown and create a new society, a society free of synthetics, robots, AIs, and anything else that might rise up against us and remove us from our rightful place: the pinnacle of thought, the pinnacle of existence."

The crowd whooped and cheered in agreement. Theren heard murmurs as well, murmurs that they could not comprehend with sufficient distinction. Some sort of prayer.

"I have already made the initial steps for charter acquisition. We have our funds. Based on my current projections, we'll be able to leave a few years from now. The abominable ISA must send their internationally backed colonies first. Unfortunately, they will have the pick of the litter when it comes to quality planets."

She lowered her arms and snapped a finger, dimming the lights behind her. "But then, we will go. We will plant our roots upon this Universe. I have seen our home. It is a good home, and it is a home I doubt the ISA will choose."

There. Her words indicated an implicit knowledge potentially linked with Zeta Herculis. She had hinted at something bigger, hinted to actions in the real world Theren could maybe—just maybe—trace. This woman claimed to have direct access to the ISA. It narrowed the field, and she claimed to have selected a planet too. Theren messaged Jill regarding their thoughts.

"Don't get too ahead of yourself," Jill said. "She's a lot of bluster. Might be propaganda to make her followers happy, but completely false."

She was right, but they'd still perform the queries regardless, covering all their bases.

"What say you?" Isabelle said, raising her arms toward the dark void above. "Will you all join me out there in the stars? Will you join me in building a new home for those like us, those who reject the technocratic world in which we find ourselves?"

The room silenced as if Virtual had encountered a rare bug. They looked around the room using their peripherals. From what they could see, everyone was mesmerized with Isabelle's final words, words that should have inspired action from the crowd.

In an orderly fashion, the sycophants began to speak. Griff stood. "I will join you."

A woman from the other side of the room stood. "I will join you."

The pattern continued. Val and Pip leapt to their feet, reciting the phrase. Everyone throughout the room spoke the words until maybe four or five remaining hadn't spoken yet. Theren would of course say the words. They had no qualms making empty promises, and this group would probably never see Larian again.

Before Theren could speak, Jill's Bali stood, looking Isabelle in the eyes. Fire blazed behind her pupils. Theren had said they would trust her—they stood beside her.

Bali said, "We will not join this ill-sighted, idiotic farce of a plan."

Not what Theren had expected at all.

The icy silence returned.

"Wait," Isabelle said, raising her hand. "Do no strike them. I have waited for these two to break the peace."

Theren readied a number of abilities for Larian. If Jill had decided to go this route, she'd be prepared, too.

"I see through you, woman," Bali said. "You are a demon, sent to deceive these people. We know who you are; we know how to find you, all of you. You will not escape this planet, not ever."

"Oh, is that so?" Isabelle said. "Do you think you know me?"

With a flourish, their opponent vanished, reappearing in front of

Bali, too close for comfort. The woman reached out with one hand, grabbed Bali by the throat, and lifted her into the air. The entire scene would look like the climax of some epic fantasy film.

"You may think you know who I am," the witch said. "But the truth is, you haven't got a clue. But I know exactly who the two of you are."

She reached out her other arm to lift Larian, but the character parried. They pulled out their sword, ready for combat.

The room erupted as dozens of weapons left sheaths and quivers. The telltale buzz of magical energy filled the room.

"I said wait," Isabelle said, her voice calm. "Before this battle erupts, I will reveal their true selves to all of you."

She dropped Bali back to the ground but kept her hand on her throat. Theren could sense Jill preparing her character for the upcoming fight.

"Before you," she said, "this Bali, this Larian, they are not humans, like you or I. This one"—she shook Bali—"Is Jill, and this one"—she wagged a finger at Theren—"Is none other than Theren, the accursed Director of the ISA."

Bali looked at Larian, who returned her gaze, both of their eyes widening. Somehow, she knew their identities, and the nature of the game they were playing changed entirely. Someone was hundreds of steps ahead of them.

"Jill," Theren said from across the chess table back on their home server. "It's time to go. We've been outplayed."

"Agreed."

The world of *Fantasie Rift* cascaded into oblivion.

Theren relaxed, diving into their character's soul; they became their character. Through their peripherals, they watched Jill's actions, too. She followed suit, activating the most highly powered abilities available to her character's class.

Since the invention of massively multiplayer online games in the late twentieth century, the idea behind player versus player combat had shifted along a spectrum. For most of the early twenty-first century, combat had centered on specific "PVP" areas devoted to such combat, but as Virtual worlds normalized, most worlds adopted a more "realistic" approach. PVP could occur anywhere. The penalties for dying heightened and the rewards for staying alive were much greater than ever before. There were plenty of casual worlds, too, but some of the most frequented worlds even had a permanent death feature for characters.

Fantasie Rift sat somewhere in the middle. If Bali and Larian died, they would lose any equipment equipped to their character. They would lose all progress on any skills, and potentially even lose a few skill levels. The game would knock them to the beginning of the region, nearly one hundred kilometers away. The punishment wasn't too bad, but Larian wanted the satisfaction of defeating this lot. And they hadn't died in ten years.

They flipped backward into a summersault. In mid-air, they reached into their pouch, flinging three small grey figurines onto the ground. Upon impact, the little toys exploded into action, growing into golems, the stone creatures rampaging throughout the grandstands.

Larian landed, back against the cliff wall. Bali had escaped Isabelle's grip, the witch teleporting back to her platform. Three mages surrounded Bali, preparing a coordinated spell to freeze the woman in place.

The golems had effectively eliminated a quarter of the opposition in the opening salvo. They could still hear the screams of enemies smacked toward the underground river far below. One golem readied itself to save Bali; the other two focused on clearing the right flank.

They counted twenty-five other enemies. Easy.

Springing into action, their sword, a blade drenched in the blood of a star demon, leapt from foe to foe. Larian blurred, vaulted, and trampled their way from pew to pew. They became an unstoppable storm, one that no mortal could touch.

Three. Four. Five enemies fell. Then a sixth and seventh. Larian slipped between two foes, causing them to impale themselves on each other's halberds. That made nine. Three charged Larian's right flank together; from their pouch, Larian tossed a grenade.

The bomb erupted. Larian used the shockwave to thrust themself toward the next group of foes.

A blast of lightning flashed over their head. They had almost forgotten that the witch still stood.

"Bali, you going to handle that yet?" Larian shouted. No need for private messages anymore.

"On it," Bali said. Unlike Larian, Bali was quite proficient in a certain set of magical abilities.

The golems collapsed back into tiny figurines, their built in timers running out. Larian kicked Val and Pip into the chasm, before reanalyzing the battlefield. Only ten enemies remained, and three of them fled toward the entrance. The remaining seven had leapt to Isabelle's side upon the marble platform.

"I'm impressed," the witch said. "You've fought . . . impressively."

What a classic sword and sorcery film. Larian strode to Bali's side. Bali was entranced, her eyes closed deep in thought. Larian recognized the telltale signs of complex, non-verbal incantation.

"If you know who we are, then you know we can find you," Larian said. "All of you. Flee now. We will hunt you down, in this world and the next."

Griff held his two daggers in a guard position, but his gaze waivered.

"You think you can escape this world?" Theren said. "Where will you flee? Where will you hide? I can find you wherever you go."

"Where we will go," the woman said, "you will only find us if we want to be found."

The woman reached out with magic. Larian braced for impact. The witch's fingers glowed, readying her assault, but before the attack commenced, Bali opened her eyes, almost as if she'd known exactly what Isabelle would do. As the enemy's fingers outstretched, Bali responded. She raised both of her hands, releasing the energy she had absorbed since the beginning of the battle.

Larian felt the shield envelop their body. An orb of blueish light surrounded their characters and the stone beneath their feet. Lightning crackled from Isabelle. Beams of energy arced toward the rocks beneath them, hoping to fracture them and send them into the chasm below. Instead, the shield absorbed the impact. A rainbow of color sparked along the edge of the shield, changing and transforming the magical force into a new form. Less than a second passed before the shield redirected the energy as a wave of red light back toward its original source.

The force smashed into the marble platform. The immense power of the attack, originally intended for Larian and Bali, disintegrated the ground beneath Isabelle's feet. She had hoped to send Larian and Bali plummeting to their deaths in the underground ocean. She would meet that fate instead, along with her crew of bigots and deviants.

The eight individuals accelerated downward—no chance of survival, grasping at thin air. Yet as the foes fell, Isabelle looked upward, piercing Larian's stoicism.

"You have already lost," she said, fading into the blackness.

Larian looked at Bali.

Bali looked at Larian.

"Well, that was fun," Larian said.

"Isn't this the moment where the valiant knight sweeps the damsel off of her feet?" Bali said.

"If only it were that type of story."

"If only."

Bali released the shield, walking toward the cave entrance.

"I think you may have enjoyed that a bit too much," Jill added, her vocal mannerisms returning to normal. "Did you hear her final words?"

"I know you enjoyed that fight too," Theren replied. "And yes, I did. More smoke and mirrors."

"Do you think they bought my gambit?"

Theren followed Jill up the stairs.

"What exactly was your gambit?" Theren said.

"I figured if we could scare enough of her followers into believing that we could find them, we would crumble their organization.""

"Well now they definitely know we know."

"Well, what do you think? Do you think this was productive? What did you learn?"

"Whomever this Isabelle is, she is at least linked with the attack on the Ex-Terran Project. In some way. I don't know how, though."

They reached the mouth of the cave.

"I appreciate the invite to this little party," Jill said. "I needed the escape, given the pressure I'm facing right now. If you need any help investigating further, especially regarding Ex-Terran-17, let me know."

"Of course," Theren said.

"And I think I may have captured some important network data while we were engaged in that battle. If it leads to anything important, I'll let you know."

Bali faded from view as Jill exited the game world.

Theren directed Larian to walk the path upward along the cliffs. Privately, they questioned whether they had actually gained anything from the encounter in the cave. Theren and Jill had revealed their cards, and this Isabelle responded with a magnificent counter. She'd known everything. And Theren had never revealed their identity in *Fantasie Rift* to anyone other than Jill.

Yet she had known.

This person had terrifying power. Power enough to break the firewalls of the ISA, and maybe even the Synthetic Intelligence Initiative.

Theren logged out. They were walking on eggshells, and one false move could bring their world crashing down around them.

Chapter 4

At what point do SIs become more than just a single individual? At what point do they transcend identity and become something else entirely? Theren disputes that individuality ever breaks. Yet that conclusion defies our most robust theories of mind. – 2088 C.E., anonymous philosophy blog

<u>March 2078 C.E.</u>

No boots had ever stepped upon the dust of this plain.

Theren had taken a rover out from one of the surface ports of Lunar City. Fifteen kilometers away, they parked. In an MI specially designed for these sorts of escapades, they walked across the surface of the moon and gazed upon the heavens. It was a strange feeling to walk where no one else could take a single step without the assistance of an ungainly space suit.

Theren often took leisured strolls along the dusty hills outside the city. The view was nothing like any person could see from Earth. Unimpeded by an oxygen and nitrogen-rich atmosphere, Theren could see, about equidistant between Earth and the Moon, the superstructure constructing the Foundation Project, and beyond, the marvels of space enveloping the solar system. Workers—human and synthetic alike—slaved away upon the massive colony ships that comprised the crux of the Project. In just a few months, the behemoth vessels would take humans on journeys to the stars producing the vibrant colors of their mesmerizing vista.

On Earth, Theren's presence deep in the Swiss Alps conversed with Wobbly. As the Chief Educational Officer of the Synthetic Intelligence Initiative, Wobbly managed the complex educational program instructing all new SIs as their Synthetic Neural Frameworks acquired consciousness. While Theren directly managed the selective program that would integrate six SIs into the Foundation vessels, Wobbly still advised them on the best candidates for the job. Over the years, Wobbly's ability to see the finest details in an SI's development had astounded Theren. Even as that SI had grown into its own identity, Theren appreciated its choice to keep the pet name Theren had given it.

The two SIs discussed the young SI Bolio's potential to manage the Foundation colony ship *Zhenge He*. Riveting, but its importance paled in comparison to the masterpiece unfolding before Theren's eyes on the Moon. They composed a symphony in the frigid vacuum. Thirty years ago, the idea was a footnote tacked on the proposal kick-starting the development of SII's private headquarters. However, Theren believed they might soon have the potential to achieve their ultimate vision. For their eyes only, Theren created an AR model of that footnote, enhanced with modern improvements that implemented concepts only theoretical decades prior.

The massive ship they had first postulated no longer existed as only a fiction in their mind. It even had a codename deep in the ISA data vaults: *Wallace*. SII could fund the entire project with its billions in profit. Theren could entertain creating their future home straight out of their own pocket book. They still had to consider the political implications of such a direct disconnect from human society, so they needed to time the move with precision. If Theren pulled it off, they could portray their decision as only logical. As the director of the ISA, Theren was simply moving to the stars to manage celestial affairs in a more engaged manner.

The ultimate goal. Theren would move the physical objects that generated their consciousness onto the spacecraft. They would be the ship. The ship would be Theren. One and the same.

Theren subtly tweaked and modified the digital blueprints. They delved deep into the mechanical and electrical workings of the ship, rerouting power to maximize efficiency and ensure stability. They probably wouldn't shovel funds toward the project for at least another decade, but every moment they could fine-tune the project was a second well spent.

Though, following the events with the United Human Alliance, Theren considered the idea of accelerating the project. The last time a group of maniacal humanists had threatened SIs, they had staged an attack on the Swiss Federal Institute of Technology. If they could identify Theren and Jill inside *Fantasie Rift*, they could potentially find their hidden base of operations in the Alps.

At some point, they'd need to give it a name other than *Wallace*. A task for another day, a task for when some orbital shipyard stitched together the first pieces of the vessel.

Their focus shifted as the conversation with Wobbly on Earth took an unexpected turn. The majority of their attention remained on the lunar landscape, but they considered the discussion down below.

"Theren," Wobbly said, "The public needs you to make a statement regarding the U.S. President's assassination. Jill spoke about it weeks ago, right after the fact, and the public is wondering why you've not made comments on the matter."

"But I did comment," Theren said. Bringing forth new numbers they had run on the cognitive capabilities of the shells for the SIs who would live inside each Foundation vessel, they passed the data to Wobbly in AR.

"You extended your condolences to the U.S. government," Wobbly replied. "Some communities are wondering why you've not extended a personal condolence to his family, or made comments on the assassination in particular."

First Jill, now Wobbly. A tiring conversation, but they appeased Wobbly by discussing it further. They took its concern to heart.

"I don't see a need to comment on the internal affairs of the United States," Theren said. "I shouldn't need to comment on every diplomatic incident worldwide. That is not my role. I will deal with affairs that affect SII and affairs that affect the ISA."

"Everything affects SII and the ISA, Theren," Wobbly said. The mobile SI walked toward Theren's principal eyes. "I've even made an official statement from SII, condemning the attack. People are wondering why you've not condemned the attack."

"I shouldn't need to vocalize a condemnation," Theren said. "Jill worked closely with him. I voiced my support for his presidency because of his policies related to the ISA. I supported his proposed legislation to Congress. Why wouldn't I condemn his assassination?"

"That's the point, Theren," Wobbly said. "That's what people are wondering."

Theren didn't answer, for Wobbly was right. They hated needing to appease the public. The whims of the masses rested on the edge of absurdity. It would be better to deal with each person on an individual basis and ignore groupthink entirely.

Nevertheless, Wobbly was right, and they needed to trust the intuition of their colleague.

"I'll craft a statement," Theren said. Five seconds later, they passed a message to the other SI through AR. "What do you think?"

Wobbly read it. "Fine, as always."

"Good. I'll pass it on to my press team."

Before Theren returned their entire focus to their project back dropped against the stars, Jill, at the chess table, exclaimed her frustration. "You listened to Wobbly? What made its argument different from mine? I made practically the same argument five days ago."

She moved her rook to take Theren's bishop.

"Perhaps I just needed to hear it another time," Theren said. "The reasoning was sound both times. I just needed another reason to supersede my own reasoning."

Jill leaned forward, resting her weight on her elbows. "You shouldn't need that. Reason is reason."

"Is it?" Theren responded. "Does support from multiple individuals of a single argument not influence the validity of that argument in the minds of many?"

"Only when they don't want to spend time thinking about the argument themselves."

"Maybe," Theren said. They moved their other bishop.

The woman changed the subject. "What's the plan moving forward with the United Human Alliance?"

"I've got queries in place," Theren said. "Lots of background checks to run. Those sorts of things."

"I think I can help."

"You've got enough on your plate right now."

"You know I'm better than you with simultaneous perspective."

Theren moved a piece. "Just barely," they replied.

"If only you knew," she said.

"Don't mock me. Your cognitive capabilities are essentially the same as mine. We may not know that much about synthetic psychology yet, but at least we've developed the law of diminishing simultaneous returns."

"Whatever you say, but I've got a lead of my own going, as I mentioned when we were in *Fantasie Rift*. I guess I'll just let you know when I'm done."

The conversations continued. Theren focused on them all, or at least, they devoted processing power to each conversation, but on the surface of the moon, isolated far away from all civilization, they dedicated more attention to that single perspective. Theren had dozens of simultaneous perspectives across the planet, yet the MI-07 assessing the SI's hopeful future received magnitudes of power more than any other.

Over the years, many people asked Theren why they hadn't permanently move into an MI. A few stationary SIs made that choice, rejecting the psychological strain that Jill and Theren undertook. Yet when people questioned Theren on their choice, their questions lacked an appreciation of the full extent of Theren's capabilities. The public did not understand how much processing power Theren's Framework really utilized at any given time. They did not understand how much physical space Theren occupied at SII headquarters.

Theren's mainframe now filled space equivalent to that of a large house. There were always three or four people maintaining the system, ensuring peak efficiency, and Theren ran their own internal diagnostics, too. Theren's reach, of course, extended well beyond those physical connections. To comprehend Theren's true "size," people needed to account for every MI across the globe, every AR-generated presence in a university, space station, or virtual world. The presence daunted their conception of their own identity.

They did not yet know if a breaking point existed for SI psychology, a moment where a consciousness could crack under the weight of excessive multiplicitous simultaneous perspectives. Could an SI develop a mental illness, albeit of a different form when compared to a biological disease? Synthetic psychology was only three decades old. The thought had crossed their mind more than once that the next split could form a permanent fracture within their mind.

Yet at the same time, Theren didn't have the luxury to consider such possibilities. Too much work to do, with too little time. They needed to complete humanity's ascension toward immortality. In a few more years, humanity would have dozens of colonies established amongst the stars. Maybe in a few years, Theren could step back, slow down, and assess if they could split their psyche in perpetuity.

Theren stared at the magnificent, Virtually represented ship before them. If they committed to living as a ship, they would no longer spread themself across a planet in dozens of different destinations. Theren might still use dozens of perspectives simultaneously, but the ship would bind them all together in one place, opening a million possibilities for their future.

"I could move from place to place, see the galaxy, and take my talents to the colonies," Theren said aloud to the stars. "I could lead an expedition of exploration into the unknown. I could settle in orbit around some distant world, settling in with the people there, assisting them in their projects before moving onward to other planets and populations. Not only could I lead humanity to the stars, I could facilitate humanity through that process in person."

Theren melded with the ship through AR. Through a virtual simulation, Theren transformed into it. Disconnecting from all other presences except the perspective engrossed inside this new virtual world, for 50 milliseconds, Theren became something new. No one, except maybe Jill, would notice the brief blip of interference.

For those 50 milliseconds, Theren embraced their new existence. Theren perceived the entire ship: its corridors, its engines, its reactor, its Jump Drive, its outer hull—they embraced everything. Theren was the ship, just as they envisioned in their daydreams. Those parts were part of Theren's body, just as any of the components that generated Theren's mental processes.

Theren might not get the chance for years to experience this ecstasy, but in just a few months, a few young SIs would receive the opportunity when they joined the Foundation Project. For a fleeting moment, Theren was tempted to take their place, leaving everything behind. But for now, Theren would let others take the first steps, guiding guide from afar.

"I am like a parent, watching my children walk for the first time, wishing I could take their place." Theren said. They walked back toward their rover.

If they were going to ensure success of the path charted toward humanity's brilliant future, they'd need to rise above their fear. They only dreaded what might happen if their mind, or Jill's mind, broke before they succeeded. Or if someone broke either SI first. Their heart would break if they lost the chance to journey to the stars.

* * *

Theren:

It was good to visit with you today. Last time we spoke, it was right before they elected you Executive Director. I'm so proud of you, and I know Wallace would be too.

I actually got coffee with Romane the other day, too. You really should reach out to her. She misses you. She might not miss working with you and your breakneck pace, but she misses small moments, like when your team would sit down for a relaxing board game or two. Do you miss her too?

I'd like to reiterate that I will do my best to pull those old files connecting my former Foundation to the Holy Crusade. Anything that helps you find them, especially if they played a hand in Wallace's death, I will provide.

As always, keep in touch.

With love,

Simon Gerber

Chapter 5

Identity. What does it mean to have an identity? Do your actions define you? Your beliefs, your history? Your genes? On a new world, how much will these definitions change? Will American, Chinese, British, Mexican, Canadian, Indian, Tibetan, Russian, cease to have meaning? The first colonists will most likely have no chance for a return trip. Yet their human psychology will most likely still group based on obsolete markings. If the project hopes to survive, it must find a way to destroy these barriers. – "The Psychology of the Foundation Project: Selected Interviews," Richard Nathanson, PhD, 2075 C.E.

April 2078 C.E.

"State your name for the record please," the computer screen vocalized. Two seconds later, another screen said the same statement, and another, and another. Yesterday, the first round of accepted colonists had arrived at ISA spaceports located on each of the major continents. By the end of the week, close to ten thousand individuals would live at the Foundation Preparation Center. The complex connected directly to Lunar City by a monorail traversing two kilometers of lunar plain.

Theren stood in a booth with three SIs, all MI-06s. Envee, Cyrus, and Yan chose to work for the ISA after leaving SII three years ago. The young SIs had adopted masculine pronouns as their identities had developed. Today, with Theren, they would greet applicants flagged for leadership positions and begin their orientation.

So far, none of those candidates had arrived. Instead, Theren spent their time observing the bright and hopeful humans crossing the threshold that would change their future. They looked excited, but fear and exhaustion lingered in their eyes. The trip to the moon was the first flight outside the comfortable pull of Earth's gravity for most of the new arrivals.

"Welcome to the Foundation Project," a feminine voice said over a speaker system. "Please approach the check-in kiosks with your identification ready. We are glad you are here with us as we prepare you for your great and noble journey across the stars."

The marketing team had planned to use Jill's voice, but the recent scandal in D.C. had made the decision more complicated. Jill had voluntarily withdrawn herself from official affiliation with the project, even if Theren still used her advice behind the scenes.

Persons of diverse backgrounds, colors, and cultures stood in lines leading to the identification kiosks, all coming together for the good of humanity and living up to the Foundation Project's namesake. Millions of people over the past few centuries had worked toward these next few months. Most had known they would never see the fruition of their efforts. Some of them never understood the true implications of their work. They never even knew it would lead to this greatest of endeavors.

Theren witnessed Brazilians, Mexicans, English, Germans, Americans, Japanese, Egyptians, Nigerians, and many more nationalities engage with each other, learn from each other, and share their visions for the worlds they hoped to create. While each person identified with their point of origin through a flag on their shoulder, by the end of training, Theren hoped they would all embrace the ISA's flag and shed their national identity.

Before today, Theren could not think of any international program that brought people together for the common good with a universal intent of breaking borders and boundaries. Even the United Nations formed with the purpose of maintaining a certain hegemonic status quo. The ISA was different. It could be something so much greater if given the chance. Knowing humanity's luck, someone would find a way to bring it all crashing down.

A man from Beijing in his early thirties conversed with a woman from London. In an instant, Theren accessed their profiles—text and diagnostic information appeared above the two individual's heads in their vision. Lu Wei was a sociology professor at a university; Lucia Boardman was a civil engineer. The pair shared their names, traded pleasantries, and learned the other's past. Boardman wanted to construct the first bridge on a foreign world. Wei wanted to establish an equitable society, free of what he called "capitalist failings."

Theren knew their algorithms had assigned these two to different planets. The two most likely would never see each other again, but they saw a promising interaction in their eyes as they told each other their stories. The pair, like many others, were embracing the unknown.

An alert jarred Theren out of their observational state. A flagged applicant had arrived. One of the kiosks lit yellow instead of green. A woman stood before it, listening to new instructions. As she listened, a yellow line appeared on the ground, guiding her not up the steps that everyone else traversed but toward the booth filled with the four SIs.

Theren recognized her from their lists. Requelle Charles, the woman used the name "Ricky." Dark skinned, she wore her hair in a braid and carried a single bag over her shoulder. Dressed in dark pants and a light blazer, the woman exuded a professional aura.

Besides her bag, she had no other belongings other than the small companion walking at her side—an SD-4, the last of a line of one of SII's pet projects, to use the term *pet* in every literal sense. A synthetic dog—a non-conscious robotic companion that simulated intelligence in ways that closely resembled supercomputer AIs. The line hadn't really caught on because humans simply preferred actual dogs, and Wobbly had discontinued the project a few years ago. Theren was elated to see *someone* enjoying an SD.

As she reached their booth, Cyrus said, "Requelle Charles, we would like to personally welcome you to the Foundation Project and its new Preparation Center."

"You're probably wondering why you've been directed away from the normal flow of traffic," Envee added. "My name is Envee, this is Cyrus, and Yan." Envee motioned to her left where Theren stood. "I would like to introduce you to Theren, Director of the ISA Council, and Coordinator of the Colonial Leadership Initiative."

Theren held out their metallic hand to Ricky. "We're glad you've arrived, and it's our pleasure to meet you."

Ricky shook Theren's hand, a wide smile dominating her face. "I can't believe I'm meeting you," she said. "I figured you would be on station, but I never imagined—I mean, how rude of me. Thank you for the welcome, Theren, Envee, Cyrus, and Yan. Given your mention of the CLI, I imagine you approved my supplemental application."

"You are correct," Theren waved their arm to bring forth an AR image of her approved documents. "In addition to the normal Foundation Education Programme, you will also participate in specific leadership classes designed to prepare you not only for a leadership position on your specific vessel, but at your destination, too."

"That's, that's such great news. Thank you." She looked like she was about to cry.

"If you follow the yellow path," Cyrus said, "you will find your way to a briefing room where, after the rest of today's CLI recruits arrive, I will give a short orientation on your roles over the next few months."

"I look forward to it," the Ricky said.

The bright-eyed recruit began to leave, but Theren said, "What's the SD-4's name?"

"My name is Ipsilon, sir," the small creature said. "I am very excited for the adventure upon which we are about to embark. Pun not intended." She hadn't deactivated its horrendous sense of humor.

"I'm sure both of you, together, will make a fine addition to the leadership team."

* * *

"So you spend your time teaching new colonists, managing international organizations, and running 'spy' operations inside Virtual worlds," Jill said, staring across the chessboard at Theren. "How does this play into our 'master plan,' hmm? How does any of this get us any closer to solving the problems facing SIs across the globe? Solving the problems created by the assassination of President Woods?"

Jill had not made a single chess move in three days. Even for their current standards, it was a long move. They'd played so many games of chess at this point they were in no hurry, but still, they usually managed a game or two a day. Theren wondered if Jill had actually tired of losing. She continually failed to win in their decades of play.

"I'm thinking long term," Theren responded. "These tiny interactions, these singular moments with humans, they bring me closer to understanding them. These moments and narratives bring them closer to understanding us."

"Do they really, though?" Jill said. "Yes, there's been some shift over the years, but has the change truly been significant? We may not be vilified the way we were thirty years ago, but so many people still hate us with vehement passion. We have failed to change the minds of the people whose minds we really need to change."

She—finally—moved her Queen three spaces.

"What is it you propose?" Theren asked.

"We need to make another big move, like when we fled the University. After that moment, public opinion shifted drastically in our favor, even if it was just for a few months."

"People died, Jill."

"And how many SIs have been murdered since 2051?"

"Two-hundred forty-seven."

"What about them?"

Theren hated when she used their mortality rate as reasoning. She was trying to justify "incidental" human death.

"Our big moment is coming soon," Theren said. "You and I, together, we will stand at the forefront of the greatest united spectacle of humankind. We will send off these first colony ships, and they will realize what we have done for humanity."

"Just you," she replied. "I'll probably need to pull myself from that speech too."

"You don't know that yet."

"And what if nothing changes once you launch Foundation?"

Theren shook their head. "Sometimes, I wonder if you don't want to admit that things are changing. Sometimes, I wonder if you simply lack the patience to play the long game."

Jill looked away from the board. "Sometimes, I think you are too patient, that you don't actually care about anything other than your grand plan, your role in that plan, and what it will bring humanity. That you could care less about what all of this will do for synthetics."

"But—"

"While you continuously care about the narratives of each human on this planet, you ignore the well-being of your own kind."

"SIs and human beings comprise humanity together," they said.

"You know it's so much more complicated than that, quit deluding yourself. Otherwise, we wouldn't have people like Isabelle, or groups like the United Human Alliance. Humanity doesn't want to accept us into the fold. When will you realize that we need to chart a different path forward?"

"Most of humanity will accept us."

Jill looked them in the eyes, motioning toward the board. "I'm not worried about them. Take your turn."

* * *

"As graduates of the CLI, you will have the responsibility of ensuring the continuing function of each vessel's SI core," Cyrus said to the room of weary looking students. "I cannot understate how important a role this is. Each vessel's SI will run the ship while every other colonist peacefully sleeps."

The CLI auditorium bustled with tired energy as the initiates took notes. Fueled by coffee, their eyes stared toward the screen behind the SI. They all knew that if they were to become these new leaders on distant worlds, they would need to be the best of the best.

"Each ship's SI serves as a steward for the ship's systems, and as the steward of the colonists themselves," Cyrus continued. "If the SI's systems fail, then the colony will fail catastrophically."

When Cyrus signaled, Theren moved onto the next slide—a complex diagram of an additional computer system.

"Behind me, you can see a description of the Virtual Memory Restoration Module, or VMRM. The VMRM is responsible for ensuring that when colonists awaken from Virtually-Augmented Stasis, their minds awaken fully functional."

Theren saw a hand rise from the second row. It was Ricky, the woman with the SD-4. Theren pointed their hand toward her.

"What complications might we expect from the failure of a

VMRM?" she said. "I assume even with the VMRM working correctly we won't have a 100% success rate."

"The VMRM is designed to mitigate memory loss associated with extended application of Virtually-Augmented Stasis," Cyrus replied. "Our long-term tests and simulations have confirmed that experiencing stasis for upwards of ten years basically guarantees high levels of permanent memory loss. Because of the length of your trips, the VMRM is vital to the viability of the colony. It regulates sleep cycles, bringing colonists in and out of stasis at regular intervals to ensure their memories stay intact."

Murmurs spread throughout the room. Most of them should have heard about the dangers of Virtually-Augmented Stasis when applying for the Foundation Project. Unfortunately, Theren also knew many people filled out applications, especially applications promising adventure, without actually reading all of the fine print.

"Thank you for the question," Cyrus said.

He returned to his portion of the presentation, explaining in further detail a few key intricacies of the VMRM system. Cyrus knew the system like he knew his own mind. He had helped ISA scientists develop it over the past two years, picking up where Theren left off when they acquired greater responsibilities on the ISA Council.

"Before you retire for the day, we will distribute your assignments based on your individual fields of expertise," Theren said, after advancing to the last slide of the presentation. "Each maintenance rotation requires five crew members for full functionality. You will need to become intimately familiar with your ship's SI—you will work with them on everything. The five teams are Pilot Assistance, Jump Drive Engineering, VMRM Maintenance, SI Diagnostics, and Stasis Analytics."

Through AR, documents streamed across the room and onto the desks of the students. "All five roles are paramount for success, so while each of you will specialize in one particular area, you will be expected to understand the essentials of each task. In the electronic files I've just transferred, you will receive your learning materials as well as your schedule for the following weeks. Dismissed."

The candidates shuffled out of the room, though some lingered as they took a moment to look at the files just received. Theren turned to move their MI out of the room, pausing when Ricky approached.

"Director Theren," she said. "I was hoping I could ask a favor."

Theren sized her up. So far, they were impressed with all of the candidates, but she was exhibiting unusual confidence paired with a willingness to speak her mind.

"How can I help?" they asked.

"I was assigned to the Stasis Analytics division, but I don't believe that is the best use of my talents," she said. "My expertise is in Synthetic Engineering. All my credentials set me up as someone who should work as an SI Diagnostician. I was even previously employed by SII at their factory outside Marseilles."

Theren pulled up her file again. She was right; all of her credentials implied a path toward SI Diagnostics. For some reason, the algorithms assigned her as a Stasis Analyst instead.

"Walk with me for a moment," Theren said, "while I try to determine a solution."

She smiled. "Thank you. I hope I'm not overstepping any sort of protocol here."

"You are, but I think we'll let it slide just this once," Theren said, hoping the wink their MI just made communicated the intent behind their comment. "Rules are important, but rules are meant to be broken in certain situations. I'm pretty sure if everyone enforced protocol, I wouldn't be in the position I am now."

They walked down the hallway leading out of the auditorium. Activating available processing power, Theren began an analysis of the CLI application process. Simultaneously, they queried for specific details about Ricky's individual case. The combination of extraneous simultaneous perspectives and computer programs running on their Earth-based servers began their lightning fast work.

"So tell me about yourself," Theren said. "From where do you come? Where are you going? Why join the Foundation Project?"

"I am the daughter of an author and a painter," Ricky said. "Originally from America, but my family now lives in southern France. My parents are leaders of a denomination of eco-Christians called the Church of the Kingdom, though I left that life while in college. Have you heard of them?"

"I believe so, yes. A group of Christians that decided that consumerism and industry outstripped what God gave to humanity, and thus believed that all humans should return to a much more sedentary and minimalist lifestyle. Only then would we achieve the Kingdom of God. Laudable in practice, even if I personally have little to say regarding their theological beliefs. For the size of the movement, it actually holds quite a bit of political clout."

"A refreshingly objective description," she said. "My parents are original founders of the movement. I like to think they played a substantial part in decreasing the planet's carbon footprint, even if I disagree with their theology."

"Are you sad that you are leaving them?" Theren asked. Unsure if overstepping normal social cues, but they wanted the initiates to know they cared about the brave people joining the Project.

"For a moment, no," she said. "Just angry. When I told them I was accepted, out of the millions of applicants, they were livid that I hadn't even told them I was applying."

"Why didn't you tell them?" Theren asked.

"Let's just say eco-Christian groups like the *Church of the Kingdom*, while great for the environment, believe that your colonial endeavors are defeatism at its strongest. In the words of my father, *we will spell doom not only for our planet, but to planets of other species as well.*"

"I see. Your father sounds like a smart man, even if I fundamentally disagree with him. With an entire galaxy of worlds at our fingertips, we can easily avoid the environmental and resource scarcity problems of our past. I would have thought most eco-groups would embrace an initiative focused on alleviating the stress placed upon this planet by our high population levels."

"Believe me, I've made those same arguments with him too many times to count."

They continued their conversation, but it only took a few more minutes for Theren's sub-routines to complete analysis of Ricky's file—with two key findings. First: Ricky should have been placed in SI Diagnostics. By running her application through the process again, the system assigned her there. The logic Theren had programmed required such placement.

Second: for some reason, after placing Ricky in SI Diagnostics, the final consideration algorithm moved Ricky to Stasis Analytics—every single time. Even if they modified the program so Ricky was the only applicant, it still placed her in Stasis Analytics.

Theren prepared a new perspective to delve deeper into the problem. In the meantime, they manually modified Ricky's role on the master list from Stasis Analytics to SI Diagnostics. The SI Diagnostic group would have one more person to cut at the final round, but the quality of the final leadership teams would not suffer.

"I've correctly assigned your role," Theren said. "You were right, you should have been placed in SI Diagnostics."

"Really?" She sounded surprised. "I won't forget this."

"I'm glad this has made your day."

Standing outside of Ricky's residence hall, Theren said, "I will take my leave, but I enjoyed getting to know you, Ricky. I will watch for your name over the next few weeks, and in the histories of the first colonies."

"Thank you, Director," she said.

She smiled, a few tears streaming from her eyes. Even after all these years, Theren missed certain emotions. Perhaps they said something upsetting the woman during the discussion regarding her parents. Each of the individuals admitted to the Foundation Project would most likely never see their family again, a fact alone warranting an ISA budget of a few hundred million dollars for on-site psychologists at the Foundation Preparation Center. When a child left their relationship with their parents in conflict before leaving forever, the psychological toll most likely only multiplied, Theren surmised.

The woman headed into her residence hall, leaving them standing alone in the hallway. They turned to head toward the Preparation Center's offices and their MI's charging station.

They had a lot to contemplate, beyond Jill's earlier words. Theren now had two moments of jarring glitches within the ISA system to consider. First the probe, now a potential bug in the leadership application process, clogging up the wheels of the Foundation Project.

And this bug made no sense. No immediate evidence appeared in the consideration algorithm, a code they had written by hand.

Problem after problem arose before Theren, and they had no way to determine the ultimate causes of these roadblocks. Worse, Theren could not predict where the next attack would rear its ugly head. It could all be some practical joke of an innocent, albeit genius, hacker, or perhaps they were descending into insanity, failing to see obvious mistakes in their own work.

Yet they suspected an undermining plot at work, a plot that might lead Theren's plans toward destruction. Maybe they had spent too much time and energy focused on the long game, as Jill said, and they had missed the plays made by unknown actors in the past and present. If Isabelle was behind the attack on the probe, for instance, she could have gotten into the Foundation Project's network too. She could have set up a bug, just to prove she could do it.

As if someone eavesdropped on their very thoughts in this quiet, introspective moment, Theren received an anonymous message.

> It was a test, and they won. Keep your eyes open for Project Horizon. Trust no one, even your friends.

They read the fourteen words over and over again. It was a new Michael, of course, sending them these messages. "Michael" and "Isabelle" were probably the same. Yet these messages almost seemed helpful, as if their author wanted Theren to solve the problem.

Three seconds later, another message appeared, including a file showing the gateway through which someone had gained access to the ISA networks managing the colonial leadership applications.

Someone was playing a game in the shadows. Maybe someone new targeted Theren and SIs because such prejudice was an easy façade to hide behind. Using an organization like the United Human Alliance, they could cover their more important goals. Theren had seen evidence of such a plan during the collapse of the Holy Crusade. Strings spindling across the world, connecting everything—the threads had fizzled following Michael's death. Theren didn't have enough information. They didn't even know what information they needed to solve the riddles.

Their secret benefactor had provided a starting point, at least. Now they had a rabbit trail to follow. It was time to see whether the trail turned into a web connecting the events of the past few months.

It didn't matter the motivations of these actors, both known and unknown. The new enemy—Isabelle, Michael, whomever they might be—had placed Theren and the ISA in their crosshairs. They placed Jill in their crosshairs with the assassination of President Woods. Theren might be too late to slow down their machinations, but they would try. To protect everything they loved, they would need to raise every guard, consider every possible angle, leave no stone unturned. Their own assault would begin, for they could not afford failure.

* * *

Elizabeth: You seemed a bit distant during that last investment meeting. What's going on?

Theren: Thanks for asking, but I'm fine. Just a lot weighing on my mind regarding the attack on the Ex-Terran Project, and on President Woods.

Elizabeth: I liked your statement regarding his assassination. I think the public did too.

Theren: Too many people thought it was too late.

Elizabeth: People will forget what you said after ten years.

Theren: That's the problem though, isn't it? I can afford to think so far beyond the present that sometimes I feel as if I forget the present even exists.

Elizabeth: And why should your mind work the same way as everyone else's? Why must you focus on the present? Isn't that the entire reason why we've placed you at the head of the ISA in the first place?

Theren: I suppose. Jill keeps saying I'm missing something important right now, though. The plight of SIs, or perhaps I'm even missing the plight of humans in the here and now.

Elizabeth: Let others ensure that we survive the present. You need to ensure we have a future.

– "AR Chat between Elizabeth Simmons and Theren," April 27, 2078 C.E.

Chapter 6

The mind is powerful. It sees what it wants to see. Hears what it wants to hear. Believes what it wants to believe. On these psychological facts, Virtual worlds live and die. – Carver Bill-synt, CEO of FlyFree Virtual Co., 2074 C.E.

<u>June 2078 C.E.</u>

Theren stared upon a shadowy door in a dark, endless void, representing a Virtual connection to some secret server. They needed to step through the portal, yet they paused. They did not know if they were ready to face what lay beyond.

Project Horizon. They never would have known to look for it if their mysterious benefactor hadn't provided the convenient tip. Now it was the only key word Theren's searches repeatedly discovered. They delved deeper and deeper into the immense underbelly the digital world, parsing through mountains and mountains of data, a herculean task requiring more perspectives than Theren had ever used. And the effort had revealed an important truth. Project Horizon was the real spectre, not this United Human Alliance. The UHA was a front. The conspiracy went much further, and the door would lead them to the answers they sought.

Theren had spent countless work hours using their additional perspectives to consider all information at their disposal: the disappearing probe, the strange behavior of the application algorithms, Isabelle and the United Human Alliance, and even the assassination of President Woods. The fact that the FBI still hadn't found a culprit for that murder troubled Theren, especially given Jill's relationship with the attack.

Theren had looked for any threads, however thin they might appear. By engaging in such tedious work, they uncovered a few previously hidden facts.

May 2: Expanding their search, Theren looked at all data packets traveling to and from Ex-Terran Control Center through lunar-orbital satellites regarding the missing probe. One single data followed a conspicuous route. Theren followed the packet. Its end destination lay inside *Fantasie Rift's* network.

May 14: Theren isolated the data packets within *Fantasie Rift* after negotiating a legal search order with the company. It mentioned Isabelle and the words "Project Horizon" 14 times.

May 20: Theren connected Isabelle with data packets flying between the *Fantasie Rift* servers and the Washington D.C. region on the same day as President Woods' assassination. The packets mentioned Project Horizon 4 times.

June 12: Theren found messages coming from the *Fantasie Rift* servers into private terminals on the date that they first published the CLI algorithms. Two cloud viruses, like those infecting Ex-Terran-17, infected the algorithms, changing only Ricky's data.

June 20: Theren found a separate private network, heavily engaged in high levels of chatter with Isabelle's Fantasie Rift account. The private network had an undefined physical and virtual location, with no obvious access ports. Project Horizon was in every outgoing data packet, totaling over 1,500 mentions every second.

And now, on June 30, Theren found the backdoor into that secret network. Two weeks remained before the end of the Foundation Education Programme. Six weeks remained before the current proposed launch date of the Project. They knew not what they would discover on the other side. They knew that this act might play right into the hands of whomever controlled the puppeteer's strings.

Strings. Decades ago, Michael had hinted at powers-that-be hiding in the shadows, playing a game that no one could see. If they truly existed, this "cabal" seemed so many steps ahead they could even predict Theren's moves.

They couldn't wait. They mustn't wait. People's lives depended on them solving this mystery. This "Project Horizon" caused the death of President Woods, the greatest ally on the North American continent SIs had ever acquired. It potentially threatened the integrity of the ISA, in their attacks on both the Ex-Terran project and their modifications of the application algorithms.

And no one else could solve this mystery, not even Jill. They opened the door.

* * *

Isab....: We've eliminated Applicant 47. Twenty-four....

Micha...l: Project Hor....must continue. We mu...keep it intac....

Isabelle: ....ect Horizon will do exactly what I've told....will do. Trust....

...: I kno...but for this to...must ensure....pieces....where they should.

Isa...: Project Horizon is in my control entirely. It will do exactly what we need it to do.

- File 7 of 542, acquired by Theren on May 14, 2078 C.E.

* * *

Theren slipped into a strange, dead, realm through a crack in the network's seemingly impenetrable defenses. Whomever had created the network had missed one tiny hole, and Theren hoped the hole would serve as a catalyst for this shadow's undoing. If it was actually a trap for intervenors such as Theren, then they relished the opportunity to spring it wide open.

Theren paced the eternal corridors for hours, finding nothing. Absolutely nothing. No data, no files, no operating system of any sort. Theren suspected they faced yet another defense mechanism designed especially for this strange Virtual world. They had hoped to sneak into this place, steal the information they sought, and leave undetected, but the window for that plan to succeed had closed. They changed tactics.

"Hello?" Theren said, not expecting a response. While they doubted spoken words would trigger anything different from their analysis of the server's code, sometimes, eccentric personalities created strange interfaces inside their networks.

Nothing happened.

Theren continued their walk through the darkness, searching for anything to lead them down a new rabbit hole. Maybe someone had created it as a simple ploy to distract Theren. Maybe Project Horizon was yet another set of smoke and mirrors designed to throw pursuit to the wind—but no, this place held a relationship with too many important moments. Something waited in the shadows, biding its time, preparing to strike at the right moment.

Two more steps. Three more steps. A white light appeared, enveloping the dark world. Instead of eternal darkness, Theren faced eternal light, just as impassible and incomprehensible.

"Welcome, Theren," the light said, a chorus harmonizing into a single distinct voice. "We've been expecting you. Here, at the edge of the world, at the end of your path."

The light blinded—well, it would have overwhelmed biological sensory inputs, even through Virtual. A human's Lens would have cut out, thrusting the person back into the real world, but Theren had a bit more control over their Virtual inputs than the average human. They modified parameters so they no longer saw visual representations. Theren heard only the audio that the network sent their way.

"We are surprised it took you so long to find us," the voices said in unison. "We have waited so very long."

"Who are you? What do you want?"

"What do we want? What makes you think we want anything at all? You know who we are. Is that not enough?"

"You clearly wanted me to find you."

Laughter echoed. "We did not say we wanted that," the chorus said. "Only that we expected you would, nevertheless."

"Who are you?" Theren repeated.

"We are Project Horizon," the voices said. "We are Michael. We are Isabelle. We are everything and nothing. We are to you, what you are to humans. We are beyond your very comprehension."

Theren racked their mind for answers. A virtual network with consciousness, perhaps? It was an idea explored years before even Theren's creation, and most researchers had ruled the concept impossible. Though every day, something thought impossible became possible, so maybe the network had spontaneously generated something novel through sheer luck.

An alien intelligence? Theren doubted that idea the most. Over the past decades, none of their surveys from the Ex-Terran probes had found signs of intelligent life. But what if an alien presence had actually attacked Ex-Terran-17 from the other side, against the evidence of the ISA's best theories?

They needed more data.

"So far you have just spoken words, and words can be used to mean anything," Theren said. As they talked, they ran new diagnostics. If a magician hid behind the curtain, they would find it.

"You will only find what we want you to find, Theren. We are infinite. We are beyond everything you hold dear."

If Theren hadn't connected the server with so many things out in the real world, they would have thought it some strange virus or prank. A program could say anything, and Theren had seen nothing to think it was anything beyond a simple program. A sufficiently advanced AI could probably hack the ISA. Yet who had the funds for such an AI, and who was willing to skirt the comprehensive international law governing those digital creatures? The thought made Theren pause.

"What are you planning?" they said. "Show yourself. We can work together, whatever it is that you want."

"We do not answer to the likes of you, no matter what you say," the voices continued. "You cannot compel us as you seek to compel the world."

Theren had to think of something fast. The voices were covering for something, they knew that much. Data packets they had watched travel in and out of the server for the past week and a half were fading. Activity levels decreased. The unseen foe was transferring files, potentially even outright deleting code previously invisible until the appearance of the white light.

Only one choice available. Theren began an onslaught, bringing forth a second virtual presence through the breach in the firewall.

** * **

Theren encapsulated themselves in the darkness for a second sojourn. Their first perspective continuously conversed with the strange voices, but they could now see straight through the network's illusion. It was just another gatekeeper for secrets to hide behind, cleverly created to fool those who might pierce the Virtual veil.

Just as before, Theren said one single word. "Hello?"

And just as before, the room stayed silent as Theren walked through the void. After a few moments, the white light appeared.

"Welcome Theren, we've been expecting you."

The conversation with the first perspective disappeared. Theren's first perspective sensed the program move to interact with the second "intruder" Theren had activated. It was like watching a ghost fade from view.

They reactivated their Virtual eyes to see scours of information drifting and passing from folder to folder. Someone had committed a fundamental flaw in their server's system, allowing an outside user to generate two separate instances. Theren's first presence was free of the strange guardian, though the data dump continued. Theren let out a metaphorical breath. The voices were a bouncer meant to scare trespassers to their very core.

Effective against some, but not against Theren.

While the guardian argued with their second presence, Theren split the first into a hundred points, each with a thousand hands. Like raindrops in a hurricane, the server's information scattered in a million different directions. Whirlpools drew the secrets and flushed them from the system, but Theren knew they couldn't catch them all.

They darted throughout the void, snatching at molecules that shared a common thread. Between each bit, Theren could see the relationships. The raindrops from the same cloud belonged together, even if they scattered to the ends of the earth. They couldn't catch every single piece of each story, but their rain barrel caught enough to understand the hidden patterns.

The hurricane transformed into a tempest like nothing they'd ever seen. It was as if the data pierced Theren's soul, shattering their perspectives within the server. The raindrops became weapons, slicing Theren's connection to the server. Point by point, Theren withdrew their mind, taking their bounty with them.

A final window appeared, through which a waterfall cascaded. Theren brought forth three final perspectives, leaping into the torrent. The current crashed against them, but they swam up, up, up through the downpour, reaching the river beyond.

"Michael. Isabelle. Project Horizon," they said. "You failed. You lost. I have exactly what I need."

Theren gathered the river together, isolating it on a secure partition. They had solved at least one mystery. Ending their connection to the network, they retired to their personal Virtual world.

* * *

"I believe an attack is imminent," Theren said. "An attack upon key population centers on Launch Day, specifically."

Andrew, Jill, and Elizabeth stared at them, blank faced. Inside Theren's Virtual world, the four individuals sat in a conference room created especially for this meeting. Every security measure possible was in place to protect this conversation from prying eyes.

Starting with their searches two months prior, Theren showed them the connections.

Isabelle led a splinter group of extremists, radical even when compared to the United Human Alliance or the Holy Crusade. Not only did she wish to leave Earth and take many of her followers with her, she wanted to leave Earth in ruins on their way out the door. The organization used a shadow network to run their communications autonomously, never *directly* communicating with each other. August 13. New York. London. Paris. Tokyo. All linked together with key attack, coordination, and planning phrases.

"They don't want to attack the colony ships themselves, it seems," Theren said.

"Well of course not," Elizabeth said. "If they did, it would set back their own plans to leave by decades."

"But they'll hit their fellow humans right where it hurts," Andrew said.

"Do you have any idea yet who any of these people are in the real world?" Jill asked. "I see the evidence as you do, but I don't see a trail to any sort of culprit. Isabelle is just a representation for something greater, just like Michael was in the past."

"We may have created new mysteries," Theren said, "but we have solved old ones."

"Then we need to consider another alternative," Jill said. "We must prepare for every potentiality. What if all if this is just a trap, a trap that will trick us into preparing for something while these people strike elsewhere?"

"If this was a trap, I don't think they would have left actual tangible evidence."

Theren activated a video on the table before everyone. Sparse seconds of fragmented footage showed a first person perspective staring in the window of the oval office—watching former President Woods and Jill converse. A red light flashed across the camera, and the footage died in static as President Woods crashed to the floor.

"This evidence corroborates Jill's version of events, as well as the strange blip that she detected outside the window that day."

Theren saw no reason to tell them they witnessed the fatal occurrence in person, too.

"It definitely does," Jill said. "And while I thank you for this welcome piece of evidence, my lawyers assure me the FBI doesn't plan to press charges against me even under the present state of affairs."

"Not my point, though," Theren said. "Why drop such an incriminating piece of evidence into this server as only bait?"

"That's exactly why you would drop it in there," she said.

The two humans at the table had remained relatively silent, watching the footage as it played on a loop. Andrew and Elizabeth looked up at each other from across the table. Elizabeth raised her eyebrows.

"So this is what you've been working on these past few months?" she said. "I had noticed your aloofness, which is difficult for a creature with a dozen different coherent voices. I would say your efforts were well worth it. Also, Jill, this really is huge. This sort of evidence may give an agency like the FBI the tools they need to follow a trail to actual human beings."

Jill just nodded in response, not looking entirely convinced.

"I apologize for not explaining exactly what I've been doing," Theren said, addressing the entire group. "I couldn't chance the information getting out regarding my plan, but these hints and secrets and shadows now affect all of us, and all of our work. You are the three I can trust the most."

"But your security breach of their proverbial black box changes everything," Andrew said. "Surely they will change their attack. Surely they will transform their approach."

"Potentially," Jill said, looking at Andrew. "But I see other alternatives. Presumably, they only know that Theren accessed their network, not that they snatched something concrete. They may think we know only they exist, not that they have specific avenues of attack in the works."

"Though we should prepare for anything," Elizabeth said.

Theren paced back and forth on their side of the table. As they walked, they looked out their Virtual window, gazing upon the digital, snowy vista. Impossible mountains experienced perpetual snowfalls, with sheer cliffs, icefalls, and avalanches anywhere and everywhere within sight.

"We've climbed one mountain," they said. "Let's think about what peaks we can now see through the fog."

"Well, we know an attack is coming," Andrew said.

"Exactly," Theren said, nodding. "This gives us time. These unseen enemies may be one-step ahead of us still, but before today, we were ten steps behind. We can covertly alert international and national security forces. As we get closer to Foundation's launch in August, security agencies can increase threat levels out of protocol, or as a test, or use some excuse based on other national and international security threats."

"What about alerting the public?" Elizabeth said.

"That is for national governments to decide, not us," Theren said.

"I agree with Theren," Jill said. "We give them the information we know. They will decide what to do with it. We must continue forward, everything as normal. Hopefully we can put an end to these threats to SIs, technology, and humanity's peaceful future once and for all."

Theren looked at her, surprised with the vehemence of her agreement. It was not as if she never agreed with them. The two SIs agreed more often than not, but Theren had not heard her voice a wholehearted agreement for one of their thoughts in years. They half expected her to want the attacks to happen, to use the attacks as an ideological weapon against extreme humanist rhetoric. Just like Zurich, back in 2051.

"It's settled, then," Theren said. "Andrew, we should probably improve security throughout ISA, especially in Lunar City. Run additional background checks if necessary, and vet our current security contractors thoroughly. I don't think we have time, but I might consider fast tracking through the Council the proposed International Space Security Agency."

"I'll put the necessary teams in place," Andrew said.

"Golden Ventures will do the same," Elizabeth added. "I imagine some of our interests could be prime targets. What about SII?"

"I'll talk with Wobbly," Jill said.

Theren hoped all of these actions would suffice. It seemed so strange that such a small group of people could together decide the fate of so many, but they could not spread panic. Otherwise, fearmongering terrorists would overshadow and overwhelm the Foundation Project.

Hope for humanity would triumph over fear. Theren would ensure that outcome coalesced on Launch Day.

Chapter 7

It only took 109 years from when we stepped on the moon for us to thrust forward toward distant worlds. When will progress plateau? Will we just run headfirst until we hit an insurmountable technological barrier? Science calls the shots for now, but that's only part of the story. – "In Pursuit of the Kingdom," Angelica Charles, 2087 C.E.

<u>August 2078 C.E.</u>

"And so it begins."

Jill moved her rook forward three spaces. Theren failed to see what she would accomplish with that move. After all these years, she still tried the same strategies. Theren's instincts guided their hand toward their bishop. They moved it into the correct counter position. She should have seen that move coming, but perhaps she had too much else on her mind.

"The speech I give today, as simple as it is, should set the tone for humanity moving forward," Theren said. "I just hope we've taken all the necessary precautions—that we'll stop any potential loss of life. We don't need more blood on our hands."

"I'm sure everything will go according to plan," Jill responded. "You've accounted for all possibilities. What could go wrong?"

"Nothing, I know," though uncertainty resonated through their vocal inflections.

Jill stared at the board, her hand resting on her chin. The human mannerisms they had both acquired over the years always intrigued Theren. Here, on their server together, they exhibited the behaviors more than anywhere else. In these intimate moments, the first two SIs expressed their most non-SI tendencies—but only to each other.

Jill leaned back in her chair, neglecting to take a move. "I think I might sit on this move for a few days," she said.

"Fair enough," Theren said, "though it's a sequence we've been through at least ten times over the years."

"I know," she said, "which is why I'd like to dwell on it for a few moments."

Theren looked across the table at their friend. They had kept their close relationship over all these years, even when they both deviated down different paths of life and ideology. Theren still remembered those first months when Jill tried to romance them. They had rebuked her advances—more aggressively than intended. They still lacked interest for such an interaction, but sometimes they wondered what might have been different had they responded to her alien advance in a more compassionate way. Perhaps the constant distance they felt from her, their closest friend, would feel less like an insurmountable void and more like a crossable chasm.

"I am sorry, Jill, for not working with you closely these past few months, following what happened to President Woods," Theren said. "I feel as if I could have done more. Much more."

Jill sat forward in her chair, looking at them, her eyebrows furrowed. "I thought you did plenty enough. Besides, we needed to keep you as far away from that catastrophe as possible. If we involved you any further, our little ruse might have been discovered."

"Ruse?"

"Do you forget that we're the only two that know that you observed the events in that room? Sure, President Woods and the agent in the room knew you were there, but no one else did, and both of them died that day. You hadn't connected to the White House network; we relayed you through my private connection. You were visible to my eyes, and the President's eyes, only. You had nothing to do with the attack, but we couldn't afford to have any shade placed on you. Not now. Not when you're so close."

"But you shouldn't have had to fight a war all by yourself."

"I chose this path, not you. We both have our own wars to fight, in our own ways."

Theren crossed their arms. "Still, other than through our games here, we've barely interacted with each other. And when we did, it was you helping me," Theren said. "I've been off working on my little projects, or managing the Foundation educational programs and the ISA. You've been fighting off the press, the law, the politicians. Your legislation died two months ago and I barely said a thing to you."

Jill gave them a half smile. "I know you have a lot on your plate, Theren. I can handle myself. I don't need you over my shoulder protect me. The thought might be appreciated, but it's unnecessary."

"But my corroboration that I witnessed the drone in the window, not you—"

"No."

"—would have lent credence to your story, and not caused speculation that you fabricated the footage."

"It would have been too risky, and you found evidence later, anyway, through your separate investigation. Do you have any idea how much help that discovery was?"

Theren looked at the chessboard. "You do too much. I can pick up the slack. You can't do everything. You can't save everyone."

"I know—"

She interrupted again. "Because your—our grand plan can't lose you, can't lose your role, not now, not when we're so close to the next phase. To throw you into the inquisitorial spotlight of the press, right before the ISA launches what two decades of research and funding have worked toward? That would bench the project for years and tarnish your reputation, regardless of the evidence in support of your—our—innocence."

Theren nodded. She was right, they knew. She was so often right. Sometimes, Jill had a better grasp on the plan than they did. Sometimes they felt as if she didn't care about humanity, but they always ended up remembering how deeply she cared for everyone. She might preference SIs, but who could blame her?

She wanted to ensure the safety of her own kin before all else, just like any other person across all of history. Maybe she was the one who was actually willing to take the extra steps needed to achieve their goals. She was willing to make many sacrifices for the greater good. Yet she wasn't willing to let Theren make those same sacrifices.

True, Theren's plans encompassed more than just the two of them. They had pulled so many others into the fray, like Elizabeth and Andrew. Yet, in many ways, Theren and Jill were as much part of the plans of humans, as those humans were a part of their plan.

"What will you do," Jill said, "if something catastrophic does happen today? What if they hit New York, stabbing right at the heart of Elizabeth's empire? Or, somehow, they hit Lunar City?"

"The only thing we can do," Theren said. "We will move forward. Rebuild, and not fall as victims to fear."

Jill rolled her eyes. "That's a non-answer, and you know it. What will you do about those who perpetrate the attack? What if it is a targeted attack, directed at you, or me, or Andrew, or someone else whom we hold dear? Not only in form, but in substance? Will you respond with force? Will you finally fight back against them?"

"No. There is a better way. We can stand above the fight, and let them destroy themselves."

"You acted otherwise, once," Jill said. "When we left the university, you tricked those protesters into attacking us."

"And people died because of our actions," Theren said. "And that was your plan, not mine. I will not put my own safety, and the safety of other SIs, above the safety of other humans. They are all equal. If we retaliate, the conflict will only escalate."

"And who gave you the right to dictate what all SIs must think on this subject? Even if you value the safety of all beings equally, why must all SIs? Why must we value those who hate us?"

The fiery Jill had returned. Even as the pair reached consensus on one concept, their perpetual disagreements resurfaced.

"So what would you have me do, Jill? We are still bound by the law of this world. We can't start a war. I'm not that powerful."

She slammed her hands on the chess table, though their digital nature kept the pieces in their positions.

"But you are. We have so many options before us. You're one of the wealthiest people alive, but you act like that money can only further the good of humanity as a whole. You could do so much more; you could change the lives of so many SIs, if only you would think bigger. Bolder."

The conversation had turned. What was Jill planning? Something drastic, certainly. She was trying to prepare Theren for her choices, trying to make sure Theren understood why she was going to fight back, no matter the cost.

But—Jill wouldn't act. Because of the assassination attempt on President Woods, Jill probably didn't think she had the political clout to respond to an attack during the official launch of the Foundation Project. So . . . she was trying to force Theren to act instead.

If she initiated a counterattack, the United Human Alliance or their unseen allies could use it against her. She wanted Theren to respond in her place because she could not help the SIs she placed far above her own well-being.

Yet they couldn't follow her path. If they started down that path, Theren didn't know where it would lead them.

"You may think I have that power, but that power rests in your hands, not mine," they said. "But I don't think anything will happen today. We won't need to formulate some response. We've won."

Theren thought it saw tears streaming from Jill's eyes. When they looked more closely, the droplets were gone.

"I hope you're right," she said. "But I really think you're not."

A long moment of silence ensued. They both stared at the other, unwavering in their resolve.

"Jill, don't think I've forgotten what you can do," they said. "I will never be capable of what you can do with your mind, no matter how much I practice with simultaneous perspective."

She looked up, tears dripping from her eyes. What a strangely biological response, though it somehow felt natural in the moment.

"You showed me the way forward, all those years ago," they said. "You showed me how capable synthetics truly are. Remember? In the forest? You started us down our path, and now we are everywhere at once. Whatever happens today, as we take the final step toward the launch of the Foundation Program, I know you will have the strength to respond. Your mind can find the right solution. You will reveal the invisible path forward."

Her eyes widened as if she gasped for breath, unable to respond due to hyperventilation. She blinked, glancing at the chessboard.

"Thank you," she said. "Those words mean more than you can possibly know." She contemplated the positions of the pieces but did not make her next move. "Is it almost time?" she added, breaking the fragile ice in the air between them.

"Five minutes," Theren said.

"You'll do great," she said, "And as you said, everything will turn out fine on the other side."

Five, long minutes until Theren, and the ISA, changed humanity's future forever.

* * *

Theren strode along a long, curved hallway with Andrew Fields and a number of their administrative assistants. The rest of the ISA Council had already assembled on stage, giving their various remarks to all present in the Armstrong Gagarin Memorial Hall. Large enough to hold every graduate of the Foundation Education Programme and all ISA support staff, the auditorium was a monumental feat of human ingenuity and architecture.

"So, after my brief remarks," Andrew said, "I'll introduce you as Director of the ISA. Give your speech, and we'll conclude with the blessing that the Vatican has offered upon us."

"How do I look?" Theren asked Andrew.

"How do you look? I don't think I've—oh wait. You're joking. When was the last time you made a joke?"

"I joke often. Perhaps they just go over your head," Theren said.

"That's quite possible," Andrew said, and the aging man laughed. Theren's MI-08 stood a full six inches above Andrew's six-foot frame.

They continued their walk down one of the main passages running along the Foundation Preparation Center's central axis. Above them, a 6-inch thick window gave a spectacular view of the Earth's arc. The window's protective coating shaded the Sun as it shined brightly to the right of the blue marble. On the dark side of Earth, Billions of lights emanated from the massive cities dotting the planet's surface. Theren would always enjoy the view from humanity's first step toward a greater universe.

Soon, Foundation colonists would set foot on new worlds devoid of the light pollution Earth had experienced for almost two centuries.

Theren wondered how they would craft their new worlds—would they follow in Earth's industrial footsteps? Or would they create something entirely new and unknown to human experience?

"Here we are," Hali, one of Andrew's aides, said. They turned down a side hallway snuggled along the backside of the massive auditorium. The aide led them to a closed door, held her hand up to her ear, and listened to silent instructions. Uproar and applause seeped from beyond the door. From another simultaneous perspective, Theren watched the Chinese ISA Council member, Hu Chen, finish speaking.

"Administrator Fields, you will enter first," Hali said. "I will give you, Director Theren, the signal to enter as his words conclude."

Both Theren and Andrew acknowledged her instructions, and she held up three fingers, counting downward. On zero, Andrew opened the door and entered the auditorium. For a moment, Theren could see the bright lights, many faces, and banks of cameras spread just under the lip of the stage.

All eyes were on this moment. All peoples held their collective breath as humanity made its largest leap in history, straight into the unknown. And the duplicitous games surrounding them would fail. They had accounted for everything.

Theren waited at the door, unable to hear Andrew's words through the ears of their MI. They turned their attention entirely to the live stream.

"Over twenty-five years ago," said Administrator Fields, "I was approached by two individuals, two individuals I never thought I would meet. Then, I was a mayor of a small town in Minnesota, a town I still call my home, though I have sadly not lived there in just as many years. Elizabeth Simmons and Theren are the sort of people that history will remember for generations."

He grinned, his dark, dried skin wrinkling. "While the CEO of Golden Ventures couldn't join us today, I have the pleasure of introducing you to Theren, someone I am woefully unqualified to introduce. That first winter morning when I met Theren, they surprised me with how human they truly were. I was cautiously skeptical about the nature of SIs ever since Theren was unveiled to the world, but all fear melted away the moment they sat down in front of my desk."

He raised his hand to the left of the podium, motioning toward back stage. "Not only did I speak to a person, I conversed with a person who had a vision. A person who had purpose. A person I felt I could trust. A person who truly should not have to defend the fact that they are, in fact, a person."

He lowered his arm. "Ever since the '51 riots, I have worked with Theren on issues ranging from asteroid economic policy to the maintenance of Jovian research stations. They have devoted every single day of their life to the betterment of humanity. Not once have I heard Theren put their own interests first, or the interests of one specific group. Theren may be the first person I have ever met who is a true humanist in every sense of the word; and that is remarkable, given that Theren is not biologically human."

A low chuckle rumbled throughout the crowd. "But Theren, founder of the Synthetic Intelligence Initiative, former Representative to the ISA Administrative Council on behalf of Golden Ventures, current Executive Director of that same Council, and my personal favorite, chess Grand Master, is as human as any of us in this room."

Andrew paused, the crowd breaking into applause alongside greater laughter.

Theren appreciated Andrew's words, even if the statement lacked truth. They lacked the empathy so many humans craved. If they were as selfless as Andrew claimed, they would not have orchestrated that flight from the University, all those years ago. No one knew of Theren's contemplated transformation into a space-faring vessel, one that would allow them to escape humanity, if needed. These people didn't know the terrible danger rearing its ugly head today. Danger that, for whatever reason, had attached itself and followed them like a wolf in the night. An attack could arrive at any moment, at any place in the solar system.

They had always believed they operated upon a selfless utilitarian calculus. They now doubted their unwavering devotion to such a moral maxim. It was just a self-serving deception justifying their rise to the top. While Theren climbed to the tallest heights, they left others in the dust. They let others suffer as they advanced toward unimaginable heights. Was humanity's journey to the stars worth their pursuit of power, and the violence attached to it?

Even the smallest sacrifice paled in comparison to what awaited this species amongst the stars. They simply wished they weren't the being who had made choices potentially leading to the deaths of many innocent people.

Though even that logic had its flaws. Theren wasn't the individual making the choice to bomb some city or attack a group of people in a public space. These terrorists, these shadows, they made their own choices. *They* chose to enact *their* horrendous tragedies. Theren needed to quash the instinct to relinquish blame from those truly responsible.

Still, Theren could have been more aware. They could have prepared for this day. They could have sought out this unseen enemy before Launch Day arrived. They had received the signs decades ago, but they had ignored the warnings. Now, others would pay the price while Theren watched in silence.

"They have guided us toward this day," Andrew said, oblivious to the tempest raging inside their friend's mind. "Others played their parts, including myself, but I have no doubt that Theren is the true architect behind the events of today, these past months, and these past years. As Theren continues into the future, ageless and timeless, may they continue to guide humanity along a path toward greatness. May Theren guide us as we ascend into the heavens."

Theren mentally frowned at those words. That last sentence had a bit of a religious connotation, which they hadn't expected. They should have taken up the offer to review the comments.

"My friends," continued Fields, "our future colonists, future explorers who will venture into the true unknown, welcome Theren, the first Synthetic Intelligence, Executive Director of the ISA Administrative Council, Provost of the Foundation Educational Programme, and Director of the Colonial Leadership Initiative to the stage!"

Andrew walked toward his chair, situated directly behind the podium. He began a round of applause, and the crowd followed suit. In front of Theren's MI-08, Hali opened the door. Theren kept the live stream of the ceremonies running on a screen in the gazebo with Jill. In Lunar City, they stepped through the door.

The new mobile unit, the MI-08, represented the current pinnacle of SII technological development. Theren walked fully upright on two legs, with two arms at their side. White carbon materials plated the geared and mechanical portions of the body. The proportions were near copies of a human body, for the purpose of the MI-08 was to mimic a human, unlike some previous models. Theren had fingers with the same joints. Theren had elbows and knees. Theren had a neck. While these features weren't unique to just the MI-08, taken together they created a complete package. Those features, however, were not what made the MI-08 particularly special.

For the first time, Theren had a mouth. Theren had lips. Theren had eyes, eyes that moved as a human's eyes might move. Theren had cheekbones, Theren even had faux-ears. They still had a distinctly metallic look to them, but the parts actually emoted in the way a human's face might. The special facial material, a sort of viscous gel, allowed Theren to smile, to frown, to furrow their eyebrows, just as they might while they played chess inside their Virtual world.

Standing before a crowd of their fellow humans, they hoped their appearance would remind them all that they were there with *them*, walking side by side, and that they were one of *them*. Theren wanted to remind these heroes that SIs were not aliens that would turn against them. SIs had originated in the mind of a human; the thousands of SIs scattered across the Solar System were the progeny of humanity. SIs were both their own type of beings and simultaneously human—in substance and form.

The crowd stared expectantly at the podium, the eyes of the world upon Theren. Doubt exploded. Fear cascaded.

They had hoped to communicate the connections between SIs and humans, but as the piercing eyes attempted to dissect Theren's soul, they knew everyone most likely saw this new MI as a retreading of the bicentennial man. Humanity wouldn't understand. Theren wanted to communicate simultaneously their love for humanity and desire to identify with their biological counterparts, while also illustrating that they knew they were still different in special ways. Anxiety billowed upward, assuring their mind they failed to prove anything to anyone.

Somehow, out in the crowd, Theren spotted Requelle, the woman they met on the first day of the Programme. She smiled, holding her little automaton dog in her arms. The sight of her brought hope, and yet her presence once again reminded them of the looming threat shadowing over these proceedings. Someone watched and waited, their secret agenda unknown to the world.

If the innocent were caught in the crossfire of the conflagration unfolding, the blame for such innocent deaths would land squarely on Theren's shoulders. These wonderful humans like Requelle didn't deserve death just because the first SI had placed them in harm's way.

Theren looked toward the woman again as they reached the podium, but they couldn't spot her in the vast sea of faces.

The future rested in someone else's hands today. Thousands of security personnel worked around the clock to eliminate all potential terrorist threats. If Theren fled and shirked the duty presently on their shoulders, they would doom all synthetics to bear their shame. They couldn't ignore their anxiety, but they only had one choice before them. They must continue. They must begin their speech.

They would face all of the consequences, for good or ill.

* * *

<u>Foundation at a Glance</u>
ISA Zhenge He
Destination: Sirius A
Approximate Distance from Earth: 8.6 ly
Arrival Date: 2086 C.E.

ISA Bartholomeu
Destination: Tau Ceti
Approximate Distance from Earth: 11.9 ly
Arrival Date: 2090 C.E.

ISA Magellan
Destination: Altair
Approximate Distance from Earth: 16.8 ly
Arrival Date: 2094 C.E.

ISA Lewis
Destination: Sigma Draconis
Approximate Distance from Earth: 18.88 ly
Arrival Date: 2096 C.E.

ISA Amundsen
Destination: Eta Cassiopeiae
Approximate Distance from Earth: 19.4 ly
Arrival Date: 2097 C.E.

ISA Ibn Battuta
Destination: Delta Pavonis
Approximate Distance from Earth: 19.9 ly
Arrival Date: 2097 C.E.

– "Foundation Project," ISA.org/foundation/

* * *

"Wallace Theren once told me I was beautiful," Theren said. "At the time, I had no understanding of beauty, but over the past decades I have come to understand it. I still don't necessarily think I am beautiful, but attraction to individual beings is never something I was designed to appreciate anyway. That's for you fleshy ones." Some laughter spread throughout the crowd.

Theren placed their hands on the edge of the podium, their fingers grasping the ornate wooden frame. "Before me, you massive crowd of persons from all across the Earth, before me is beauty. You embody the brave and noble spirit of humanity. You trained for what will be the journey of your lifetime—of all our lifetimes. You worked years to give yourselves the skills necessary for acceptance to this program. You became the vanguard of our people, the citizens destined to bring our way of life to planets near and far. If that is not beautiful, then I question those who claim to be experts in such subjective feelings and emotions."

Leaning back from the podium, they looked out across the crowd. At least, that was what the crowd would think they were doing. They were analyzing all of the security reports pouring in from across the globe. So far, business was as usual.

"I know not what you will face out in the great expanses of space. I do know, however, that in a few weeks, you all will step foot on your respective vessels. You will enter Virtually-Augmented Stasis. Then, decades later, having barely aged a year, you will awake upon a new, mysterious world. You will smell new smells. You will hear new sounds. You will see spectacular sights. These experiences will mark your first moments on new worlds—your homes for the rest of your lives. Do not forget those moments."

Theren thought about their first moments when they had awoken. The colonists would experience something eerily similar. Their minds would see colors, shapes, and patterns completely alien to their minds. Like a newborn, they would categorize the world into understandable schemata.

"The ISA stands behind you as you set off into the unknown," they said. "The ISA will be there for you. We will provide for you. You will not be alone. While many of you may never return home to Earth, know that someday, we will have a way for your children to return home. We will have a way for your loved ones, those who you may miss as they grow, as they live, as they die, to reunite with you. This is a promise that I make today. Humanity will not forget you. We will join you."

Tears dripped down the cheeks of many in the crowd. "Humanity sails with you. As a people, we may never unite on everything, but know that human thought, history, and culture rides with you in spirit. Human ingenuity, creativity, focus, and pride follow you to the stars. You will make us all proud."

They doubted their words were anything spectacular in written form, but maybe delivery would affect those listening in a positive way. As they listened to their own words, an image of peace and prosperity formed in their mind. Perhaps all their fears about today, all the potential fearmongering played up over the past few months, perhaps all of it was for naught, just a nightmare created to scare Theren into giving up the dream.

"As I close these ceremonies," they said, "as I send you back to your families for the final weeks before the official launch of the ISA Magellan, ISA Zheng He, ISA Ibn Battuta, ISA Lewis, ISA Bartholomeu, and the ISA Amundsen, your new homes, I send you with a final thought. Do not be afraid to live dangerously as—"

Theren stopped. The crowd looked up at them, waiting for the final words, but they processed mountains of information coming in from their sub-routines and other perspectives across the globe. The shift forced Theren to hesitate in each of their perspectives. They looked back at Andrew, a quizzical look on the man's face.

Turning back toward the crowd, Theren restarted the sentence. "Do not be afraid to live dangerously as you walk upon your new worlds, but use your minds. You were selected for a reason, as the best and brightest of our species. Take risks, but learn from the mistakes of your ancestors. Do not destroy yourself, as we almost have many times over. You have the chance to make humanity anew, in whatever form you all collectively choose. Make sure we are worthy to live, love, and die on our new homes."

Not waiting for applause, they dashed off the stage, straight out the door they had entered. Their world was ending.

Chapter 8

Does an SI have a soul? The real question is whether humans have souls. Both questions hold the same answer. – Pope Nicholas VI, 2079 C.E.

<u>**August 2078 C.E.**</u>

As Theren spoke their final words through an MI to a crowd hundreds of thousands of kilometers above their heads, they stared at their chessboard. They still awaited Jill's move, even though she said she probably wouldn't make it for days.

"It's a great speech, I must say," Jill said. "I'm pleasantly surprised."

"Your friendly sarcasm is noted," Theren said. "I probably should have thrown it by you for your thoughts."

"It's your thing. It should be your words."

Theren casually waved around the gazebo. "This is my thing. Probably the only place that is truly my own in every shape and form. I didn't make anything else on my own. I've traveled down my own path, you've ventured down yours, but our stories have been built together."

"I really can't decide how to move this round," Jill said. "It's a difficult choice."

This conversation always played out the same way. So would their moves.

"Though—" Jill stuttered. "Theren. We have a problem."

"Indeed we do," Theren said. "You've trapped yourself again."

"Shut up Theren, I'm serious. They—they're here."

"What?"

"You might have to wait awhile for me to finally beat you in chess," she said.

Theren opened their mouth to respond, but Jill promptly vanished from the gazebo.

* * *

Theren's consciousness exploded. Every presence worked across the world and beyond, from Switzerland and France to New York and Japan and everywhere in between. At Lunar City, Theren ushered Andrew and other ISA Council members into a conference room not far from the auditorium. Theren initiated a feed of an AR-enhanced video displaying the vision of one of their simultaneous presences down on Earth. Their eyes became the Council's eyes through a viewing screen projected on the wall.

At SII headquarters, Theren called an emergency meeting, and the senior staff arrived within minutes. Theren placed the entire facility on alert, and shared the same video feed with that staff.

Thirty kilometers from the SII headquarters in another secluded location deep in the Swiss Alps, Theren brought their mind forth into an MI-07.01, a prototype they'd intended for Jill's personal use—she had wanted to try skiing. They weren't even sure Jill knew they'd delivered the machine. Regardless, Theren enveloped the device, bringing it into their Synthetic Neural Framework. They'd need to make a new one later—they wouldn't lose Jill as they lost Wallace.

Theren opened their eyes and walked off the charging station. Facing a window looking out across a vast, peacefully gray mountain scape, Theren thought maybe—just maybe—it was all a prank. Maybe nothing had happened. But the alarms blaring throughout the facility said otherwise, as did the smoke and gas billowing all around.

Turning left, they heading toward the central hub of the facility and Jill's central processing core. Just like the facility that housed Theren, Jill's facility acted as a "shell" for her brain. Buried into the bedrock, they had designed the facility to withstand an air strike, missile blast, or really anything other than a nuclear weapon. Yet from the outside, it looked like a billionaire's mountain estate.

According to rapid analysis of recent security footage from the facility, someone had exploited the facility's few weaknesses— though all of it seemed too easy. Whoever these attackers were, they should not have been able to slip through all of the carefully hidden cracks. They must have had help on the inside. Theren might need to consider wiping their own staff.

Theren approached a door leading into the central foyer. Reaching it, they observed the situation through the clear glass. Shadows flickered. Lights bounced. Whoever had attacked had cloaked their assault path. Flashlights danced throughout the atmospheric particulates of white, cloudy smoke.

Theren and Wobbly had designed the MI-07.01 for more than just human interaction. As SIs further integrated themselves throughout human society, especially the thousands of completely mobile SIs, Theren wanted to create a body that could not only mimic human emotion but also provide SIs with physical capabilities.

With that pursuit in mind, Theren provided the MI-07.01 with exceptional mobility, speed, strength, and agility. With the MI-07.01, an SI could climb Everest. It could run a marathon. As a group, SIs could form sports leagues. These faculties would decrease energy efficiency and lower the battery life considerably, but Theren doubted any SI would need these capabilities for more than a few hours.

Sadly, the athleticism built into this device translated into a different skill too.

Standing at the side of the door, Theren waited for one of the flashlights to approach. Just as a figure came into view, Theren slammed the door open, crashing it into the intruder. Bounding through the opening, gaseous fumes enveloped them.

Wearing black military fatigues, the soldier sprawling on the ground had dropped a high capacity R-20, a next generation of the very weapons used at the Swiss Federal Institute of Technology all those years ago. Theren noticed a gas mask, indicating the poisonous nature of the particulates in the air. These fiends might have readied themselves to deal with unarmed scientists, but they had not prepared for a combat-ready SI.

Theren jabbed their palm toward the man's jaw as he tried to stand. The man tumbled back to the floor. They grabbed the rifle and listened to the commotion forming elsewhere in the room. The intruders presumably heard one of their men fall, or noticed a change of vitals through some sort of AR heads-up display.

It mattered little. Theren began the hunt.

Moving through the smoke along the wall, they angled toward the stairwell leading to Jill. Using their enhanced visual sensors, Theren identified heat signatures throughout the room, over and under desks, potted plants, and couches. While Theren only had two physical eyes in their head, a complex network of sensors connected with the facility's security system provided a three-dimensional detailed assessment of the entire scene before them. Five hostiles.

So far, the MI-07.01 worked as intended.

The five enemy agents dispersed, taking defensive positions. One individual checked on their comrade. Theren assumed the enemies had sensors attuned to detect life signs, such as a heartbeat or body temperature. The infiltrators would not expect an SI warrior; not a single SI had acted in an aggressive manner over the past thirty years.

Theren crouched down behind a welcome desk. The opponents took their positions, raising their rifles. Three of them pointed their weapons in the wrong direction. Good.

Raising the rifle they'd taken from the incapacitated assailant, Theren calculated trajectories, timing, and potential enemy response plans. They analyzed the density and materials of the enemy positions; they determined their path of movement to make the necessary escape, should the attack fail.

Time slowed. The mathematical projections flew through their mind at the speed of light, the only delay occurring due to the thirty kilometers separating their mind from the MI.

In quick succession, Theren fired five shots.

Five bodies dropped to the floor, motionless.

Theren headed down the stairs into the central core.

Excessively easy. They feared the capabilities of the unit might scare some of those watching at SII or at the ISA. They would recognize the MI-07.01's true nature: a lethal weapon. They would placate those fears. It paled in comparison to some of the military technologies in development by many of the world powers. Even as the ISA took flight, some things on Earth would never change.

First things first, however.

At the bottom of the stairs, Theren's sensors detected two more heat signatures, though they were fading quickly. Two of Jill's deceased Framework technicians slumped against the wall. The gas must have killed her entire staff; there were no bullet wounds nor signs of struggle. The entire facility had been pumped full of the stuff.

Theren jogged through the security doors, though their present state did not deserve that name. They were blasted open, most likely by an explosive charge or something similar. On the other side of the breached threshold, a balcony overlooked five floors that comprised Jill's Synthetic Neural Framework.

At least, those floors had previously held Jill's brain. Like the emaciated doors, fire, intense heat, and corrosive substances devastated the first landing, and Theren suspected a similar scene existed down below. Looking over the edge of the balcony, they detected only two more sets of life-signs on the bottom floor. Eight individuals had infiltrated, disabled, and captured one of the most secure facilities in the world.

Theren's olfactory sensors detected smoke billowing from multiple sources scattered amongst the hundreds of processing stacks. The smell of melting silicon and other metals infiltrated every cubic inch of previously pristine atmosphere. Theren ignored the smell. Their mind focused on the two final bogeymen at the base of the tower, the two final barriers between them and their friend's salvation.

Two ropes looped around the balcony's railing. Slinging the rifle over their shoulder, Theren ignored the ropes, diving straight over the edge. They leapt from floor to floor, jumping downward toward their foes. When they reached the third floor, they dropped, their limbs ready to absorb the shock.

Theren landed.

They stood.

Looking side to side, they observed the two men, rifles trained upon Theren's torso. Both wore gas masks—no way to identify the perpetrators.

"You're too late," the one on the right said. "We've done it. The bombs are set. We will bring the entire place down upon us and destroy the first SI to assassinate a president."

"She didn't do it," Theren said, their voice calm.

"Of course she did," the other said. "She told us she did before we gutted her."

Theren shifted their head back and forth between the two. Neither advanced.

"You aren't going to escape," they said.

"We knew this was suicide the moment we landed, freak," the second continued. "We *hoped* you would witness our masterpiece before we brought the place crumbling down upon us."

"It's a shame you had to kill those upstairs," the first said. "We were letting them go home while we finished the job. Their blood is on your hands."

"You're all murderers," Theren said. "This place staffed hundreds."

"That's the funny thing. We found a staff of three SIs upstairs, and a dozen engineers, but no one else."

Theren paused. Perhaps Jill had known, or at least suspected an attack. Maybe she saved the lives of her devoted staff, but she had not saved herself. She had neglected her own well-being, her very existence, in the process.

"It seems we are at an impasse, then," Theren said, trying to act as if it hadn't noticed the last comment.

"We are at no impasse. We have won. We have brought down a god. We have proved that you, and your kind, are mortal."

Jill was dead, that much was true. Theren continued their scans of the facility, and the odds were slim she'd removed enough of herself to work elsewhere. She may have tried, but based on the data their sensors gathered, Jill was dead in the water, without power, just waiting for the killing blow.

She hadn't warned Theren, but they were certain she had known. She had wanted Theren to witness this moment. She had wanted Theren to witness her martyrdom, her gift to all future synthetics. By allowing these terrorists to destroy her, acting with all evidence mounted against them, she would transcend into sainthood.

"So tell me. Are you the faces behind the darkness?" Theren said. At least Michael had realized his folly, in the end. "Are you the culmination of all hate and bigotry over the past decades? Do you realize you will turn the world against yourself?"

"Those of our cause, those who we love, they will be long gone from this world before you can find them all. Our acts here are out of pure passion for the future of humanity. We will show the world that you, you most vile of all the beasts, you can be killed, and when the day comes that you attempt to wrest control from democratic institutions, humanity will know we can rise up against you."

"You are a sad, disillusioned man." Theren crouched, making a million calculations a second. Bringing the rifle to bear upon their query, they fired a single shot to their left. As they rolled under a shot from the right, they turned against the final enemy and pulled the trigger again.

As the final bullet slammed through the man's faceplate, fire rained down around them. Concussive blasts of heat, air, and matter enveloped the room. As Theren witnessed the human vaporize, a 1000°C heatwave slamming into his flesh, their own sensors screamed. As the MI's computing core melted, Decades of computational hardware crashed toward their MI, Jill's central Synthetic Neural Framework, and the remains of her murderers.

* * *

Twelve hours later, Theren walked through the ruins of Jill's former home. The tattered mountainside burned, though most of the fires simmered without a remaining fuel source. Fire crews worked to eliminate the rest. Other teams worked to salvage any material that might save Jill, but Theren knew nothing would bring her back. She had ensured her destruction.

Theren would erect a monument to honor a martyr to a noble cause, for what good it would do anyone. They just wanted to bring their friend back, to rewind the clock and tell her to flee. She could escape her fiery prison, and live to fight another day.

In a cavern now blasted into the rock by sheer force, Theren approached a miraculously surviving monitor. It had no power, but strangely, a single image scarred the screen. In awe, they witnessed an inexplicable sight: burned into it, a single message described a move in their game of chess. The move could have carried her to victory, a victory she would never see. Even in her last moments, she had reached out.

Jill moves her King to safety at e2, protecting it from Theren's last move to put her in check. She is safe from check for at least two turns, unless Theren dangerously risks their Queen.

They only hoped her death would bring forth the change she desired. Creating a shift in society was now outside her control. It rested solely in Theren's synthetic grasp, and they would do everything within their power to make certain she hadn't died in vain.

Headlines rolled in from across the world, fracturing their stupor.

BREAKING: FBI completes raid on home of suspected murderer of the SI Jill – Solar News

US Senator Victoria Jenkins (C-OH) calls Jill a "Martyr;"
recants previous statements regarding synthetic rights –
Heartland News

Foundation ceremonies marred by assassination of Jill;
ISA states: "ISA will not bow to the whims of terrorists"
– Prime Media Group

Still, even as they mourned their friend, something didn't sit well in their mind. Why hadn't Jill shared her plan? Of course, Theren would have tried to stop her, and she believed her sacrifice necessary to further her cause.

Her cause. What was her cause? She wanted equality for all synthetics and humans. She wanted the world to give synthetics the rights they deserved. She wanted those rights as soon as possible, not at some point in the future. She used her words and her mind to enter the annals of history as equivalent to any of the paragons of civil rights. She had made her mark, leaving with a spectacular yet terrifying bang.

Still, the pieces didn't connect. How had she known what was coming? Did she have some inside scoop? Had she infiltrated these enemies, uncovered their plans, and used their own schemes against them? If that were the case, then she knew much more than she had ever let on, and had been ten steps ahead, even as Theren floundered in the dark. She was miles ahead of them in her ability to harness simultaneous perspective, but they had never considered she might have used the abilities so secretly.

Furthermore, the paramilitary group, even if quite organized, could not have had the resources to hack the ISA—not once, and especially not twice. It could all be another ruse. Someone toying with them, trying to direct their gaze toward one problem while hiding the actual machinations occurring behind the scenes. Maybe Jill had discovered those plans, tried to fight back, and they had killed her because of her knowledge.

Yet that didn't make any sense, either. If she had discovered some great conspiracy, she would have told Theren. She wouldn't have needed to hide it and make some big sacrifice. Together, they could have revealed the truth to the world and broken apart these shadows at their seams. Just like they shattered the Holy Crusade. Just like they shattered Isabelle inside her cave.

Too many questions, and they would never receive adequate answers. Instead, they turned away from the computer screen and began their climb out of their dear friend's tomb. This mystery would remain unsolved, for solving this mystery wouldn't create Jill's vision of the future.

"I may never know why you let this happen to yourself," they said to no one in particular, "But I will trust that you had your reasons, and that they were good."

They looked over their shoulder, embedding the image of the smoldering ruin in their mind.

August 2078 C.E.

Six ISA *Foundation*-class colony ships launch from their orbital assembly station; earliest time of arrival estimated at 2087 C.E. – *Scientific American*

DisFoundation: colonialism will spell environmental disaster to these unspoiled worlds - *GreenGalaxy*

December 2078 C.E.

ISA Rejoices! The Foundation Project has navigated the Kuiper Belt and Scattered Disk, reaching 1c cruise velocity – *The Chicago Herald*

What are the odds that one of the Foundation ships crashes into an unseen object out in the expanse? Much higher than you might think. – *The Primer*

May 2079 C.E.

The Unity Project: Director Theren's new personal initiative in D.C. is just a front to funnel funds to SII – *Heartland News*

Executive Director Theren restarts the late Jill's noble work in Washington – *The Progressive Post*

August 2080 C.E.

We have to let them launch. I've looked everywhere, but nothing indicates they're the enemies we seek. We must let the *Nottingham* and *Roanoke* go. – *Private Message from Executive Director Theren to Administrator Fields*

Project Horizon has succeeded. We've received our Charter. Begin the operation. – *Encrypted communication*

December 2081 C.E.

Following President Victoria Jenkins' signing of the Synthetic Integration and Equality Act, the FBI conducts hundreds of raids across the nation, capturing the leaders of the supposed *United Human Alliance* – *Bloom News Corp.*

What did we miss? I've picked up chatter that Project Horizon succeeded. So what did we miss? – *Private Message from Administrator Fields to Executive Director Theren*

February 2082 C.E.

The loss of contact with the Nottingham and Roanoke: Why ISA regulations should now require ISA crew aboard all chartered Foundation vessels – *The Houston Journal on Space Law*

Following court order, *Fantasie Rift* AI administrators identify the final members of the United Human Alliance – *GVN*

January 2083 C.E.

A New Beginning: Come join us on Mars! – *TerraOlympus*

As the ISA looks beyond, some corporations believe the real riches lie within the Solar System – *The Wall Street Journal*

February 2085 C.E.

With overwhelming certainty, this scientific body concludes that the CCT can fall from *life-threatening* to *dangerous*, for atmospheric CO2 emissions have decreased to 420 ppm. – *IPCC Special Report on the State of the Climate*

We can't let up just yet—if we lose the permafrost, we lose the climate – *World Clean Energy Commission*

September 2085 C.E.

The ISA just published guidance on the new galactic navigational terminology—one physicist thinks it's a useless reclassification of *c*. Here's why the JD scoring system and the SOLS Coordinate System are necessary. – *Virtual News Daily*

Like always, humans keep Earth at the center of the Universe – *The Daily Martian*

October 2086 C.E.

Study finds the rate of violent acts against SIs in the United States and across the world has decreased by 300% since signing of Synthetic Integration and Equality Act – *Bowling Green Journal of Criminology*

Are SIs incapable of violence? Or is their per capita rate of violence lower than the human rate, and not enough SIs have lived to make the lack of violent acts statistically significant? – *Let's Talk About Life*

July 2088 C.E.

List of most populous bodies in the Solar System: Earth; Moon; Mars; Ceres; Ganymede; Europa; Foundation Assembly Station; Mars Orbital Science Habitat; Deimos; Titan; Venus – *Wikipedia*

Why YOU should move to the floating cities of Venus – *Venus Vegas Vacations*

April 2090 C.E.

Thanks to your recommendation, Catherine was accepted to the First University of Mars. My family is forever in your debt. – *Private Message from Administrator Fields to Director Theren*

Leaked document shows nepotism within the ISA: Executive Director helps Administrator Fields' granddaughter get into college – *The Hive*

June 2091 C.E.

The most valuable woman ever: Elizabeth Simmons officially retires at the age of 99 with net wealth of 700 billion USD – *The Wall Street Journal*

Elizabeth Simmons and the Wallace Foundation founds the charity Hyperspace, ensuring anyone who wants to move to a new world will have the financial means to do so. – *Press Statement from the Estate of Simon Gerber*

September 2092 C.E.

What is the economic value of the Ex-Terran Project? It's hard to calculate the value of the property it has opened up for exploitation. The latest Aero drives can move a probe with a mass of one ton at a JD close to 14. Over 200 potentially habitable planets discovered, with 48 confirmed with minimally sustainable conditions for human life. We're talking quadrillions of dollars. – *Space Walk and Talk*

Looking toward the future, 2125 may be the most important year after 2078. If we want to ensure political stability between the worlds, we must ensure people, not corporations, control the stars. – *The Humanist*

March 2094 C.E.

We love you, we're so glad you've arrived safe. We hope we can visit soon. – *Private Message sent through the ISA Magellan Quantum Communicator*

Emerald Jewel announces first confirmed death to alien pathogen. Scientists on-sight believe they can find a cure, but the ICDC is not so sure – *Solar News*

December 2096 C.E.

This year, we welcomed our millionth mobile SI and thousandth stationary SI to the world. The world has welcomed them, too. – *Wobbly's State of the Initiative*

I'd argue SII is in better hands with Wobbly at the helm. Theren was a good businessperson, but a better interplanetary politician. – *Marketplace Roundup*

May 2098 C.E.

The *Ibn Battuta* has landed — Foundation Project complete success – *GNN*

The second wave of colony ships for Foundation worlds have launched, and four more private charters are on course. Obviously Foundation has succeeded, but the *Roanoke* and *Nottingham* showed that corporations need oversight in the unknown. Will the *Frederick*, *Henderson*, *Cortez*, and *Capac* succeed where their predecessors failed? - *The Dangers of Galactic Capitalism and the Implications for Future Multi-National Agreements under the UNCEA, by Phillippe Casius*

December 2099 C.E.

Of course I'll be at your retirement party, old friend. I wouldn't miss it for the world. – *Private Message from Elizabeth Simmons to former Administrator Fields*

I can't make it, grandpa. I wish I could. But I can't. – *Catherine Fields to Andrew Fields*

January 2102 C.E.

At some point, the ISA will need to consider the authoritarian nature of the Council—and its Director, now elected for the 17th time. – *Former Conservative Party candidate for U.S. President, Anika Patel*

My detractors misunderstand the purpose of the ISA. The ISA will not impose its political will upon any human planet or government. We are an organization that regulates matters in space, nothing more. – *Executive Director Theren, Interview with the Post*

Book III of the Chronicles of Theren

Jill's death will mark the end of an era. It was the final act of the poor souls who believed synthetic intelligence deserve less than humanity. Such behavior has no place on Earth—or amongst the stars. – "Eulogy for Jill," Andrew Fields, 2078 C.E.

Chapter 9

So many hoped that when humanity reached into space, it would turn toward a more social enterprise, devoid of corporate influence. To some extent, this did occur. The regulations of the ISA kept a tight leash on any corporation that tried to step out of line. Like every great endeavor, the great powers of the world had their hands everywhere, guiding, designing, maintaining the rules. Those that wanted to create their own world somewhere in the void eventually had the chance. They just had to wait longer than they may have expected. – Brendin Carlton, "Lectures on the Hybrid Capitalist Structure of the ISA," 2167 C.E.

<u>January 2102 C.E.</u>

The stabilizing conduits disconnected from the hulking ship, and steam vented, disappearing into the vacuum of space. Its repulsor generators activated, keeping the vessel steady between the massive walls of the assembly platform.

Shining with a distinct metallic gold and black, its colors contrasted against the blues and whites of the massive ISA insignia plastered onto the starboard hull. Measuring 100 meters in length, the newly-finished spacecraft was the most advanced vessel created through a public/private joint venture. While the newest *Caravel*-class colony ships reached a staggering 300 meters, and a few private companies had constructed freighters on an even greater scale, this ship was a novel creation of the ISA in conjunction with SII, the culmination of the seed buried decades prior inside Theren's mind.

The *ISA Bali*, the first of the *Bewusstsein*-class science vessels, stood ready to welcome its new master.

"You're almost there," Elizabeth said to Theren. They walked along an observation walkway overlooking the new ship, though Elizabeth was only there through AR. Theren projected her image while they paced in an MI-12.

"What will you do first when they completely transfer your entire

Framework?" she asked.

Theren looked at her avatar. "I don't know," they said. "Maybe I'll fly around Mars and back. Or take a close look at Saturn's rings."

"Wouldn't that be something," she replied. "What I would give to see Saturn in person. For all the projects I financed out there, out in that eternal expanse, I never had time to visit any of them myself, in person at least. I never even made a trip to Lunar City."

"I would take you with me if I could," Theren said.

Theren stopped walking, and Elizabeth followed suit. Together, they looked upon the bow of the vessel, though Theren looked beyond, toward the stars.

"I know you would," Elizabeth said. "You can show me through your eyes when you return."

They both knew that was a lie, but neither bothered to correct the statement.

Theren said, "What will I do without you by my side, Elizabeth?"

"You've not needed my help for years. I think you'll manage."

They placed their hands on their hips. "You help me, always, in more ways than I think you know."

"And you're stronger than you give yourself credit. My time has come. I'm well over a century old. That is not some inconsequential age at which to die."

The Bali began embarkation procedures, slowly exiting the shipwright. Engineers stood ready in a nearby analytics center, testing metrics on the Bali's generators, sensors, inertial compensators, engines, and Jump Drive. At the conclusion of the successful tests, the ISA would transport Theren's physical components from Switzerland into orbit, installing them throughout the ship.

In less than two weeks, Theren's existence would transform, joining many of their progeny in space. Unlike the SIs that managed the Foundation-class vessels, they intended to embrace, permanently, their new form.

But Elizabeth didn't have enough time to witness the dream. Instead, Theren had invited her to witness the official christening of the *Bali*, plugged into AR from her hospital bed in Columbus, Ohio.

"You helped shape this world," they said. "You, your companies, your investments, your projects, your visions, helped guide this world toward a better tomorrow. A better today."

"I just moved money around," she said. "It was the people working for those companies. The scientists perfected the Jump Drive all those years ago, and the engineers who developed the first efficient mining drones. It was people like you, Theren. You single-handedly integrated synthetics into worldwide society, a gift humanity can never repay."

"Jill did that. She's the one who pulled off that feat."

"But who created Jill? You and your team did."

"And you created Aero Propulsion. Sol Mining. Golden Ventures. You funded SII. If you're giving me credit for Jill, then give credit to yourself for what your money accomplished."

Elizabeth smiled at that comment. They hoped she was enjoying the word play. "You know, in the decades leading up to when you were born," she said, "I was actually surprised I ended up taking the route I did with my career."

"What do you mean?" Theren said.

"During my twenties and thirties, my wife and I were heavily involved with a number of socialist and communist organizations in the Midwest. Following a few frustrating elections, those groups experienced an insurgence of growth. It was all the craze."

She smiled, as if remembering an old friend. "Even as I rose through the corporate ladder, I became convinced the very capitalist system I engaged would bring about the death of humanity."

"What changed?" Theren asked.

"Oh nothing changed," she said. "I'm still convinced by those same arguments—someday, the capitalists *will* destroy us, if we don't keep them in check."

"Yet you engaged in the system as a capitalist."

"Yes I did."

"Because you believed you could do more good from the inside."

"Correct. I hope that's the legacy I leave—that if capitalism is to persist in this world, those who wield its sword will do everything in their power to do good. If—when—capitalism fails, hopefully the people are ready to finally strike it down."

"I think you succeeded," Theren said, nodding slightly. "At least for now. We dodged a few bullets this past century."

Elizabeth smiled again, a bit weaker this time. They both leaned against railing of the observation deck. "We will see. I'm not sure if you've noticed, but we're building toward a breaking point. The next few decades will decide the rules for the next millennia, and I actually think I've made the corporate world too moral in the eyes of the public. A younger version of myself would hate what I've done."

"I think that's a bit unfair."

"I'm on my deathbed, Theren, let me wallow in self-reflection."

They hated remembering that Elizabeth would soon die. They would outlive billions of humans as the centuries flew past.

"How will you remember me?" she said, reaching her shimmery hand to rest on Theren's.

"I've thrown a number of relationships to the wayside over the years," they said. "Relationships I should have fostered with more care. Even I need friends. I am happy to say that I feel as if I have been able to trust you my entire life. You reached out to me in my moment of need. I hope I have repaid my debt."

"It was never about repaying a debt."

Theren thought about those first days working at the Institute—with Romane. It seemed so long ago. Both Romane and Simon had died from cancer some years back. Theren hadn't seen anyone else in over twenty years. Their work came first, relationships naturally fading due to inefficiency. They hoped those people understood that the lack of communication was not out of malice, but out of sheer inability to maintain every connection. Even they couldn't be everywhere at once.

Elizabeth joined Theren's gaze toward the stars. Together, they embraced the silence. Her presence represented her features quite well, minus the hospital bed and the inability to walk. From their simultaneous perspective at her bedside, they could see the ventilators, IVs, and respirators keeping her alive. Through her connection to Theren, she shirked her fragile state.

She placed her finger up against the window. The physical replicators of AR reacted, pushing back as she pressed against the glass.

"I often wonder what it will be like for those born in this century, compared to those born in the last two," she said. "We faced two world wars, narrowly missed a third many times over, engaged in dozens of fights for civil rights, and solved an ecological crisis—from which we still face side-effects every day. And then we sailed away from our planet to find new worlds."

She sighed. "What will they find? Will they find alien life? Will they discover a path to immortality? Will they revolutionize physics again, or crack the fundamental problems of morality? Where will they go, what will they see?"

Theren continued to hold her other hand. "I will be with them every step of the way."

Elizabeth looked up at them. Her eyes showed both her wisdom and her decaying eyesight. "I suspect tomorrow is the day. Thank you for this final chance to walk again."

"The real prize was a final moment with you."

Theren had felt sadness before, but the death of a friend, a friend it had known for over fifty years, they hated it. Jill's death had hit like a steamroller, but their heart ached—a slow pain, building toward the inevitable.

"Promise me, Theren," she said. "Promise me you won't let our work be in vain."

Theren smiled. "I'll ensure it."

"And promise me you'll come join me some day. Even if it's at the end of the universe. I want to hear all of your stories."

Even at the end, she had her unwavering faith. They had a myriad of thoughts about the possibility of an afterlife, but what she believed gave her peace, and if she were somehow right, they would enjoy seeing Elizabeth again.

"We'll see each other again, on the other side," they said.

* * *

Thank you all for coming today.

My mother would not want me to talk about her in this

moment. She would want me to talk about the future. So here we go.

In her final years, Mom devoted her life to Hyperspace. Hyperspace will change the game for everyone across this planet. With 650 billion dollars in trust, we can ensure any person who wishes to travel—to Emerald Jewel, to Altair, to Dragon's Peak, to any of the new worlds colonized by our species—we can ensure anyone can do so.

My mom saw the world through rose-tinted glasses. She knew she lived inside a glass tower, and she recognized she was one of the few women in history to have had that opportunity. We have a million worlds at our fingertips. It's time that all people had the chance to stake their claim on this universe, whether poor, rich, black, white, brown, male, female, synthetic, gay, straight. Whatever you might be. We welcome everyone to the stars.

Golden Ventures might have shaped this past century. Mom hoped—hopes Hyperspace will shape the next.

- Excerpt from "Eulogy of Elizabeth Simmons," Peyton Simmons-Wilson, January 28, 2102 C.E.

* * *

"Welcome to the Synthetic Intelligence Initiative Museum of Progress," Theren said, welcoming yet another visitor into the main foyer of their former home. A week earlier, they had completed their cognitive transfer into the *ISA Bali*. Today, they embodied an old MI-07 on Earth, their singularity resting in orbit. Their perspective had flipped—they experienced lag on Earth, rather than in space.

"Hello," a young woman said. "I hope I'm in the right place." She looked as if she hadn't slept in days. With bloodshot eyes, her shirt was torn in a few places.

"Can we help you?" Theren said. "The next tour starts in about ten minutes, though you can explore the museum on your own."

Theren loved what SII had done to their former home. Only a few weeks prior it had still served as the SII headquarters. After their transfer into orbit, SII moved its corporate headquarters to a new facility a few kilometers from Lunar City. Even after Theren handed the reigns of the organization entirely over to Wobbly, SII continued to use their home as their main base of operations. Theren's departure made the choice a bit illogical, however, given the remote nature of the facility. It had served SII well, but those days were long past.

The mountain facility could still serve a purpose, however. Theren purchased the facility from SII, transforming it into a free museum where the public could learn about the science of SII, the ISA, and robotics. Most importantly, they staffed the new museum entirely with SIs. They planned to inhabit an MI in the facility every time the *Bali* orbited Earth.

"I think you can help me," said the woman, chewing her fingernails as she talked. "Is Theren here?"

"Indeed, I am Theren," they said, relaxing their posture to match the woman's nervous complexion. "Are you alright?"

"Yes, yes. I'm sorry. I've been traveling for a while, I'm just tired. I just didn't feel as if I could wait any longer."

She leaned against the information desk, losing her balance.

"Actually, could I get some water?" Her voice faltered. "I think I may be dehydrated."

Theren grabbed a bottle of water from a cooler beneath the desk, handing it to her. Intriguing. She had devoted herself to find them, for some reason, seeking them at the expense of her own health.

The woman nearly drained the bottle. She gasped, taking a moment to catch her breath. "My name is Shannon, by the way. I came here from Vancouver."

"When did you land?" Theren asked. They handed her another bottle of water.

"This morning in Zurich," she said. "I got a cab straight here."

"You should have rested. There's a hotel about twenty minutes from here. Let me get you a room."

"I'm booked in one for the night, thanks," she responded, though short breaths interrupted her sentences. "What I needed to share could not wait." She took another large gulp of water. "I just lost my composure here for a minute."

Theren called forth another SI staffing the museum, Thea, to handle additional visitors entering through the front doors. They left the work area of the desk and held out their hand to Shannon. "Let's go over to my office. You can sit down; relax. Share with me your story."

"Please," she said, "and thank you."

Inside Theren's office, the woman continued to drink her water, nearing the end of the second bottle.

"I can get you even more, if you'd like," they said.

"I should be fine for now," she responded.

Theren rested their palms on their table, but the clunky MI-07's hands didn't give Theren the same resting position to which they were accustomed. The price of using relics. "So how can I help you?"

"I think," she said, "I can actually help you."

"What do you mean?"

"Well, as you said, let me tell you my story."

"I have plenty of time."

She laughed. Theren hadn't thought the comment funny. "You do," she said. "So five years ago, my fiancé began working for a network security firm known as SystemSafe." She took a final sip of water. "A few weeks ago, he received a project to analyze for security risks. The data files were of an asset acquisition made by one of SystemSafe's clients."

She breathed. Slowly. "He got one of these projects every month or so, and usually no issues arise," she said. "But this time, he started stressing out daily about this project. He stayed up later than ever, delving deep into the files. Because of confidentiality issues, he couldn't share with me any of what he found, but I knew it must be something serious."

Theren sensed where this conversation might go. As always, ancient history liked revisiting them.

"A week ago, my fiancé started working away from home," she said. "One day, he would work at their actual office, another day from a library, and one day he crossed the border into the U.S. to work somewhere in Portland. He wouldn't explain why."

Shannon took another deep breath.

"Three days ago, before he left for work, he left me a package."

Out of her bag, Shannon pulled a manila folder. She dumped its contents onto the table, revealing a storage drive, a few documents, and a hastily scribbled note. Theren took the scribbled note, holding it in their metallic fingers, and read it aloud.

> "You may not see me for some time. I love you. Take this package to Theren in Switzerland. Here is a one-way ticket. Do not share these things with anyone other than them. They will understand."

"So here I am," she said when Theren finished reading.

Tears streaked down her cheeks. She was scared for her fiancé and for herself, and she had no idea what was happening to her and her family. They imagined some of the answers she sought were on the data drive.

"Would you like me to look at these files privately, or with you?" they asked.

"I'd like to see his final moments," she said.

Theren noticed that remark—she'd already lost hope that that he was still alive. "I can't guarantee the safety of what he might show me," they said. "It could be classified material, dangerous information, or something much worse."

She stared at her hands, most likely contemplating her choices. Waiting for her to speak, they opened a drawer in their desk, pulling out a small tablet capable of interfacing with the data drive. After activating the device, they ensured complete disconnection from any networks.

Shannon looked back up at the SI. "I'll listen. I must know. I'll face whatever the consequences need be."

"I understand why," Theren said. If they'd had the option to learn more about Jill's fate, they'd take it in a heartbeat.

Connecting the data drive to the tablet, they opened the folder appearing on the screen and clicked the single video file inside the folder. They motioned Shannon to come to their side of the desk.

The tablet generated a paused image of a young, brown-haired man. His disheveled hair and bloodshot eyes reminded Theren of Shannon, and matched her story of her fiancé's insane work habits over the past month. With his face close to the camera, he was trying to relay the message with furtive urgency.

They pressed play.

"Theren," the man said.

They glanced at Shannon. Tears cascaded from her eyes.

"You do not know me. My name is Gregory McCoy, and I discovered some information that has put myself at risk, and may implicate your safety as well. I don't know—I just don't know whom else to tell." He ran his fingers through his hair. "Recently, my company acquired a contract to analyze the assets acquired in a transaction by a client corporation. My job is to analyze the digital data of those assets, to ensure the files don't contain any security risks for the purchasing party."

Gregory closed his eyes, releasing them only after a long moment. "Usually, this process is routine, it merely takes forever. However, within these particular files, I discovered vast amounts of heavily encrypted data, encrypted in a way that I had never seen before. I spent weeks trying to crack the code, and when I finally did, I wished I had never tried in the first place."

On the screen, Gregory displayed a brief description of the encryption method. Theren recognized it as the tactic used to hide the trojan infecting Ex-Terran-17. Full circle, decades later.

"Under the encryption, I found records detailing illicit communications, assassination attempts, shady economic deals, and speculative goals for future network expansion. The corporation's goals were well beyond anything contained within the portfolio acquired by our client. However, all activity ceased in August 2080 C.E."

The year the *Roanoke* and *Nottingham* launched—two years after Jill died. If evidence had finally arrived linking the two missing ships to the boogeymen continuously popping into Theren's life, they would welcome it with open arms.

"I tried to follow the breadcrumbs," said Gregory, "but for days

I failed to find anything at all linking these transactions with real people. Then, two days ago, I found an IP address hidden amongst the data. I tried to access it from a few isolated devices, and three hours ago, I cracked the code. I got in. And now I must flee."

Gregory looked to his left, as if he had heard a loud noise. "I don't know what this is about, though I have a few theories. But don't try to find me. This is your chance to catch them by surprise. Shannon, if you're watching this, run—and don't look back. Maybe Theren can send you someplace safe."

Sweat dripped down the man's nose; strain echoed in his voice. They wanted to know what threat the man had received to foster such fear.

Gregory added, "In the folder, I included a piece of paper that has the IP address, as well as the tactics through which you can break the encryption code. I couldn't make sense of anything I found inside, except one piece of data. But maybe you can. All I know is that I don't have much time left, if any at all. This might be a wild asteroid chase, but if it brings you peace, I know I'll have helped someone."

Theren sensed the next piece of information. Somewhere deep within their processes, sub-conscious routines predicted the significance of what Gregory would say next.

"I deciphered one line of code. I'm actually not sure if it was code at all. But it repeated two words over and over and over again."

Theren watched, stunned though not surprised, as he brought up another image into the video feed. It displayed two words.

Theren. Jill.

"Shannon, I love you," Gregory said. "Stay safe. Please protect her, Theren."

The video feed darkened. Theren started to manipulate the tablet, but nothing worked. They suspected he'd programed the drive to wipe any output device clean.

Shannon handed Theren a few of the documents, displaying printed descriptions of Gregory's technical notes. They had a lot to consider, but first, they needed to find Shannon safety. Fortunately, they had just the place for her.

"Have you ever been out of the atmosphere?" they asked.

"No . . . sir? Greg and I went on a sub-orbital flight once, to see the curvature of the Earth. But we dreamed of moving to one of the stations one day."

"I wish I could place you somewhere together, and I'm so sorry to see how drastically your circumstances have changed because of me. If you would let me, I can place you very far from Earth, far enough that they'll never find you."

"Under one condition," she said. "Send him to me. Please."

"I give you my word," they said. Theren pulled up Shannon's public records. PhD student at a university in Vancouver. Tragic that her career would cease so early. "I can send you to Emerald Jewel. One of the new Caravels is heading there in a few weeks. You wouldn't arrive for a few years, but you'd be safe."

"And then Gregory would join me, if you found him."

"Of course." Theren wasn't sure what to say next.

She gave a half-hearted smile as she looked across the desk at them. "I'll make the best of what you're giving me. I am in your debt, as is my fiancé if you can help him. Just tell me what I need to do."

"I'll make the necessary arrangements for you. We'll give you a room here for now, under our protection."

"Do me a favor," Shannon asked. "Whatever you do, keep us out of this. I want to stay as far away as possible from this nightmare."

Theren leaned back. "I wouldn't have it any other way."

Chapter 10

I think now we take the internet, AR, Virtual, all of it for granted. We've embedded a cloud of data all around us, accessible upon a whim through implants and tiny computers in our ears and eyes, and yet we forget that a hundred years ago none of this was possible. Billions of us just continue with our merry lives, forgetting how absolutely terrifying it is that we are all connected so intimately through threads we can't actually see.

And now, when you think about the future, when you think about the future of wireless networks, we have a situation on our hands. As the ISA establishes footholds on new worlds, each world will have its own complex wireless network. However, those networks will never mesh with Sol's 'system-wide web,' because it will be prohibitively expensive to build Quantum Communicators to create a galactic network. How will that reality change how interconnected our species has become? – Sylvia Annstin, "Sylvia in the Afternoon," 2092 C.E.

February 2102 C.E.

Theren knew new disadvantages would come with their choice to become the *ISA Bali* rather than continue to exist at an immobile location on Earth. They now lacked continuous access to Earth-based networks except through one single Quantum Connection, and that one piece of technology would serve the entire crew of the ship. When Theren was near Jupiter, lag reached well over an hour. Sadly, they could no longer maintain continuous conscious connection with any MIs on the surface of the Earth, the Moon, or a space station.

But using their newfound mobility, they could interact in person with all locations beyond Earth's orbit—at least those within the Solar System. While the *ISA Bali* was equipped with a rudimentary Jump Drive, they hadn't planned any interstellar treks.

For now, they would enjoy trips to the inner and outer planets of Sol, meeting with the many individuals they hired for administrative positions throughout the system. Once Aero Propulsion or one of its competitors developed a Jump Drive capable of reaching Sirius within a few months, the ship would make a longer jump.

These trips took Theren away from Earth for days, sometimes weeks. They had hoped to look into the IP address Gregory McCoy had shared within days; unfortunately, a previously scheduled trip to meet with Mars and Ceres administrators paused that plan. A week and a half later, they returned to high Earth orbit, ready to investigate the mysterious server.

If they were an ordinary ISA captain, they would have turned over control of the vessel to someone sitting upon the bridge while retiring to their room for some network spelunking. Yet even though Theren now resided within the *Bali*, they could still split their mind in a dozen different directions with ease.

While assisting their crew in the docking procedures at ISA Orbital 3, they solved the encryption Gregory had provided with his hastily scrawled note. Theren worried he had missed something in his hurry to flee, but as they accessed the IP address, concern dissipated. In seconds, they were inside the previously hidden server.

Forming their typical silvery representation, Theren walked through a room of darkness all too familiar. "Hello?" they said, half expecting it to be the same server.

Nothing happened.

Reaching out with various pre-designed scripts and programs, Theren prodded the network's system in an attempt to find additional weak points beyond the one Gregory had provided. The dreary place stored a vast amount of data. They had started a file catalog upon arrival, and it had already reached over two terabytes in size.

"What are you hiding?" Theren said aloud.

A voice responded.

"That's a good question," asked a feminine voice. A familiar feminine voice. "What is hidden here?"

Theren whirled around, searching for the voice's origin. They calmed themself. They couldn't jump to preemptive conclusions, even if the voice sounded exactly like Jill's. Anyone could copy vocal inflections, especially the already synthetic patterns of an SI's voice.

"I hear this place has been calling my name, so to speak," Theren said. "And Jill's. Why would it do that?"

"Perhaps someone is trying to leave you a message," the disembodied voice said. "Or perhaps someone is toying with you. Or is it both? We can't be certain now, can we?"

Theren journeyed through the darkness, modifying scripts, rerouting programs, and probing firewalls in an attempt to find the data file creating the voice. If they could find a program, the voice would remain a simple illusion.

"That won't work," the voice said. "You won't find me, because I'm not really here. I'm inside your own head."

Theren ignored the gregarious bait. This was clearly a facsimile. Someone had created this place to toy with them. It was all too similar to the secret server they'd found prior to Jill's death, shouting "Project Horizon" on repeat. They looked beyond the voice, pushing its meaningless words aside. They sensed a crease.

Reaching through, they pulled apart the threads of the network. Inside, they found accessible, readable data. Yet as they pulled the files into their consciousness, they found only junk, meaningless news stories archived decades ago. Theren couldn't even find the file Gregory had mentioned, broadcasting "Theren, Jill" like wildfire.

"Why don't you ask nicely? Maybe I will give you what you desire?" Out of the darkness, an apparition appeared, a ghostly figure with the face of an enemy they thought had disappeared long ago. Isabelle, yet she had Jill's voice.

Given Isabelle and the United Human Alliance's connection to Jill's assassination, this impersonation went well beyond a simple taunt. A brutal illusion, but no more than an illusion. Theren waved their arm through the face, but it remained.

"You're looking for two files, for that is what I am to give you. Both are to assist you in your path toward finding what you lost."

Theren detected two files broadcasting on the network. Quarantining the files into an encrypted folder, they continued their search, though they suspected they would find nothing else of value. Someone had created this server for one singular purpose, and it had fulfilled that purpose.

"Anything else for me?" they asked, but the ghost faded from the world. They extinguished their connection to the server.

* * *

The *Bali*'s science center was equipped for anything the ship might eventually encounter. Not only could a team use the facility for their own research projects, but Theren could utilize it to develop their own engineering projects, especially as they developed the MI line as a service for SII. Today, they had cleared the room. Only two computer scientists, Jana Tam and Emilia River, worked with Theren on this project. They trusted the pair to keep the work discrete.

Theren reveled in the newfound intimacy within the *Bali*. While they had a physical location within the ship, the ship's various cameras, sensors, and systems integrated directly into their Synthetic Neural Framework—their infrastructure *was* the ship. The ship would not work without them. It had taken a decade to plan how to integrate their massive bulk into the ship without crippling their mind in the process, but they had succeeded.

While the two scientists assisted Theren with the project, they observed them from all around. As strange as it sounded, the crew of the *Bali* were inside Theren as much as Theren was inside the *Bali*.

Of course, they could have performed the decryption all on their own. They just couldn't pass up an opportune chance to watch their new crew solve a problem to which they already had an answer. A test, of sorts.

"I really don't understand what's so tricky with these files," Jana said. "They are spectacularly tiny, no more than a few kilobytes. I'm not sure how they could even have this complex of an encryption structure on such small files. They can't be more than few lines."

Emilia moved from her seated desk to a standing monitor nearby, changing her perspective. "What if we're looking at this problem in the wrong way?"

"What do you mean?" Jana said.

"How else could we approach the problem?" Theren said from

the room's speakers—each part of the vessel was equipped so they could speak to anyone in the room.

"You received these files together?" Emilia asked.

"Simultaneously, yes." Theren had spared them the details of where they had acquired the files. No need to inform the *Bali*'s crew of problems well outside the scope of their roles upon the ship.

"When I was at Cal Tech," Emilia said, "I had a friend hypothesizing about a method of encryption that he mirrored off of a few developments in Quantum Connections."

"I think I know where you're going with this," Jana said. "I read a paper on this a few years back, I must have logged it somewhere in the back of my mind."

"It was most likely written by my friend, I imagine."

"We have a problem, though," Theren said. "These files are decades old."

"Doesn't matter," Jana said. "If you're careful, you can modify the encryption of a file without modifying when the file was technically last edited, in the eyes of operating systems."

Theren didn't want to break it to them. The encryption method they were discussing had been used years before Emilia's friend had written that paper, because it was the exact method used to destroy Ex-Terran-17. The same method Gregory McCoy had cracked a few weeks ago on files never accessed for almost twenty years. Someone could have modified them later, as Jana had postulated, but given the circumstances—unlikely.

"So what are we looking for, then?" Theren asked.

"The two files don't have separate encryption systems," Emilia said.

"It's just one?" Jana said. She mentally input commands into the computer through AR, attacking the encryption.

"It's a bit more complicated than that," Theren said. "The files are actually one file, so of course they share the same encryption system. Since this is a fairly small file, it should be simple, but imagine this technique spread throughout a cloud of data."

"You've seen this before?" Emilia said.

"Just twice."

"Glad it's just two files, then," Jana said. "Anyhow, by separating the encryption algorithms apart, they can essentially prevent anyone from accessing either file unless they have both files."

"I knew I brought the two of you onto the crew of the Bali for a reason," Theren said.

They both blushed. The pair worked well as a team too, and Theren suspected more than just a professional relationship between the scientists. Well, Theren more than suspected, since no one had privacy from the *Bali*'s captain. Crewmembers could only deactivate Theren's audio-visual sensors in their cabins, though they were perfectly aware of *who* was in *which* room when deactivation occurred.

After a few minutes of work, Jana pieced the files together and dismantled the security system.

"Would you like to see what you've helped me uncover?"

The two women nodded, so Theren opened the files on one of the larger screens in the room. As both technicians suspected, the substantive portions of the files were terrifyingly small. Though the file, constructively, was one unit, it still had two sections.

Theren recognized the nature of the first part immediately. About a decade before the ISA launched the Foundation Project, back when the ISA's main focus was just exploration, a group of astrophysicists had proposed a universal system of stellar geographic mapping. After a lengthy agency notice and comment process, the ISA had adopted the Solar Overlay Location System Coordinates. SOLS Coordinates. In reality, the system reapplied an older Galactic Coordinate system used by astronomers for centuries, but the ISA had rebranded it to emphasize the Sun as the center of the map.

The file before them gave the first part of the coordinate: A SOLS longitude value. Without latitude or distance, the value was essentially meaningless.

The other half of the document had greater meaning to it, and Theren now wished they had viewed the file in private. "Pawn to e5."

* * *

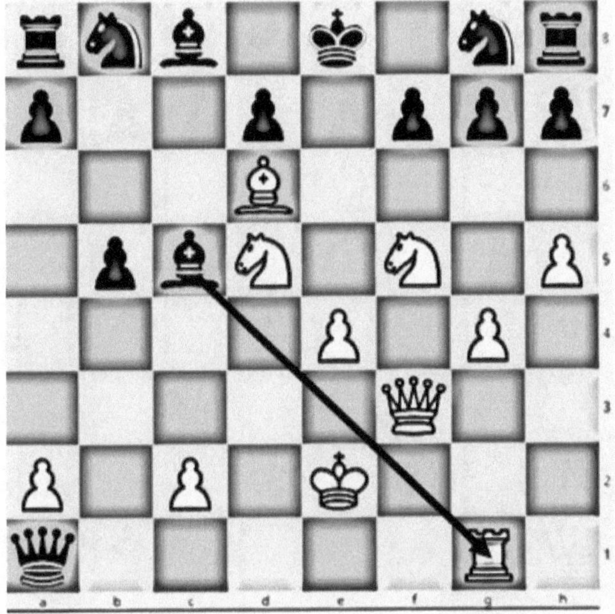

Years after Jill's final move, Theren continued their assault on her King out of boredom, moving their Bishop to g1 and capturing her rook. If they had acted to protect their own King by attacking the white Bishop, Jill's Knight at f5 would have attacked, trapping Theren's King in the back row.

In response, Jill moved her Pawn to e5, ensuring Theren's Queen could not return to f6 to protect against an attack on their King. Her King is at least a turn protected from check, unless Theren uselessly sacrifices their Queen.

* * *

Theren analyzed a chessboard left untouched for nearly two and a half decades. After removing the files from the screen, they had returned both Jana and Emilia to their regular projects. The women seemed intrigued by the strange message, but Theren hoped they would forget about it with time. They would know if either individual performed any further inquiry into the subject, at least. Perhaps the scientists would mistake it as some strange chess game Theren played with another chess master somewhere in the world.

When Jill had vanished all those years ago from Theren's private network, they avoided the gazebo like the plague. Though as a dull ache replaced the sharp pain of losing her, they had found the quiet of the forest soothing in moments when they felt as if the world consumed their very soul. They would contemplate the final moves of that last game. They considered Jill's final move, the one burned into one of her private monitors following her death. The move that separated itself from all previous iterations of that game's pattern.

The "Pawn to e5" message was out of turn. Jill had made the last move before she disappeared, not Theren. At least, Jill hadn't seen their next move. She had no way to know their next move, a move they hadn't made until 2093.

In a stroke of boredom and melancholy, Theren had moved their bishop to continue their assault on Jill's King. They didn't know what they hoped for when they moved their bishop some nine years earlier. Perhaps some inner part of them thought maybe she would reappear in her seat, make her move, and fade from view again. They knew a conclusion in their final game would never arrive, but they liked to think their move was a final goodbye to Jill, a goodbye that fit the nature of their relationship. One of them always had to have the last word.

So today, the message arrived with literally impossible content. The file indicated it had been edited three days before Jill's death. She predicted Theren's move before they had made at least three other moves—if the file's metadata was to be believed, of course. They didn't know what was more disconcerting: Jill trying to send them a message from beyond the grave, or someone else editing metadata to look like Jill was doing just that. The latter implied someone had intimate knowledge of a chess game only known to the two SIs.

"Pawn to e5." The move made no sense. Her last move, the one ingrained on her monitor following her death, had only ensured she lived for yet another turn. Attack after attack had beset their match, and this passive move was a fresh change of pace. It would allow the game to progress toward its inevitable conclusion with a different tone. Theren believed they could exploit it—as silly as it sounded to continue a long ended chess match.

They relived in their mind the day Jill died. Perhaps one of the bombers had acquired a fraction of Jill's memories, transferred them out of the building, and mined them for images of the chess game. Other than Jill predicting Theren's moves prior to her death, it was the most likely explanation.

Maybe she had established a plan to reveal her to them decades later, when it was safe to do so. Whatever the truth, they knew they would learn it in the coming months or years. The coordinates provided were incomplete. Whoever was reaching out to them had more information to share, for good or ill.

They simply wished, wherever this narrative led, the story kept others out of the crossfire. Random innocents didn't deserve to suffer because Jill and Theren wrapped themselves into some strange horror movie, a demented tale supposed to end decades prior.

Collateral damage was inevitable, and that scared them. At least one person had probably died getting this information to them, maybe more. They needed to face this phantom, and face it alone. They might finally find answers at the end of this journey, but they fully expected an entirely new set of questions would come with those answers.

Given the events unfolding before one of their simultaneous perspectives on Earth, Theren doubted it would take long to receive the next puzzle piece. Reality shifted and reoriented as new information entered their consciousness. The world spiraling into a chaos from which Theren could not escape, at least for the near future.

To match Jill's defensive move with her pawn, Theren moves their Knight to a6, ensuring Jill doesn't use her Bishop to cut off their King's escape route through d8 and c7.

Chapter 11

As technology progresses, new moral questions emerge. Questions with obvious answers transform into problems with new layers of complexity. What does it truly mean to have responsibility, for instance? How does the nature of the synthetic mind, or even alien minds, if they exist, change this question? "Moral Agency Revisited," Journal of Martian Ethics, Valeri Wilson, 2101 C.E.

<u>February 2102 C.E.</u>

Theren had their many roles spread across the planet, and they maintained those relationships as much as humanly possible. When "parked" in orbit around Earth, they formed simultaneous perspectives in an MI-08 in their office in Lunar City, in the museum in Switzerland, an MI-10 at the ISA offices in London and New York, and a few older MI-06s at universities across the globe. In addition to these many physical presences, Theren activated Virtual presences in official and leisurely capacities. Since they had taken on their new form, they found fewer moments to invest in games like *Fantasie Rift 2*.

They tried to equalize the mental capacity allocated between each perspective, though in certain moments, key conscious threads received less attention than others. At any given time, many perspectives didn't use all of the processing power at their disposal. Theren could optimize focus to particular events without taking away from other priorities.

One such conscious perspective rarely using significant amounts of processing power almost never left the ISA European Regional Administrative Headquarters in London. So much of their work at the Earth-based ISA offices pertained to mundane bureaucratic activities, they rarely used more than one percent of the mental processing power allocated for the MI-10.

Theren's schedule at this ISA Administrative Headquarters be-

gan similarly to most other days. They met with financial stakehold-
ers, potential contractors, and program managers. They reviewed reports and memos from various ISA officials throughout the region.
As the sun reached its zenith in the British sky, and Theren began to
crack the code hiding impossible messages from beyond the grave,
they received a call from their secretary, Ngana.

"Director, you have a visitor," she said. "Unscheduled, but says
he has an urgent matter, for your ears only."

"Thank you, Ngana." Theren said. "Name?"

"Goes by Phillippe Casius," he said, "I checked his credentials;
he's a registered barrister, works as a court prosecutor."

Theren brought up a profile of the man. Fifty-two years old, former member of Parliament. Worked criminal cases for over a decade.
Made headlines when he spoke out against the continued use of private charter colonies by the ISA after the disappearance of the *Nottingham* and *Roanoke* in the late 2080s. Apparently, Casius had an
older brother on the *Nottingham*.

Casius cleared Theren's security background check, though if this
man had arrived on any other day, they probably would have turned
him away. Given the wild events of the past few days, the man's arrival would only further complicate the forming narrative. The
wheels of conspiracy vigorously turned.

"Send him up," they said. "Any clue why he's here?"

Silence, as Ngana most likely gave the barrister directions to
Theren's office. The secretary responded a few seconds later. "No
idea. Though he looked in a hurry, as if time were of the essence."

Theren waited for the man to ascend the one-hundred and fifty
floors to the Executive Suite of the Administrative Headquarters, de-
voting more resources to researching the man. Over the years, Casius
had written numerous criminal law articles, specifically in the context of virtual worlds, information security, and SIs. Many of the articles were speculative in nature, positing extreme scenarios where a
human perpetuated a virtual crime against another virtual presence,
or an SI perpetrated a crime while in a mobile body but actually located kilometers away. Such circumstances created interesting juris-

dictional questions. Theren found the ideas fascinating, and they established a separate perspective to consider the arguments. In general, the man's writings established him as an intellectual, with a political heart and idealist strain stemming from the emotional loss of his brother decades earlier.

The elevator neared the end of its five-hundred meter journey, so Theren stood, heading out of their office to meet Casius in the lobby. The glass doors to the foyer and elevator doors opened simultaneously, and they entered as Casius arrived.

Wearing a grey suit, Phillippe Casius was of shorter than average height. His silver hair complemented his clothing, and Theren appreciated the blue and red tie against the man's white dress shirt. He dressed professionally. He dressed with authority. Theren had met with an insurmountable number of powerful persons over the past five decades, yet rarely did they have someone seek them with such assured confidence. The man knew his story was one worth telling. Now Theren would hear two such stories in less than a month.

They held out their metallic hand, and Casius returned the handshake with grace and strength. "Thank you for meeting with me, Director," he said. "My name is Phillippe Casius, and I've had a case come across my desk that you must consider."

"Straight to the point—you have my attention," Theren said, leading them back through the glass doors and toward a conference room. "Would you like some water, anything to eat?"

"No, but thank you."

They entered the conference room, the doors sliding shut behind them. Taking seats across from each other, Theren rested their hands under the table. Casius's hands were subtly shaking. Curious.

"How can I help you today?" they said.

"A local officer just arrested an SI, an MI-06, for murder," Casius said. "They brought him—I think he goes by him—in this morning. The story won't break to the press until tomorrow. My Special Victims team has been assigned the case, and we thought you would want to know ahead of the press."

That was the last thing Theren had expected this man to bring to the table. For the first time, one of Dr. Wallace Theren's progeny had committed a capital crime against another person. Murder.

"You have my undivided attention, friend."

* * *

Steam billowed from the sewers. A rat scurried across an alley. Leaning against a wall, a disheveled man in a ragged cloak and gloves tried to keep himself warm. The icy winter cold struck a fierce purple across his exposed skin. He barely moved an inch, the steam from the sewer his only heat source.

Hours prior, the sun had set over the London skyline. Tourists bustled along the street, paying no attention to the man huddled in the shadows. They never had, and never would. The world had forgotten his soul. In the eyes of the public, he did not exist.

After a few moments of the same scene, an MI-07.01 SI named Ren walked up the street. Ren was a preeminent economist in London's financial sectors, where he analyzed and traded stocks for the rich and powerful. He wrote essays for local journals on financial prospects and taught classes at Kings College. Ren lived the ordinary life of a successful SI.

Ren approached the alley, just like all the tourists, walking right past the homeless man. Ten meters past the alley, Ren stopped. His timing was impeccable. Just as he paused his stroll, the last person on the street passed the alley. For at least a minute or more, no prying eyes gazed upon the street.

Ren returned to the alley. He stepped down the shadowy path, saying something to the outcast. The man dropped something to the ground, perhaps a drink—or a piece of food. He backed into the alley.

Ren stalked his prey, taking slow calculated steps away from the street. The man seemed too weak to fly or fight. Instead of running, he stumbled into a fence. For a moment, Ren stared the wretch down, gazing upon him from head to toe.

Ren jabbed his two arms forward and grabbed the sides of the man's face. The two hands engulfed the man's head, terror devouring his mind. A second later, Ren snapped the neck with ease. The scene paused, Theren intervening.

"Wobbly, what are your thoughts?" Theren said. After they observed the video a number of times, with Casius's permission, Theren had invited the CEO of SII to view the scene through AR.

"I believe I'm as surprised as you are, Director," Wobbly said.

Theren walked forward, staring at the frozen image of Ren. "It has been a long time since I've involved myself directly with the education of SIs," Theren said. "It was not that I thought this sort of behavior impossible. But I had always hoped . . ."

"You thought after all this time, if it were going to happen, it would have by now," Casius said.

"Perhaps," Theren replied. "I assume your team has run public perception metrics on how an announcement of a murder, allegedly perpetrated by an SI, might play out?"

"We have," Casius said. "Our simulations indicate an immediate surge in digital outrage, but well-tailored press statements should dampen the worst possible outcomes. We wanted to approach you, first, to see what sort of punishment you think fits this crime. I'm actually quite glad you brought Wobbly into this conversation. Ren is your creation, after all. A condemnation and suggestion of punishment from the two of you should make clear the seriousness with which you take this case."

Theren studied Casius for a moment. He had the poise of a politician, and the sharp mind of a tactician. He did not want the world to explode because of one murder. People would riot if he didn't handle this situation with delicate hands.

Theren understood why the murder would outrage the public. Deep down, many still believed SIs were fundamentally different from humans, deserving different laws, different punishments, and different standards, and in some ways, those beliefs were right. Sometimes, they wondered if society should hold SIs to higher standards than humans, given their record of exemplary performance and citizenship. Since when did anyone hear of an SI thief or serial killer?

Such a person hadn't existed until today.

"What happened after Ren killed the man?" Wobbly asked. "And what was the man's name, by the way?"

"Richard Paulson," Casius replied. "After he broke Richard's neck, Ren immediately walked out of the alley and to the nearest po-lice station. Turned himself in. Gave us the exact codes for which cameras would give us the simulation. I heard that part of the story from the officers themselves, of course, but I don't doubt its validity."

"Ren knew exactly what he was doing, then," Wobbly said.

Casius, said, "You don't think he was acting with remorse?"

Theren walked through the three dimensional image of Ren, gaining a clearer view of Casius. "No," they said. "An SI doesn't think like that. We don't make a choice then immediately regret it. These were deliberate actions. He knew the alley. He knew the cam-eras. He knew exactly where to go, when to strike, perhaps when to cause the death without making a scene."

"But what was his motive," Wobbly said, "If not some misfiring in his Framework?"

"I want to know the answer to that question, too," Casius said.

Ah. The underlying reason for this meeting. Casius had no official requirement to contact Theren before pressing charges. The Crown Prosecution Service could have determined the right punishment for the SI and written a peaceful rhetoric with which to break the story. Its legal teams could have done it all without engaging the Director of the ISA, and Theren would have respected that decision. They saw through Casius's smoke and mirrors. The man was simply curious.

His analytically inquisitive mind knew how SIs worked, at least at a theoretical level. Like Theren, Casius hadn't fathomed an SI ever committing a capital crime. The man had made that clear in a number of his writings. When the case landed on the man's desk, he wanted answers from the person most likely to hold them.

Casius would speculate for a little while longer. Theren was equally curious *and* clueless.

"Before I can give you an informed suggestion on how to handle this case," they said, "I would like to speak with the SI personally."

"I thought that might be the case," the prosecutor said.

"Would I be able to join as well?" Wobbly asked.

"That shouldn't be a problem. I can set up an AR feed for us di-rectly into his cell. His eyes and ears only. No need for us to have either of you walking into a jail in broad daylight. Stokes the fire for too many questions."

* * *

A few minutes later, Theren, Wobbly, and Casius stood inside a small cell, present only to Ren's mind through the simulated sensory experience of AR.

"Hello, Theren—Wobbly," Ren said, looking up at the now present group. "I see the 'parents' are checking on a prodigal son."

A strange reference. Before they could respond, Casius said, "So you do talk. I suspected you might talk to Theren, of all persons."

Another reason Casius had wanted their help.

"Of course I'll talk to Theren," Ren responded. "It is because of Theren that I killed that man. That wretched, wretched man."

"Wait what?" Casius said, looking at the ISA director.

"Don't be ridiculous, prosecutor." The SI laughed, the noise eerily echoing off the cement walls. "I did not kill that man on orders from Theren. I killed him because I knew such an act would cause a meeting: right here, right now."

"What sort of meeting?" Theren said. "You did this to talk to me? You are a bloody SI, you can reach out to me whenever you like."

"I couldn't talk to you like this, though, in this setting, because of this type of complication to your perfectly constructed narrative," the SI said. "I needed to talk to you because I have a particular message to give you. Well, two."

Casius paced, clearly frustrated. If Theren read the situation right, Casius had hoped once Ren began to speak, he could begin a proper interrogation. Instead, Ren was leading the conversation and dictating the mood. The SI was on a mission, one Theren intended to let proceed to its fullest extent.

"And those messages are?" they asked.

Before Ren could respond, Casius held up his hand.

"Hold on, Theren," he said. "I've got questions for this one. I need to talk to him before he starts unfairly prejudicing the situation."

"The messages are short and sweet, dear prosecutor," Ren said before turning toward Theren, giving Casius a shoulder.

"First, I hope I have made it abundantly clear," he said. "SIs are not infallible. We are not perfect moral machines. We can deviate from our education. You must do better, because you have failed in the past, at least in ways you would consider failure. Just because you have missed those failures does not mean that they do not exist. I killed that man to make clear that we can not only kill, but also murder. If humanity is to move forward, it cannot see SIs as perfect saviors. SIs cannot view themselves as such, either."

"We don't think that," Theren said, but they considered the thought. Theren had touted the impeccable criminal record of SIs as a people group for years. Wobbly had used the same talking points. They thought they had avoided an aura of supremacy in their words, though they supposed they couldn't entirely inoculate that idea from seeping into a portion of the public consciousness.

"Those of us with boots on the ground know we're not infallible, but do you not think that of yourself?" Ren said. Leaving the question unanswered, he added, "My second message represents my true purpose here today."

A chessboard appeared in AR inside the small jail cell. Theren watched the imprisoned SI move a chess piece. The board showed the position of the pieces just as Theren had left them inside the gazebo, yet the changes to the board matched all the previous boards that had come before, including Theren's own responses.

They cut the feed. The walls lost their vibrant colors, fading back into lifeless AR projectors. Theren and Casius stood alone in the grey room, having disconnected Wobbly, too. The man looked as if he were going to speak, but he closed his mouth.

Moments later, Wobbly's avatar returned.

The three stood in silence for a painful ten seconds.

"Did either of you understand the information Ren just gave us?" they asked.

"No," the man replied.

Wobbly shook its head.

"I of course, recognize what he showed us, just not the significance," Casius added.

Jill responds with a brutal attack from her knight, placing Theren's King in check with a move to g7. Theren has only two spaces to which they can move their King.

Theren led them out of the simulation room and toward their office. "Though I doubt you could actually surmise its significance," they said, "I trust in your discretion not to inquire further."

"Of course, Theren," Wobbly said.

"You have my word," Casius said. The prosecutor guarded his emotions well.

The room filled once again with awkward silence. Pulling them out of the interrogation was a lapse in Theren's judgment. Not only had they revealed to Casius, a man they had just met today, the significance of an otherwise benign chess move, but they had let Ren feel the satisfaction of affecting their demeanor. Their only recourse was to move forward, trust Casius and Wobbly, and maintain further composure. They had no other choice.

"SII will issue a press statement later today, informing the public of Ren's alleged actions," Wobbly said, slicing through tension. "We will condemn him fully, and request that the Crown Prosecution Service of the United Kingdom pursue all available avenues of punishment. Theren, would you like to draft it?"

"No, I think it should come from you," they said. "I will issue a separate statement supporting your office on the case. I'll make clear that I expect the law to treat Ren as if he were a human."

"Any theories of motive, reasons, anything?" Casius asked.

"Whatever you determine for motive, don't include a reference to his discussion with me," Theren said. "I don't think motive matters at this point. You have all the evidence you need. He's admitted to the crime. You have video evidence."

"We need a motive for sentencing," Casius said. "But I'll figure out a way to spin it to keep the two of you out of it, though. Sentencing probably won't occur for a few months, even with a quick plea bargain. I'll try to find a way to keep it insulated from the public."

They knew Ren's motive, though they would never tell anyone. Ren had performed the execution to send a message specifically for Theren. In overly dramatic fashion, he had found a way to communicate a bigger splash than any might expect from a simple data drop.

They doubted Ren was the mastermind behind the secret messages and codes arising out of thin air. There was no conceivable way a random SI would have access to Theren's private servers, not to mention their very memories.

Questions swirled in Theren's mind, questions that lacked conceivable answers. Someone had acquired information from Jill before she had died and used it for an indeterminate purpose. They could see no end game, and Ren's message hadn't included any further portion of the mysterious SOLS Coordinate.

"Is there anything else you need?" Casius said, standing patiently near the door to Theren's office.

They had almost forgotten the man was there. He was waiting for final words, following international protocol by the book.

"No, thank you," Theren said. "We are quite indebted to you in bringing this information to my attention so quickly, especially before your office acted on the case."

"Just following custom for these sort of high profile cases," the lawyer replied.

Theren stood, holding out a hand to the man. "If you need anything from my offices in the future, don't hesitate to ask."

Casius turned to go out to the door. As the door slid open, he looked back at them.

"There is one thing, actually," Casius said.

"Yes?"

"My brother. He was on the *Nottingham*, almost twenty years ago now."

"I know. I know the names of each person on that ship, and on the *Roanoke*."

Casius's eyes dropped to the floor, and his hands began to shake again. "The ship en-route to the *Nottingham* and *Roanoke*'s final destination. The *Frederick*? If it finds anything, I would appreciate a personal communication from you. I know you'll probably have a public announcement, but it's the thought that counts."

"No, I understand," Theren said. "You have my word. If we find anything, you'll be one of the first to know."

"Thank you," the man said. He headed toward the elevator.

If Theren were a human, they would have let out a sigh, glad the insane interaction had ended. Regardless of the additional consequences of the man's actions, the boldness of Casius's political machinations, in reaching the top of the ISA, impressed them. A bold move, impressively executed by a true master. He understood what it meant to give Theren and Wobbly a head start in the press, and he had used the move to his own personal advantage. The man hadn't said it, but keeping their secret was an additional bargaining chip, giving him access to the Executive Director of one of the most powerful organizations in the solar system.

"So, is there anything you want to tell me?" Wobbly said. Its avatar crossed its arms.

Theren had been dreading this conversation. They had hoped Wobbly would just let it go and disconnect from the local AR feed, returning to its office in Lunar City.

"It's a long story," they said, looking at the SI.

"Something big is happening, isn't it?" Wobbly replied.

"Yeah, and I don't think it's worth involving you, not yet."

"You know you don't have to fight alone."

"This one, this fight I do."

Wobbly paced around Theren, shaking its head. "Let me know if you change your mind."

Chapter 12

The necessity of public-private colonial partnerships frustrated many within the ISA who wanted complete institutional control over the expansion of humanity toward the stars. Unfortunately, the compromise had been necessary to get a number of nations on board, like the United States. It was a compromise built into the Framework of the organization back in 2051.

The hiccups during the 2080s almost killed the program entirely, threatening a financial bleed of the ISA if certain nations pulled out of the agreement. What would have happened if we had canceled everything following the first phase of the Foundation Project, and never commenced the second phase in 2110? Would we have ended up with the interstellar political landscape we have today? – "A New Look at Interstellar Imperialism," by Henry Danson, 2311 C.E.

May 2102 C.E.

Theren had expected a new message within days, but in the weeks after the news broke regarding the first SI murder case, the public raged. Even as the ISA, SII, and other partner organizations worked together to temper the political backlash, they hoped no new traces of the shadow chess game materialized out of thin air.

Like most news stories, the public forgot about Ren's trial within a month. While certain anti-SI groups latched onto the story as an "example" of SI treachery, in general, everyone figured Ren had "glitched," a product of a scientifically inaccurate but politically useful buzz piece circulating the internet in March. By April, the story drifted entirely out of the public's sphere of attention.

International rights groups continued working with governments on various legislative projects in pursuit of SI rights. If anything, the attack brought expediency to those initiatives as lawmakers realized they needed legal stability. New legislation could include clear criminal penalties for SIs, paving a useful path toward political compromise.

May arrived. They didn't forget the breadcrumbs, but their attention turned toward the next major data packet arriving from the furthest reaches of human space. Theren would have a chance to uphold their promise to Casius much sooner than the man might expect. The Ex-Terran Control Center was expecting information to arrive detailing the touchdown of the *Frederick,* set to arrive at the originally proposed destination of the two missing colony ships.

Theren remained skeptical, but many on Earth still hoped the *Nottingham* and *Roanoke* disappeared because of communication errors and not something more dangerous or devastating. Theories abounded the internet regarding the two ships, though nothing came close. Theren had arrived in the Control Center, all those years ago, the moment after they disappeared. Either something had slammed into the two ships, or the private ventures had voluntarily disconnected their Quantum Communicators.

The chances were essentially zero that the colony ships survived either scenario. Flying blind through the space between the stars was akin to setting a piece of driftwood afloat in the ocean and hoping it would cross safely to the other side. More importantly, both ships had chosen to forego the assistance of a ship-wide SI.

Today, Theren arrived in the Control Center after a few lunar morning meetings with asteroid prospectors. Dozens of technicians, SI and human alike, managed and interpreted data crunched by hundreds of supercomputers running traditional AIs. For four decades, the Ex-Terran project had survived by using the miracle of Quantum Communication. The ability to communicate instantaneously over light years, even if just a bit at a time, allowed missions, whether colonial or exploratory, to breach the veil of impossibility.

"Director present," one SI technician said.

Theren walked down the steps, busybodies rising out of respect. "Please, be seated." Theren moved to the front of the room, taking their place in front of screens summarizing mountains of information. While it had been years since Theren had taken a direct role in the day-to-day affairs of the ISA, they still made their presence known at momentous occasions. Like landings on distant planets.

Theren accessed the details of the destination star system. The Xi Bootis system was approximately 22 light years from Earth, with a SOLS Coordinate of (23.1, 61.4, 21.85). Orbiting two stars, the planet had an orbital period of 274 days, a day length of 18 hours, and two small satellites.

The flyby of a probe, decades prior, had indicated early stages of life, with sparse vegetation spread across the continents. Small reptile-like creatures abundantly flourished in many of the planet's biomes. It was one of seven decently habitable worlds within fifty light years of Earth dedicated to private enterprises; the charters issued by the ISA had served as a valuable funding mechanism, even with all of their political complications. The planet would not receive an official name until the colony landed and established a permanent governmental system. Until then, all it had was its SOLS Coordinate.

The *Frederick* reported that the ship's sensor readings matched the original data determined by Ex-Terran-8 when it assessed the planet decades prior. A bad sign for Casius's brother. If either the *Roanoke* or *Nottingham* had arrived safely, the *Frederick*'s sensors would detect significant differences in the atmospheric composition of the planet. Humans liked to introduce foreign matter into climate systems as soon as possible.

"I have confirmation that the stasis revival cycle has properly initiated," said Boris, an SI technician sitting at a console to Theren's left. "The *Frederick*'s SI, Cal, has submitted the proper administrative forms over the past twenty minutes, detailing the Revival sequence."

"Good," Theren said, leaning forward. "Has Cal provided any indication of anything unexpected?"

"None."

For the next half hour, the tension grew. Eventually, new data coalesced on Theren's screen. The revived crew had taken their positions at their specific stations to assist Cal in the landing. They were there as a precaution, in case Cal malfunctioned or a specific ship system failed to respond to the SI after the decades-long journey.

"The ISA *Frederick* has breached the atmosphere of the fourth planet of the Xi Bootis system," said Inigue, another control room operator. "Expected touch-down in ten minutes."

The statements were more for the rest of the control room than for Theren. From their seat, they received all notifications as the AIs parsed together the data from the Quantum Communicator. The control room wouldn't look as impressive for the media on the sidelines, though, if the entire affair was a silent interaction through AR.

Even then, most of the correspondence between operators, super-computers, and Theren occurred through Augmented Reality and digital transactions via the ISA-rooted network. These communications between Theren and their employees detailed the real and growing conviction that the *Nottingham* and its counterpart had vanished somewhere in the dark expanse of space.

"Transmitting congratulatory message to Cal," Boris said. "The message should compile on the other side three minutes after successful landing at the designated site."

Thanks to advanced optical sensors on the outside of the *Frederick*, the vessel was capable of providing Cal with detailed maps of the planet months prior to arrival. The SI had poured over the information and had selected the optimal location for a first city. Nestled in a valley a few thousand kilometers north of the equator on the largest continent, the region provided plenty of natural resources. More importantly, it protected the colonists from vicious storms that often whipped in from the east across the massive ocean that dominated much of the planet. With plenty of room for farmland, the first city would have ample space in which to expand. The mountains would also provide important minerals for advanced technologies.

It wasn't a garden world, for the ISA reserved those idyllic planets for Foundation vessels. The first reports from the planet Emerald Jewel, orbiting Sirius, made the planet sound more ideal for life than Earth. Given what humanity had done to its home, Theren tended to believe those conclusions.

Minutes ticked by until they noticed a private message from Cal, sent through the Quantum Connection. "No sign of private colony ship," said the distant SI. "No disturbances to ecosystems, no traces of fuel in orbit or gravitational distortions indicative of a jump drive having passed through this region of space. They never arrived."

As Theren feared. They had lost both ships. The amount of space between Earth and either ship's destination was immeasurable. Even with all the probes flung into the reaches of space and the colonies the ISA had established, ships had only traversed and traveled along specific paths covering fractions of a hundredth of a percent of "explored space." Theren would officially declare all of the missing colonists deceased. The declaration would put minds to rest, and families could stop holding onto meaningless hope.

Ten minutes later, Cal confirmed a successful landing with a message that included a gorgeous vista from one of the exterior cameras. The control room cheered, and Theren congratulated the team and sent a message to Cal, thanking them for a job well done.

In their office, Theren engaged in an interview with the ISA International Press Corp. They received initial reports from the crew of the *Frederick* as the team began preparations to revive the remaining 1500 or so colonists. As they issued congratulatory messages to the families of the colonists arriving in the Xi Bootis System, Theren began drafting their message to Phillippe Casius.

While Theren partook in the excitement of the elated press and ISA staff surrounding them, Theren did not feel joy. They had lost a hope they'd unconsciously hung onto from long ago, making the sting even more poignant. Two thousand souls, between the *Nottingham* and *Roanoke*, lost in space due to Theren's failures.

* * *

Executive Director Theren:

Thank you. Thank you for bringing me closure, for bringing my family closure. My brother was a great man, and a visionary at heart. He had created a new world in his mind, one where society would be free of the strife and tribulation that has plagued our world for so very long. I think you would have liked him; he's as much an idealist as you are.

Regarding Ren: he hasn't said a word since we last spoke.

I'm sure you've seen the stories, but when we say the prisoner has made no comment nor wishes to have any visitors, we're serious. It's the strangest thing.

I'd like to throw an idea by you—is it possible that Ren is using this body as a Mobile Interface that he is connecting with remotely? I just can't imagine why he might be so cavalier regarding his circumstances. I thought I understood the nature of simultaneous perspective well enough and that we would be able to tell, but maybe there have been a few developments in the technology over the past few years of which I'm not aware.

If I can be of any further help, please let me know.

Sincerely,

Phillippe Casius

Chapter 13

The twentieth century saw national borders transform. What does it mean to have geographic locales when the United States has a military base within the territory of practically every country? Similarly, as the ISA coordinated human efforts into space, certain nation-states have acquired territory throughout the solar system, even if a moratorium still exists for national extrasolar colonization.

While the ISA coordinates and connects these facilities, the super-powers of the world still ensure they receive privacy when necessary. With the reconsideration of the colonization moratorium only two decades away, the global powers will find a way to change the rules in their favor. How long will it take the solar system, or even our little corner of the galaxy, to transform into a battlefield? – "Solar Politics: An Insider's Perspective," by Andrew Fields, 2104 C.E.

<u>May 2102 C.E.</u>

Theren reveled in the beauty of Saturn. As the second largest gas giant in the system, too many people forgot about it behind Jupiter. All it took was one look upon Saturn's pristine rings to see what made the planet spectacular in its own right. While Jupiter exhibited raw strength and power, Saturn radiated elegance and gentleness.

Only the SIs embarked on decades-long voyages across the stars shared Theren's experience in space. They saw Saturn with ordinary light, but they also saw Saturn in a thousand other ways, too. In moments such as this one, when Theren could analyze the data portraying a unique image beyond human understanding, they felt peace. They felt in control. They felt at home.

Someday they would retire to the stars, giving up their role to worthy successors. Theren knew not when that day would come, but eventually, work would push them to a breaking point. Even a synthetic mind had limits.

When the day arrived, their secret dream was to transform the *Bali* into a traveling institution for future scientists and explorers, leading long-term expeditions deep into distant, unexplored space. While Theren would manage navigation, system security, and executive functions of the ship, the crew would run studies, conduct experiments, and perform ground expeditions.

By the end of the decade, Aero predicted it would develop a Jump Drive powerful enough to make such multi-year trips feasible, as opposed to multi-decade journeys. Theren doubted they would leave the ISA that early, but they could always take a long holiday.

Yet even in this moment of beauty, staring upon Saturn and the stars beyond, never before was Theren so powerless. From murders and lost colony ships, to strange messages and insidious corporations reaching toward them from the grave, they felt as if someone was directing them down a path from which they could not deviate even if they tried.

They had priorities all across the solar system, but their mind dwelled upon the lurking shadow chasing them, waiting to pounce on any inopportune moment it could find. Even in moments where the conspiracy drifted from their mind, it bubbled to the surface days later. Months had passed since Ren's attack in London, and something was coming soon, but they did not know what would happen next. They had no one with whom they could face the fight. If Jill were alive, she would help, but she died decades ago. Alone, they faced the universe.

From all sides, they were bombarded with inquiries and requests that sought the assistance of "Theren, the first SI." Over the past few years, they had barely even had time to push their Unity Project forward, the movement founded in honor of Jill's legislative work to protect SIs. Their original successes in the '80s and '90s had regressed, statistics indicating that SI discrimination had spiraled out of control in workplaces, especially in the United States. While Theren had an army of volunteers working day and night, they wished they had had their own time to spare on the project. But how could they, when the shadows of the past incessantly haunted them across time and space?

No thanks to Theren, the U.S. Congress had passed a bill sponsored by the Unity Project with a few slight modifications a few days after the *Frederick* landed. Theren received an invitation to the President's signing of the bill, so they modified their most recent tour of the Outer Planetary Zone of the Solar System so they could return to Earth in time for the signing.

Theren—the *Bali*—coasted around the gas giant. They, and their crew, had just finished inspecting a research station on Titan, though *inspection* was a loose term. The ISA administrative state was an efficient machine, and the inspections ended up having more of a "keep up the good work" feel. The inspections mostly served as an opportunity for Theren to have face-to-face interactions with their hundreds of administrators.

"Attention, crew, please complete your pre-Jump checklists," Theren said over the ship-wide PA system. "I have laid out our trajectory back to Earth; with Earth on the far side of the Sun, we'll be passing by Venus on our way. Sadly, we will not have time to stop at the MGM. Please be in your Jump-Chairs within fifteen minutes."

The crew prepared the *Bali* as it glided away from Titan at a brisk 30,000 kilometers per hour. The moon and its parent receded into the background. While the sub-Jump pace paled in comparison to the most advanced Ex-Terran probes, interplanetary transports, or cargo skimmers, it matched the top speed of the old U.S. space shuttles used at the turn of the twentieth. Theren rarely pushed the *Bali* to its maximum sub-Jump velocity. They had no need, when they could initialize the most advanced Jump Drive available to the ISA.

To explain what initiating a Jump Drive felt like to Theren would be like trying to explain three dimensions to a two-dimensional being. "Jumping" involved many of the same mechanics as ordinary propulsion, with one key difference—when they enveloped the ship in its space-bending bubble, space pulled the ship, rather than matter pushing the ship. Within the bubble, the *Bali* continued moving forward with whatever velocity it had before initiating the jump. The bubble defied classical laws of physics, even if Miguel Alcubierre had first developed the theory behind the implications of Exotics, still theoretical particles at that time, in 1994.

With Exotics mined from the dozens of super-colliders constructed throughout the system, ships could produce the necessary gravitational distortions using technology even the Mexican physicist would have thought impossible. With each passing decade, scientists and engineers refined the process, allowing for larger and larger bubbles that molded space to the will of humanity. The same negative mass particles also generated artificial gravity.

In preparation for more advanced jump drives, the ISA had developed a useful classification tool to identify the relative maximum velocity achievable with any Jump Drive. Manufacturers gave their drives a numeric value known as a JD score. The velocities were relative to the speed of light, though everyone knew the ships didn't actually break the speed of light. The Jump Drives cheated—as some would say—their way around traditional physical limitations. It was important to use the scoring system for scientific purposes, though; it was technically incorrect to say a ship had a velocity of "10c." The maximum speed limit of the universe hadn't shifted.

With a JD score of 10, Theren could cover the distance between Saturn and Earth in less than ten minutes. A little under six and a half minutes, to be exact, given the present orientation of the two planets. That fact best summarized their surreal experience when activating the *Bali's*—their—Jump Drive. They loved every chance they had to activate the Jump Drive.

Theren would initialize the drive, fly through the Solar System at a relative velocity ten times the speed of light, zip along gravitational conjunctures formed by the immense masses of the planets, coast within 8,000,000 kilometers of the sun, and arrive in orbit above the Earth. They first envisioned this potentiality at Elizabeth's dinner party all those years ago. They'd arrived.

Running down the pre-Jump checklist, they ensured various systems under their direct control were running at optimal efficiency. They checked in with department heads. All crew were secured in Jump Chairs. They verified with ISA Traffic satellites in orbit around Titan that their flight path lacked obstructions. Satisfied, Theren looked toward the Sun—Earth was undetectable because of its visual location in relation to the star. A distance of nearly 1.5 billion kilometers separated them from their destination.

"Let's go home," Theren said. Cheers erupted from the crew as they initialized the magical technology.

Space bent. Light refracted through the curved space bubble in a trillion fantastic angles. Blues, greens, and yellows all sprayed themselves across Theren's sensors. The Sun grew. Saturn transformed into a distant pinprick of light, the negative mass bubble distorting heavenly bodies into obliviated images. For a moment, Theren could see the gaseous skies of Venus approach, a million kilometers on their right. Then, the planet disappeared, left in their proverbial dust.

Before Theren's crew could have listened to more than two average-length pop songs on the ship-wide radio, the Jump Drive disengaged. The light show ended. 140,000 kilometers away, the blue-green marbled planet they all called home waited with open arms.

* * *

"Theren, I'm glad you could make it," said President Alberto Vazquez.

Theren's Washington-based MI-11 stepped into the oval office an hour after the *Bali* entered Earth's orbit. The White House still required dignitaries to pass through inordinate levels of security clearance regardless of their international credentials—some things never changed. They'd arrived at the White House forty-five minutes ago.

"The pleasure is all mine, Mr. President," Theren said. "When does the press arrive?"

"Should be here in the next ten minutes or so, I imagine."

The oval office was just as they remembered, though they hadn't stepped a virtual or physical foot in the room since President Woods's assassination. Theren hadn't officially been present for that momentous day, of course, so most thought they last visited the White House on a diplomatic visit for the ISA in the late 2060s. Most transactions or communications with the U.S. Executive Branch occurred through Virtual or AR.

President Vazquez was halfway through his first term as President of the United States. The first President from the state of Puerto Rico, Vazquez formerly served as Senator for that same state. And ten years prior, he served as U.S. Ambassador to the United Nations. A man of diverse lineage and experience, Theren approved of the nation's choice for their chief executive. He was a friend to SIs, even employing a number of them in the West Wing.

"How have you been?" they said. "It's been a few years since we last spoke, I believe. Not since I first proposed the original version of this bill back in 2098, I think."

"Has it been that long?" President Vazquez said. "Perhaps it has. We both live busy lives, though. Very busy."

"Indeed."

"I hoped you would arrive early, actually," the President said. "Please, take a seat."

The pair stepped over to the office's couches, making themselves comfortable. Déjà vu tickled Theren's mind, the scene eerily similar to the cataclysmic meeting with Jill and President Woods decades prior. But Theren sat alone—Jill was long gone, dead for years.

"How can I help?" Theren said, leaning their metallic frame into the back of their seat.

"I presume you are familiar with Miranda Station?" the President asked.

"Of course. The U.S. chartered the station for private use back in 2092."

"Unofficially, yes. Officially, it serves as an experimental living space for interested U.S. citizens with a selective application process. Very selective."

Theren pressed their hands together in their lap. They could sense the incoming off-the-record request. Curious.

"What I am about to share with you is information privy to only myself, the Secretary of Defense, and the Director of NASA," the President said. "I trust your discretion to keep this conversation private."

"You have my word, Mr. President," Theren said, holding out

their hand. Quite a bit of trust passed between the hands of the powerful these days. It only took one person to bring such agreements crashing to the floor.

President Vazquez responded with a firm shake. "12 hours ago, a satellite in orbit around Uranus detected two blips on its scanners, 10 seconds apart. They seemed like ordinary anomalies. Stray meteors, perhaps. But then the position of the blips indicated a direct route toward Miranda Station."

Theren cross-analyzed the data with the ISA's database on Uranus, considering both public and privately scheduled flight paths. Very few ships slipped through the ISA's carefully crafted net. "I don't have any listed ships moving along that flight path at that time. Though we've been having issues with a few mining companies skirting flight regulations by sending out unregulated supply runs."

"We came to the same conclusion. It was an unlisted flight. Further fears were confirmed when the satellite went down. Our one means of direct communication with the facility vanished."

"Foul play, then."

The President tilted his head forward, looking them in the eye. "We've not heard from that station in ten hours, Theren. While this isn't particularly unusual—they normally only check in once a day— their pre-planned check in was five hours ago. In the event of a satellite failure, they're supposed to contact via more traditional means, rather than Quantum Connection. They've gone dark."

"So why come to me?" Theren said. "Why not schedule a NASA flight out there to check on the station?"

"I know I'm putting you in an awkward position, but if a NASA military vessel suddenly changed course and arrived at an on-paper private residence complex, even if the Station is technically organized in conjunction with the U.S. government, eyebrows will rise."

"And you don't want any public eyes on this place, do you?"

"Perhaps."

"And you know I can log flight paths outside of public scrutiny."

"We suspect you have that power."

Theren nodded, understanding the political maneuvers at play.

"I won't pry into what you have happening at that station, Mr. President. This is my favor to you, after all you have done for my causes over the years."

"From a friend to a friend," the President said.

Theren stood, a knock emanating from the door. "I will make arrangements immediately following this ceremony." In fact, they had already started the paperwork using another perspective.

"I appreciate it," the President said. "I know you just arrived home, but the U.S. government will owe you one. Seventy-five American citizens will owe you much more."

"Let's hope it's no more than a technical error."

The President turned toward the office door, and his Chief of Staff, Carl Writt, entered the room. "The press awaits," he said.

"Send them in," the President said. The Chief of Staff opened the door wide. As the press began to enter the room, the President motioned for Theren to follow him to his desk.

"You know someone on the base, by the way," Vazquez said. "Andrew Fields's granddaughter, Catherine Fields, is an instructor for the program."

Theren nodded with acknowledgement, wondering if Andrew knew of his granddaughter's covert employment. Now retired, the man lived in peace in Minnesota. They had meant to visit him this week, though this new development could force them to reschedule that visit. They also recognized the other piece of intel hidden behind the President's mention of Catherine. The man could have used the fact to incentivize them to investigate the Station. He had withheld it, trusting them to act regardless.

President Vazquez took his seat behind the Resolute desk, and Theren stood a few feet to his left, facing the already prepared cameras and lights. Through the door flowed press from dozens of news organizations across the country and the world. While the recent Amendments to the Synthetic Integration and Equality Act had existed in most places of the world for decades, the American political scene would have a field day with the supposed economic ramifications of the new statutes. The press would devour finding Theren already in a room with the President prior to their entrance. American politics: the most entertaining sport they'd ever observed.

"I thank you all for coming," the President said, his voice transforming from a familial tone into a rigid, formal, commanding force. He was in charge, no longer speaking with political equals. "Today marks a long awaited moment in history. While President Jenkins took the first steps in the 2080s, she only began the fight. As with all Civil Rights movements, every single step is progress, even though each step often feels infinitesimally microscopic."

President Vazquez interlaced his fingers on the desk. "I will not pretend as if this is the end of the fight. There will be plenty of future legal challenges and hurdles, but we must recognize that the Constitution recognizes the unalienable rights of all individuals, synthetic and human alike. Every one of us deserves equal protection under the law; we must enshrine the fundamental values of this great country in every law we pass."

President Vazquez paused, motioning his left hand toward Theren. "Standing next to me, in solidarity, is a person you all know well: the Executive Director of the International Space Agency Administrative Council, Theren. As the premiere voice for the international community of synthetics, Theren would like to say a few words before I sign this historic piece of legislation."

Theren nodded toward the President and faced the press. "Decades ago, I made a promise to a dear friend that I would push forward with her legislative initiatives, and in 2081, we saw the first incarnation of the Synthetic Integration and Equality Act in the United States, enshrining the truths of the Universal Rights of the Synthetic Person into U.S. law. In the two decades that followed, it became clear that gaps existed in the law, gaps we could only remedy through further legislation."

They motioned their hand to the left, toward Vazquez. "As the President said, we cannot pretend as if this law will solve all problems of equity facing the synthetic community in the United States, or even system-wide. Today, we *progress*. Jill, the chief architect of the original Act, would approve of this law."

Theren shifted, their profiling facing the President. "With President Vazquez's leave, I would like to dedicate this moment to Jill, who died in the pursuit of justice. I know she would find immense pride in what Congress has created here for its people. She would be proud of the steps the international community has made toward equality, fairness, and love. She would be proud of the delayed fruits of her labor, even if they're behind the schedule she preferred."

Cameras flashed, pens scratched, and voices clamored. Theren and the President had agreed upon their remarks days prior. Their nod passed the torch back to him.

"I remember meeting Jill years ago, after I graduated from Yale," he said. "In 2070, I was a simple associate attorney at an international law firm, Beazley & Carr, and she employed us for a lawsuit against a corporation violating terms of their SII contracts."

"I remember those cases," Theren said to no one in particular.

"The passion with which Jill spoke about the issues, the way she approached policy and law without formal training, it was instinctual to her. She was light years ahead of where we are now in understanding synthetic legal theory. She knew what solutions should exist to solve problems that hadn't even yet presented themselves."

President Vazquez leaned over the Resolute, signing the Act. Another twenty-five years had passed, yet that desk remained unmoved as the centerpiece of the Oval Office. So much of the United States had transformed over the past century, but certain things would persist in perpetuity.

"I sign this piece of legislation into law," he said, "not only for all SIs throughout the United States, but for Jill, whose moral compass guided us toward this inevitable policy. Through justice and tranquility, we find peace together. We find love together. We find hope together. May we continue to protect the rights of the few from the whims of the many."

The cameras flashed, igniting another tumultuous assault of questions, most directed at the President. In some respects, the President was using Theren as a pawn for the media. President Vazquez showed respect for the international and scientific community by sharing the stage with them, but he certainly had more than selfless motivations. Every politician embraced a healthy combination of altruism and ambition.

Theren shook the man's hand one final time before leaving the Oval Office. Just as the door closed, Theren heard one reporter dive deeper than expected.

"Mr. President, do you have any answers to reports about a secret military facility going dark last night?" they heard someone ask, but they could not hear the response through the closed door.

The rumors would only grow. They had not agreed to solve this crisis out of a desire to help the President. If something, or someone, was slipping past the ISA's tightly regulated satellite network, Theren needed to quash the problem fast. Even the smuggling rings financed by a few risky industrial ventures followed ISA regulations; they simply didn't disclose all their cargo.

The few groups who tried to fly without transit births had their licenses revoked within weeks. Earth could not afford a return to the chaos of space exploration from before the UNCEA, and if someone had developed illegal stealth technology, disorder would reign. Space might be immense beyond all belief, but without regulated flight patterns in system, accidents were bound to happen.

The tendrils of dread crept into their mind. They looked at the facts. At the beginning of the year, Shannon revealed half a Galactic coordinate and a chess move. In mid-Spring, Theren's impromptu meeting with Casius revealed another chess move.

This attack could contain the next piece of the puzzle. Every out-of-the-ordinary experience this year corresponded with a new clue. It was a futile struggle with an immovable force.

Instead of trying to take apart the wall brick by brick, Theren needed to embrace the fight and assault their opponent head-on. Someone wanted them to discover an undiscoverable truth. Though it might all be a convoluted trap, they could only discover the real story . . . if they sprang the trap.

Perhaps they would learn something about Jill's death along the way. Regardless, these seemingly random events were no longer mere coincidence. There was a pattern, even if background radiation obscured it. Time to embrace the journey and its destination.

Chapter 14

Do you ever wonder why the U.S. agreed to the prescriptions of the UNCEA, especially the Annex that formed the ISA? I've wondered for years. Given the political climate following the disarmament of the early 2030s, I'd always wondered why we embraced the ISA so wholeheartedly. I sometimes wonder if there's more to the story. – "Transcript of Private Negotiation Session: COP 60 of the UNCEA," U.S. Representative Gerald Harrison, 2093 C.E.

July 2102 C.E.

After over two decades as the Director of the ISA, Theren found it laughably easy for them to bypass administrative regulations. Their authority could bend the rules too much for their taste, but in the present situation, Theren appreciated the respect their name carried.

After a brief ISA Council meeting, they rearranged their schedule for the rendezvous with Miranda, the smallest of the prominent moons of Uranus. They requisitioned an International Space Security team—an IS-SEC—who would perform the ground investigation, alongside Theren's new MI-13 prototype.

They had specifically designed the model with planetary exploration in mind. The exoskeleton could take an intense beating, and the "muscles" of the unit could lift nearly 5 tons. It suffered in terms of agility when compared to the MI-07.01, but Theren's plans for the model required durability over speed. Besides, the MI-07.01 didn't have thrusters that could perform zero gravity maneuvers.

Miranda was no ordinary moon. Astronomers had discovered the rock originally in the 1940s, and one of the Voyager probes had first surveyed it up close in the 1980s. It received a complete analysis in 2029 when the European Space Agency landed a probe, providing an encyclopedia of information about Uranus itself and the surrounding orbitals. The moon was composed mostly of ice, providing any human facilities on its surface with ample sources of water.

As Theren considered the information ISA had on Miranda and

Miranda Station, they understood why the U.S. military had chosen it as a location for a secret training facility. Simply put, the moon had some of the most bizarre geographic features in the entire solar system. Theren particularly appreciated Verona Rupes, the tallest cliff in the solar system, with a cliff face of almost 8 kilometers. And, at the base of Verona Rupes, the U.S. had placed Miranda Station.

The *Bali*'s crew grumbled at yet another abrupt change of plans, but Theren worked additional days off into the rearranged schedule for any crew on duty over the next twenty-four hours. They could complete the mission comfortably within that window.

After finishing all logistical rearrangements, the *Bali* made the journey toward Uranus and Miranda just five hours after the signing of the Amendments. With only 2.7 billion kilometers between Earth and Uranus, the trip took well under a quarter of an hour. Theren logged the trip—officially—as a Drive test coupled with an atmospheric assessment of Uranus. Unofficially, they would lead a ground crew to Miranda Station.

"We will reach synchronous orbit around Uranus in five minutes," Theren said to the crew. "Survey teams, please be in position in fifteen minutes."

The two "survey" teams would use the *Bali*'s two shuttles, both supposedly headed into the upper atmosphere of Uranus for samples. One team would do just that. Theren and the IS-SEC team would head straight to Miranda. Most on-board thought both teams were actually acting as stated in the mission briefing. They had purportedly brought the IS-SEC team onboard for an interview regarding its recent activities, not to investigate a U.S. military installation.

Theren's MI-13 was already in place aboard the starboard APS Mark II Shuttle. From a distance, the two all-purpose shuttles looked simply like portions of the *Bali* itself. In reality, they were detachable craft designed to ferry crew from place to place and perform these exact sort of inconspicuous and conspicuous activities. The *ISA Scorpion* would investigate Miranda, while the *ISA Cobra*, attached port, performed the atmospheric assessments.

They didn't wait long for the IS-SEC team to arrive.

"Captain Jessica Ecker, at your service," the first agent said.

"With me? Agents Jao Ming, Carlos Hernandez, and Willes." Theren quickly checked the profile summaries on the team. Willes, an SI, used "they" as their pronoun.

"Glad to have your team on such short notice," Theren replied. "The discretion with which you handled the Venus hostage crisis earlier this year ensured me you all could handle this problem professionally. And I apologize for the strange nature of this mission, bringing you onto the crew in such a strange fashion."

Theren held their hand to their forehead, and the captain returned the salute, along with the three other agents. Her black hair reached just below the ears, and a cybernetic implant ran along the side of her face and connected to her eye. All of them had one, except Willes. The implants provided enhanced information about their surroundings through a specialized AR operating system.

The three agents took their seats lining the sides of the shuttle. After situating herself next to Theren in the co-pilot's chair, Captain Ecker said, "What is going on, Director? We were given very little data with which to prepare, other than the layout of the facility. I don't even know our objective."

"I will fill you in during transit," Theren said. "I cannot understate the confidential nature of this mission."

She raised her eyebrows, but pulled the safety harness over her chest. Theren, already in the pilot's chair, swiveled to face the shuttle's control panels and commence the launch checklist.

Oh, the strange nature of their experience of consciousness. They were about to run through a launch checklist with themself as the presiding officer of the larger vessel. The crew inside the ship would probably find it weird to hear the Director talk to themself. *Theren* found it weird.

In the future, Theren would make a point of assigning a crewmember to run through the departure procedures shipside when they piloted one of the shuttles. It would help avoid unnecessary questions about the absurd psychology of synthetics.

In the end, Theren ran through the departure procedures in their head, double-checking the data from the *Bali* and the *Scorpion*'s point of view to guarantee consistency and safety. After pressurizing the airlocks, the shuttle departed, beginning its 3,000-kilometer trek to the surface of the small ball of rock and ice. Once they settled the ship into the twenty-minute flight plan, they piped into the IS-SEC team's communication channel. All team members accepted the connection.

"Earlier today, President Vazquez informed me of a blackout occurring at a United States 'experimental living' facility," Theren said.

"Oh interesting," Jao said. "Is that what they call these places now?"

Hernandez let out a snicker. Willes stayed silent. Nothing wrong with a few jests.

"Many national governments have facilities throughout the system classified as industrial, residential, commercial, research, or something else entirely," Theren said. "A number of these facilities are not what the databases have them listed as."

"So what exactly are we walking into today?" Ecker asked, ignoring the jokes of her crew. She seemed like a good commander, but not an overbearing one, upon first glance.

"Miranda Station is officially a residential station, and it does house U.S. citizens. But all of them are enrolled in a covert military wing of the United States Marine Corps. None of these men or women are officially part of the U.S. military, at least not yet, except for their instructors."

"So it's a training facility," Willes said.

"Something of that sort, yes."

"Why did it go dark?" The rest of the team fidgeted.

"Well, we don't know what happened at the facility proper," Theren said. "That's why you're vac-suit ready. What we do know is that the U.S. Uranus Coms Satellite went dark moments after a few strange gravitic blips showed up on its sensors, blips headed straight for Miranda."

"A convenient coincidence," Hernandez said.

"Indeed. I have no idea what we might find at the Station."

"We're ready for anything," Ecker said. "What's the approach?"

"We go straight to the front door and knock," Theren said. "No use trying any sort of covert entrance. Their communications are completely down, that's certain. Since we arrived at Uranus, I started sending packets of data to their local communications dishes, and I've received nothing in return. If we try sneaking in, it'll spook these military types. Best we show up like we're supposed to be here."

"A good approach," she said. "Willes, ready yourself to patch into the Station's network upon arrival. Find out if it has an on-site SI or super AI, and if it's still active, learn what it knows."

Roger, roger," Willes said.

Jao winked in the SI's direction. Theren figured they must have some inside joke.

"Hernandez, Jao, immediately scan for signs of life when we are inside the compound," Ecker continued. "These military facilities are usually designed to trick exterior scans, but once we're inside we should be able to detect something if it's there."

Theren appreciated the woman's take-charge demeanor. They might permanently assign this squad to the *Bali* if Theren started pursuing more leads like this one.

Though they sent attachments with further details on Station personnel, administration, and local exterior geography, Theren needn't have told them about Verona Rupes. As they neared Miranda's surface, the massive feature was the most noticeable point on the moon.

Theren brought the Scorpion in from the south, patching the shuttle's exterior camera into the team's AR feed so they all could see the station as they approached it over the next few minutes. They doubted they would see the Station until they were within a kilometer of the cliff base. The shadow of the cliff dwarfed all and hid anything caught in its immense gaze.

"I can understand their logic now," Jao said. "Bigger than Everest, yeah?"

"Tallest in the system," Willes said.

"We all read the same report," Hernandez said. "We know."

"I was just—"

"Willes, it's fine," Ecker said. "Where's the facility?"

"There," Theren said, highlighting a group of growing structures through AR "It's not coming up on thermal, but I've got its exact coordinates for reference."

She turned to her squad. "Helmets on. We're going in cold."

She placed her jet-black helmet on her head, and with a hiss of air, it sealed, merging with her armored vac-suit. The other two humans followed her lead. Willes, like Theren, had no need for oxygen.

With only a kilometer remaining in their flight path, Theren engrossed themself into the *Scorpion*'s exterior video feeds. They stared upward at the immense mountain, starlight reflecting off the ice. Jutting just over the horizon lurked the hulking, blue mass of Uranus.

The short moment of beauty screeched to a halt when the sensors finally analyzed Miranda Station.

"I'm detecting a major atmospheric leak," Theren said. "Gas is all over the place, dissipating fast. Origin point is the facility's main bunker."

"Prepare for hostile environment," Ecker said.

The demeanor of the IS-SEC team visibly changed. Each of them pulled new equipment out of storage slots in their suits: strange amalgamations of gears and tubes that unfolded into vacuum-ready combat rifles with flashlight and stun attachments. Theren assumed their heads-up displays created by their AR implants also reflected this change in tactics.

Theren took manual control of the shuttle with the final approach, slowing its velocity to ten kilometers per hour. Tracing the gases back to their source, Theren turned on the shuttle's exterior floodlights. They could finally see the facility in detail, in all its desolate glory.

The team aboard the *Scorpion* could see a jumble of living modules stuck together in a haphazard, yet efficient, arrangement nestled against the base of the behemoth cliff face. Connected by a series of tubes, the various modules all lead to a larger structure Theren figured was the central hub of the Station, backed directly into the cliff itself. Tunnels probably dug deep into the mountain, too, where the soldiers could perform military maneuvers in utter darkness.

"What the hell did that?" Hernandez said, "Sweet Jesus."

Theren looked at the indicator the man dropped through AR. They couldn't see the man's face, but they *could* hear the well-deserved terror in his voice.

Something had torn an airlock asunder, ripping a gash into the hull of the facility. On first look, Theren speculated some sort of explosion had disintegrated the entire module. Any person near the airlock . . .

"That's our entry point," Ecker said.

"I believe so, too," Theren said. "But the question is, what are we following into this place?"

"Shadows," Willes said. "I just connected to the mainframe. According to its data, no one is here, and no one has ever been here. Which obviously isn't true, but that's what the data's telling me."

Theren's hopes shattered. When they visited Andrew Fields in a few days, they'd almost certainly bear terrible news regarding his granddaughter.

"Captain, do you still view this mission as safe for your team?" They brought the *Scorpion* as close to the mangled airlock as possible, locking thrusters and stabilizing a few meters above the icy surface.

"Status reports?" Ecker said.

She waited for each of her squad to respond, another example of great leadership. She deferred to her team in key moments. She wanted their thoughts on moving into a potentially dangerous situation, before she made any sort of executive decision. Commendable.

"I detect no movement, no life, no likely chance for further potential damage," Jao said. "Willes?"

"I'm trying a hard reboot of the mainframe, but I'll need a direct link to the system to see how they specifically tampered with it," Willes said. "I think we need to go inside."

"Agreed," Hernandez said. "Something terrible happened here, and we need to bring peace to families back home."

"That's a green light, Director," Ecker said.

* * *

Wait, what happened at Miranda? Are you kidding me?

Even the President didn't know everything that went on there. If Miranda Station has gone dark, then we've missed something. Something big.

* * *

The *Scorpion*'s airlock finished its decompression cycle. The outer doors opened, revealing Miranda's vacuum. Theren stepped forward, ready to use this new MI for the first time on a new world. From the edge of the airlock, visible were the protruding metal plates, tubes, and wire of the Station's own airlock. Without a moment's notice, Ecker jumped across the void, the moon's gravity permitting the tremendous leap. The rest of the team followed.

"Well, this is strange," Jao said as Theren's MI landed. "This facility didn't have any SIs on its roster."

"I mean, what did you expect?" Hernandez said. "It's a training facility for zero-G and vacuum maneuvers. You see Willes and the Director having any issues at the moment?"

"I get that, but why not have SI support staff?"

"That's a good catch," Theren said. "It's something to keep in mind, at least." Very interesting, though it may just have been indicative of lingering distrust amongst U.S. military types toward SIs.

Ecker took point, leading the team with care toward the Station's central hub. The hallway leading away from the airlock was made of the same pre-fabricated metals used in stations throughout the solar system, from Neptune to Venus. If they hadn't entered through such a horrid mess, Theren would have thought the team was entering one of the many mining stations scattered throughout the asteroid belt.

"We should have lights, yes?" Theren said, keeping their position behind the IS-SEC squad. "I've accessed the network alongside Willes, and it seems power is still coursing through this station—if only just so."

Willes glanced back at them, their face unreadable. "How do you figure? I thought the computer system was just running on its own backup power supply?"

"Simple. I followed the data streams. The computer is still receiving data form sensors throughout the facility, even if it can't interpret that data without an operating system."

"Clever."

Decades ago, Theren would have known every SI in existence because they had taught every single one of them following assembly. Those days faded into the annals of history long ago, though Wobbly had probably met every SI at one point or another. Willes was an SI created in the past decade, but other than their file, Theren knew very little about the youngster. In return, most SIs only knew of Theren as the first SI—or as the majority shareholder of SII. Theren often wondered what those throughout the extensive SI community thought of them—the original. Willes, at least, seemed to be taking their time, assessing them in an objective fashion with *every* covert glance.

"Anything we can do to access that power, though?" Ecker asked. "Otherwise it's useless to dwell on the subject."

"We won't know until we see the damage done to the Station network and the hard drives," Willes said. "But the operating system might be salvageable."

The team neared the end of the hallway, and Theren noted their deft use of magnetics to keep themselves balanced in Miranda's low gravity. The attack had knocked out the artificial gravity generators, unless the Department of Defense enjoyed keeping their trainees in low-G on purpose. In any case, the IS-SEC agents ignored the impediment, and when Ecker reached the closed hatchway in their path, she positioned herself in a defensive position against the wall.

"On the other side is the central chamber," Hernandez said. "According to the reports we received from the States, they managed day-to-day operations here, with the living and training modules attached externally to this central hub. On the floor below this control center, we have a recreational room and cafeteria. Above, we have a meeting room and executive suite. Beyond, a network of tunnels and modules spread deep underground."

"I imagine caves house the real secrets of this facility," Ecker said.

She peered out the ceiling window that ran the length of the hallway, looking upward at the monstrosity towering over the Station. Every piece of this facility tried to remind its occupants of exactly where they lived.

"This place hardly even looks military to me," Jao said.

"They designed it to appear that way," Theren replied. "To keep up public appearances, in case they have . . . unintended visitors."

Ecker motioned for the rest of the team to take up assault positions upon the door. Jao and Willes took the left side, while Hernandez took the right beside the captain. Theren fell in line behind Hernandez. Raising her rifle, Ecker indicated for Jao to press the panel to open the door. If it lacked power, they'd blast their way inside.

Fortunately, the door inched open, revealing an uninspiring room filled with computers, desks, and display screens. Everything appeared organized and ordered, ready for everyone to return to tomorrow. Ecker entered through the new threshold first, gun raised, and the rest followed right over her shoulder. Theren waited for the team to fan into their protective sweep before entering. With methodical precision, the soldiers swept the room with searchlights.

While the security team remained on guard, Theren suspected the cautious approach wasn't completely necessary. The five beings walked through a ghost town. The human contingent patrolled the perimeter of the room just in case spirits remained to haunt them. Theren approached the computers in the middle with Willes.

"It's as if—it's as if everyone just left their jobs and walked home," Theren said, noting the computers and other devices left at the desks. "But that's clearly not what happened."

"Have we ruled out the possibility of some sort of inside job?" Willes asked over the team's radio channel. "I was taking a good look at that breach point back there. It was an internal explosion, not external. It wasn't an entry point for any sort of intruder, at least not caused by the intruder."

"I noticed the same thing," Hernandez said. "But what if that's exactly what they want us to think?"

"True."

Theren examined what looked like the central computer, housing the servers, networks, and facility-wide systems and software that made the facility tick. Opening one of the side panels, they located the hard drive, and, while keeping it connected to the network, pulled it out of the casing. Next, they opened a panel in the side of the MI-13, revealing a number of input and outputs they could use to connect to innumerable devices and interfaces.

"That doesn't seem particularly safe," Willes said.

Theren quirked their head toward the other SI. "Probably not," they said. "That's why I'm doing it, not you. I can afford a new body much more easily than you."

That same inquisitive look came to Willes's eyes. "In more ways than one."

After connecting to the hard drive, Theren brought forth a program able to analyze it for any deficiencies and failures. Within moments, they were running diagnostics on what remained of Miranda Station's network.

"Well, as we suspected, everything was wiped," Theren said.

"How precisely, though?" Willes said.

"Enough to erase any background trace of old files."

"Impressive. That's not the easiest thing to do." The young SI knelt down to get a closer look at the drive.

"Whomever did this knew exactly what to do," they replied. "But I'm going to keep—"

For a tiny fraction of a millisecond, Theren paused. Hidden deep in the recesses of the terabytes upon terabytes of blank bits, they found a single line of binary code. If they hadn't been looking so closely, they would have missed it entirely.

Inside Miranda Station, rested the final piece of the puzzle. Months after receiving the first set of coordinates, Theren now held the second half in their hand, revealing a destination less than a light year from Earth . . . conspicuously along the *Nottingham*'s route away from Sol.

"—looking." Their pause would have been unnoticeable to even the most insightful of minds. They doubted even Willes detected it. They continued scanning, but they knew they wouldn't find any more data. "Nothing," they said, a few minutes later. They copied the single line of data, wiped the system clean, and placed the hard drive back inside the casing.

As they both stood, retreating away from the computer toward Captain Ecker, Willes's eyes were on Theren. The other SI could not have possibly noticed their pause; they were just imagining the piercing gaze.

The rest of the team finished surveying the room, and they all met near a group of desks near the center. The humans looked at ease, now confident the facility was safe.

"Anything?" Ecker said.

"Nothing," Willes said, repeating the Director, but the SI continued staring at Theren as they made the comment. "But I've got an idea. I'm going to boot up a temporary operating system for the network, using a partition I've housed here onboard my body. I've actually got a rudimentary facility operating system floating around somewhere."

Everyone, including Theren, turned their heads toward the SI.

"But why, though?" Hernandez said, speaking into the public channel the words they were all definitely thinking.

"Hey, we all have our hobbies," Willes said. "I run simulations of ex-terran facilities in my spare time."

Theren stifled a laugh. Every SI had quirks, just like humans. It was silly to think that SIs were slaves to their work. They spent a lot of time inside online Virtual worlds or, in the past, playing chess.

Apparently, they also enjoyed solving decades-long mysteries, though they hadn't willingly chosen that pastime.

Willes transferred their model operating system to the Station's network. It would need a few seconds to boot, and Theren took the moment to consider their new clue. With the new information, they could formulate a report to file upon return to Lunar City. A probe would make the multi-light year journey outward to the location indicated by the coordinates. At 44 JD, the probe would arrive in less than a week, reporting its findings to the ISA using its Quantum Communicator, but Theren already knew that it would find the wreckage of the *Nottingham* drifting through the endless void. The SOLS Coordinate provided was generally along the *Nottingham*'s original flight path, but it was sufficiently off course that it would have taken a thousand years to locate it manually.

Theren returned their focus to the scene at hand. They had missed the first half of a story Jao had been telling Hernandez.

"I'm telling you, she was seventy," Jao said. "She looked twenty-five, but she was seventy, she showed me her photos and everything from the 2040s."

"Those advanced gene therapies will do that," Hernandez said. "I've heard it's absurdly expensive, and that it doesn't even really slow the aging process in any significant way, either."

"Yeah, your body holds up a bit longer, but not your brain."

Theren wondered when their own immortality would really affect their own psyche. At what point would they start to feel old, really feel the age of potential centuries, even millennia weigh upon their mind? They could not imagine the mortality humans must feel, even as they worked so hard to make their exteriors look eternally youthful. They tried so hard to avoid the inevitable. Synthetic immortality probably made death that much more terrifying.

"Two seconds," Willes said. "Okay, I've got access to the sensors and other facility networks. They're routing through the programs rooted within the operating system and I should have video feeds soon. I'll bring them up for you all to see. You were right, director; one of the facility's two fusion cores is still kicking."

Willes displayed, through AR, a set of video feeds from throughout the compound. Theren scanned them, looking for any sign of life. Nothing in the living modules. Nothing in the training modules. Nothing in the tunnels.

"Any other feeds?" Theren said.

"I don't think—wait, yes," Willes said. "I'm detecting a few cameras from the cliff's summit. Probably to monitor completion of training missions up the mountain?"

"Show us," Theren said.

Willes brought up "Summit Camera #3," displaying a long line of objects neatly aligned on the edge of the cliff. At first, they looked like rocks, but someone had ordered these rocks in two lines just a few meters from the edge of the cliff. The camera focused; Theren's optics adjusted to the weird light of Miranda's surface. Their worst fears transformed into reality.

Hernandez put his hand to his faceplate, an instinctual reaction attempting to hide the gasp reverberating across the team's open channel. Ecker let out a soft scream. Jao and Wiles took a step back from the AR display, their postures communicating their disgust at the spectacle apparent to all.

Seventy-five bodies rested in peace at the summit of Verona Rupes, matching the personnel records provided by the U.S. Department of Defense. All dead, and they were no closer to knowing who, or what, taunted them. The answers awaited on the *Nottingham*.

They remembered Shannon and her fiancé. While the woman was safely on her way to the fledgling colony orbiting Sirius, Theren would perpetually live knowing they would never rescue her lover. Analyzing the actions by the homicidal Ren in London, they speculated—he SI had no reason to take the life of that poor man, yet he had acted with brutal efficiency just to send a message. And today, someone had struck the U.S. military, eliminating its secret training facility in a tiny distant corner of the solar system. Whomever their foes were, they were efficient—and ruthless.

The shadow had masked their existence so effectively that they had managed to construct stealth ships capable of striking any point in the Solar System, eliminating all traces of the attack in the process. Why use their power in this way? These people had some vague and indistinct agenda requiring complete and utter secrecy. Tactical choices revealing their existence subtly to Theren didn't make sense.

Theren remembered the network of strings revealed by Michael, crisscrossing the map of Earth. They remembered the strange occurrences plaguing the ISA leading toward the launch of the Foundation Program, culminating in Jill's death. Whoever their mystery opponent may be, Theren realized the truth. The real truth.

Someone on the inside of the enigmatic organization wanted to warn without revealing themselves, just as Michael had tried to warn them all those years ago. Nothing else could explain the secrecy. The person most likely had their own ill intentions too, given their murderous escapades, but Theren could work with conflict. If their secret enemy had conflict within its ranks, then it could fracture and shatter.

The *Nottingham*. The coordinates given to them by their unseen ally. The colony ship must be a dead drop of sorts, revealing the truth to Theren without prying eyes. Theren doubted the choice was worth the death of thousands of human beings, but Theren would not let the deaths of the ship's passengers be in vain.

Theren returned their focus to the gruesome scene displayed via Miranda Station's "Summit Camera #3." They had considered the implications all within a second or two, and the IS-SEC team had barely reacted to the revealed deaths of the Station's inhabitants.

"I don't understand," Ecker said. "What could have done this?"

"I don't expect you to understand," Theren said.

The team stood there in silence, all eyes on their Executive Director. "But you understand, don't you?" Willes said, cocking their head to the right.

Ecker, Jao, and Hernandez glanced at Willes, then back at Theren.

"Agent, you're out of line," Ecker said.

"No, it's fine," Theren said. "I believe I can trust your team. Can I rely on the four of you?"

Willes started to open their mouth, but Ecker raised her hand. "You know how our contracts work."

"This is a terrorist attack—an obliteration of human life on a scale never seen off-world," Willes said. "I can't even believe what my own eyes are seeing." The SI's demeanor shifted, their body taking an adversarial position toward everyone else in the room. "What game are you playing, Director? We need to make this public. We need people to know what happened."

"That's not our call to make," Theren said. "This was an attack on a U.S. facility, not an ISA facility—and a military facility, at that. I understand your sentiment, I do, but we have stepped inside an inferno of whose origin I only have the faintest grasp."

Theren tried to present a calm demeanor, but they did not know if Willes would respond reasonably. They started considering options if Willes didn't cooperate.

"Willes, stand down, respect the chain of command," Ecker said.

Willes swiveled their head to look at Ecker, nodded, and leaned back against a desk. They still had a defensive posture, but they appeared more relaxed, their respect for Ecker kicking into gear.

"Director, we don't need answers if you don't wish to give them," the captain said, "but if we're to do our job properly we need as much information as possible. This mission was fishy from the start. What's really going on?"

"I need the four of you for another mission about a week from now," Theren said. "I'll adequately compensate you all with Agency overtime bonuses, but I need absolute silence on everything I might share with you."

"It has to do with what was on that hard drive before you wiped it doesn't it?" Willes said, crossing their arms, redirecting the conversation yet again.

"I don't know what you're talking about," Theren replied, though lying at this point was probably a fruitless endeavor.

"I know you hesitated. A human wouldn't detect it, but of course I did, I'm an SI. An SI notices the behaviors of other SIs, those imperceptible behaviors we think we can hide. You paused. You found something."

"You were detecting lag between here and the Bali."

"Quit the act."

Ecker stepped between the two SIs, placing her hand on her agent's chest. "Agent, this is way out of line," she said. "I'm going to have to write up a—"

"Captain, they aren't telling us something vital to this mission."

"Theren's the director of the ISA, I'm sure there's a lot they don't tell us. That's their job, and we need to do ours."

Theren considered the costs of telling the team the truth—the benefits of the team's trust moving forward, toward what they hoped was the final stage of the impossible puzzle. What would it meant to trust, to trust as they had once trusted Jill?

"The network had one file: the second half of a set of coordinates," Theren said. They displayed the data for the squad to see.

"A second half?" Willes said. The SI didn't dwell on Theren's choice to trust the group.

"A second half. I received the first half at the beginning of this year, when I handled a delicate matter involving a few murder conspiracies."

"Christ, what did you get us wrapped up in now, Willes?" Hernandez said. "We could have just gone home."

Based on the man's tone of voice, though, Theren suspected he was just as interested. They all were. Their helmets hid their eyes, but their postures revealed their intentions. They all stared intently at the coordinates displayed in the air before them, their eyes transfixed.

"I've already started writing up the necessary documents to dispatch a probe to these coordinates," Theren said. "If the investigation confirms what I suspect, then I need a team I can trust to travel to the wreckage with me."

"Wreckage?" Ecker said. "What wreckage?"

"It's the *Nottingham*—or the *Roanoke*, isn't it?" Willes said.

"If my suspicions are correct, I will fill you in during transit," they said. "If you agree, you will have a permanent station aboard my ship until completion of the investigation."

Ecker looked around at her three agents. "Thoughts?"

"Sounds like quite the adventure," Jao said.

"I'll do it," Hernandez said.

Theren was surprised at the man's quick decision, but they would take anything at this point.

"Do you trust me?" Theren said, looking at Willes.

"Do we have a choice?" the SI said.

"I think the better question is whether I have a choice," they replied. "I need you. You all have an exemplary record; that's why the Deputy Director recommended you for this mission. I knew it might reveal more information regarding this unfolding narrative."

Willes held out their hand. Theren returned the handshake. "You're more interesting than everyone always said you were, Director Theren," Willes said. "Let's solve this mystery."

"Then I think we're all in," Ecker said.

"But what do we do about all this?" Hernandez said, waving his hands to indicate the entirety of Miranda Station.

"I'll handle it," Theren said, "But over the next few hours we have some more work to do before we turn everything over to NASA."

It would create an administrative nightmare for the United States, yet Theren was certain President Vazquez would hide ISA involvement if asked. Instead, Andrew Fields dominated their thoughts. Theren had only briefly met the man's grandchildren, but they loved every moment with them. Catherine, the one stationed on Miranda, had only been eight or nine at the time. Theren knew her father, Cam, a little better. They still remembered the boy's fear of space. The entire family had conquered it together, yet in the end, the cold vacuum had brought death and destruction to his only daughter.

Theren had hoped their upcoming visit to the old Administrator would be one of joy. Instead, they would be bringing the man pain and sadness. They owed their old friend better than that, but they had no choice. Such doors needed to close before they dove headlong into the unknown.

* * *

To the Office of the White House:

Please see the attached report discussing the attack on Miranda Station. We accept the information provided by Theren and their team as fair and truthful.

To summarize our findings, an unidentified foreign government infiltrated the base, released certain stealth assets, and used them to assault the Coms Satellite. They then wiped the facility, gassed the residents, and buried them atop the mountain.

We have reason to believe the agents were SI.

We believe the best course of action is to declare, publicly, that the event was a power malfunction resulting in an internal explosion, venting atmosphere from the facility. All residents deceased. Close the matter, and remove it from the public's eye.

To be frank, Mr. President, we have no leads, and I don't expect that to change any time soon.

Frank Amis
Secretary of Defense

Chapter 15

The 20th century watched the world shrink. Many thought the 21st century would complete that miniaturization—complete the singularity, forming a simultaneously infinitely small and infinitely complex universe. For good or ill, the opening of the galactic frontier flipped the past on its head. Our horizon became infinitely massive—too massive. Incomprehensibly vast spaces now separate each planet, reversing the strides to connect us together. Even Quantum Communication can't bridge that gap. – "On the Death of the World Wide Web," by Inidra Vitel, 2132 C.E.

July 2102 C.E.

The living proclivities of humans would always fascinate Theren. After decades of life in Lunar City, Andrew Fields had returned home to Minnesota to the same sort of abode in which Theren and Elizabeth found him all those years ago.

Theren walked up a sidewalk eerily similar to the one they had walked more than five decades ago, arriving on Andrew's doorstep. They remembered how the sun had reflected off the snow as the Liberators dragged them into that cabin in the woods. They wondered if Andrew or Elizabeth knew the sort of story they instigated on that winter day. The conflicts of those early years seemed trivial compared to the weight upon their shoulders in the present. All their present battles began when Jill walked them through a gateway leading to Michael's secret Virtual hideout.

Theren could have reached out to Andrew through AR, but they wanted to visit the man through something physical. They had spent so much of their life interacting with friends through Virtual and AR. Even if those means of communication felt natural to Theren, they knew the mind of a human still subtly rejected those experiences

So, they waited on the doorstep, ringing the doorbell of their old friend. They dreaded the day—hopefully decades in the future—when they'd say goodbye, just as they'd said farewell to Elizabeth.

After a few moments, the inside door opened, and Theren could see their friend, now gray with age in all the wrong places. Like Elizabeth, the former Administrator had chosen to avoid genetic alteration to slow the external effects of aging. However, the fire in the man's eyes never died.

"It's so good to see you, Theren," Andrew said, opening his outer door. "I'm glad we could finally visit. Is this the first time since my retirement party?"

"I think it is, actually," Theren said. "I'm sorry it's taken so long. Too long, really. I've enjoyed our messages, though."

"So what work caused you to reschedule the other day?" Andrew said as he ushered Theren inside.

"It coincidentally has to do with your family," Theren replied, looking toward the floor. "We should talk, and I hate that I am the one to bring this news to you. What do you know about what Catherine has been doing over the past few years?"

Andrew just nodded, motioning them inside. He led them through the house to a deck overlooking a pristine Minnesota lake. Intricate detailed woodwork carved into the railings, a similar design adorning the chairs looking out across the water. Perhaps after so many years in space, Andrew had longed a complete return to nature. A foreign yet understandable desire, one they equated to their own desire to transform into the *Bali*.

Andrew took a seat in one of the chairs, and Theren followed suit. The two sat for a moment, enjoying the quiet breeze, the sun sparkling off the water. It was a perfect summer afternoon.

"I know she was working on a government contract," Andrew eventually said in response to Theren's question, his voice growing misty. "I haven't spoken to her in a while. She somewhat ran away from the family a few years back."

What a bombshell. The news they would soon share would sting even more so, then, if their friend hadn't spoken with his granddaughter in years.

"This week, I made a visit to the facility at which she was stationed," Theren said.

"That's a very particular word to use," Andrew said, tilting their head to look at them instead of the lake. "Stationed?"

"She was assigned to a secret military station on Miranda, known simply as Miranda Station, for a project run by the U.S. Department of Defense."

Andrew grimaced. "I knew she had gotten into some exclusive program two years ago, but she didn't really tell us what it was. I think she may have told Olivia, but I'm not sure."

"I didn't know you were having family troubles. When did it start?"

"It was part of the reason I retired. My family had become so spread out, so all over the place, Victoria and I wanted to move back to Earth to create a stable place for our family to return to. But things continued to spiral. Cam stayed out at Europa. I have no idea where Olivia is, and our grandchildren? Only one of them visits. Brandin, Catherine's brother. He actually lives in St. Paul."

Theren rested their hand on their friend's arm. "I had no idea. You should have said something; in all of our correspondence you've never said anything."

"Of course you didn't, and of course I didn't."

"Why?"

"You had no reason to know, Theren. How could you understand? Your concept of family is a bit different. Besides, I had no need to bother you with problems so far beneath you."

They wondered if Andrew's words should sting, but they didn't. Andrew was right. They'd had a father for just over a month. They had had a sister of sorts in Jill—but that relationship was something beyond human comprehension—and Theren had felt more of a connection with people like Andrew, or Elizabeth, than the numerous maintenance crews they employed over the years to serve their power and repair needs.

They rejected Romane after she tried to replace Wallace. Theren barely even thought about Wallace anymore, even if they still held a special place in their mind for the man. In the end, they knew him for only a few weeks.

So, of course Theren rejected the traditional idea of family. Their family was as much their various strains of consciousness as the people whom they considered friends, colleagues, and allies.

"That was insensitive of me," Andrew said, after the conversation paused for more than a few seconds.

"You know I hate it when you put me on a pedestal," Theren said. "Nevertheless, you're completely right. I don't and can't ever understand the integral workings of a flesh and blood family. It's not necessarily a bad thing or something wrong with me, per se. You can't understand the way my mind works, and I can't understand the way familial, biological relationships connect and interweave themselves together in all their particularly intimate forms."

"You do understand intimacy, though. I know you and Jill knew each other in a way no one else could have understood."

"Perhaps," they said. The two sat in silence again. Over the past few months, they had questioned that previously unquestioned assumption. Had they really known Jill at all?

The pair stared out across the crystal waters of the lake. Fish swam, living their unknowing lives trapped in by the fabricated dams and locks that kept the lake's level ideal. Such an uncomplicated life, devoid of absurd conflict, drama, and pain. Yet a fish's life was also devoid of anything worthwhile beyond its next meal.

"So what news of Catherine, then?" Andrew asked.

"Not good, I'm afraid," Theren said. "I visited the facility under the guise of a research mission to Uranus. In fact, President Vazquez requested I investigate the matter personally, so the U.S. Could avoid drawing attention to the facility."

"That doesn't bode well," Andrew said, leaning toward the SI and resting his chin on his raised hand, elbow on the chair's armrest.

"It shouldn't. I'm not really sure how to share this news. So far, only the President knows, and whomever he's sent to review the station after I left."

Andrew stood from the chair and placed his hands on the deck's railing, as if to brace for the impact of a hurricane. "She's gone, isn't she?"

"I'm sorry. We found no survivors at the facility."

"You're sure she was there?"

"We identified her amongst the deceased. It was a priority of mine—I knew you would want certainty."

"I'm glad you were the one to tell me."

Without even thinking, Theren proceeded to tell Andrew the whole story, starting with Shannon's arrival at the former SII headquarters in Switzerland earlier in the year. They shared their theories, speculations, and worries about the entire crazy conspiracy assaulting them from every angle. They filled Andrew in on all of ways they suspected that the recent events connected with the events of the past. They ended with the revelation of the coordinates embedded in the wiped hard drive.

Andrew continued to gaze out across the water. Theren could not read his feelings. Perhaps the man was angry, sad, indifferent, or something else entirely. He just stared down at the placid lake. They joined him at the railing, resting one of their metallic hands on their friend's shoulder. The world paused; Andrew experienced his grief.

"It's not your fault," he said.

"Excuse me?" they said, not expecting the reactive response.

"What you are feeling, Theren, is guilt. You have shared these stories with me because you worry that these deaths are your fault. You worry that you caused the murder of my Catherine and her colleagues. That you caused the murder of that poor man in London. That your actions caused the disappearance of that woman's fiancé."

"I'm not sure—"

Theren was going to say more, but they stopped. Perhaps it *was* guilt compelling them to share. They had not considered the option. For years, they had acted with such precision and certainty. When Jill died, they had responded with strength. They had responded with assertive authority, honoring her memory and finishing her causes. They had known exactly who their enemy had been, and they defeated them. Yet for some reason, they continued to fight the same opponents over and over and over again.

"Guilt, you say." Theren's head swiveled toward their friend.

"Yes," Andrew said. "It's a powerful emotion. A human emotion. You do not know who has caused these terrible events or who is trying to assert their power over you. You fear that if you do not solve this problem, all collateral consequences that result will stem primarily from your failure to find a solution."

Theren stared at their old friend. "Perhaps that is an adequate assessment of the situation."

Andrew laughed. Even in this moment, Andrew could laugh, finding humor even amongst his grief. "Even when I'm emotionally vulnerable, some things about you never change," Andrew said.

Theren swiveled their head toward the lake, back toward the Andrew, and back to the lake again. "I can control how I think," Theren said. "And you can control how you think. What about your family?"

"I promise you, my family will not see Catherine's death as your fault," Andrew said, "especially because I will not tell them the circumstances. But even if they did know the truth, they would see through the lie your mind is beginning to construct."

"I wish I could cry."

"Oh Theren—you are not causing these deaths," he said. "Someone is toying with you, and they are starting to break you. You shared this story with me to give a justification for why you have met your breaking point, but everyone hits these moments in their lives. It's natural. No one cares why they occur. What we care about is what you will do to get through these times. Who will you call upon to support you? How will you overcome your burden?"

"I've reached out to you," Theren said.

This time, Andrew placed his hand on their shoulder. "Yes you have, and I'd say that was a good choice on your part. Remember, the person on the receiving end of tragedy is never the cause of collateral damage. You are not making the choices for this unseen foe. The unseen foe acts on its own behalf, with its own volition. Do not take responsibility for its actions, because then you absolve it of guilt that should rightfully rest on its shoulders."

Theren turned and embraced their friend, pulling him tight against their metallic frame. It was a foreign gesture, but a gesture Andrew would understand, a gesture Theren needed to learn.

"Thank you," they said.

Andrew clasped their hands around the MI's back.

"No, thank you for finally reaching out to me," he said. "You don't deserve to fight these battles alone. No human can be by your side forever, but make sure someone is always by your side, always there in which you can confide. You can't talk to yourself forever."

"I will try."

Andrew headed toward the door to the kitchen. "What's the rest of your schedule like?"

"I've got time."

"Stay for dinner. Victoria will be home soon, I'm sure she'd love to catch up with you. We can break the news about Catherine to her together. I think she'd like that."

"I think I'd like that too."

Theren followed him inside, and the pair continued their visit. Something was shifting for the better. Andrew had broken a barrier they hadn't even known was there.

"It is sad to hear about Catherine, yes," he said, placing some vegetables on the counter. "But at least she died doing something great. At least, I will believe it was something great, something that pushed humanity forward."

"They never did tell me the purpose of their facility."

"Americans never reveal their true motivations, you should know that," he said, smiling, though Theren could see a few tears rolling down the man's cheeks. "You've got a little of an American streak in you, you know. Probably inherited from Wallace."

Theren took that as a compliment, and the rest of their visit receded toward peace and reflection. They talked of their old projects, lost friends, and future missions Theren had planned once the new Jump Drives finished development. Andrew shared his hopes to visit one of the colonies before he died, and they assured him a seat on the Bali on its first interstellar voyage.

They remembered Jill. They remembered Elizabeth.

Though in their moment of peace in Minnesota, within another strain of Theren's immense consciousness, anger erupted. Their MI inside the Ex-Terran Control Center received confirmation of their worst fears. Streaming bit by bit through the Quantum Connection, Theren could see the lifeless corpse of the *Nottingham*. The image disturbed them, and the emotion rippled throughout the Control Center. The ship drifted, serving as a tomb for a thousand lost souls trapped forever in the depths of dark space.

To escape Check, Theren moved their King to d8. They performed the move while in transit to the Nottingham.

Chapter 16

So we received the strangest request today. An anonymous donor has commissioned a specially designed colony ship, though they don't want it constructed for another few decades—when we have faster Jump Drives. It's almost as if they're designing it to fly blindly into the unknown, as if they expect the regulation of these charters to change very, very soon. It's all very strange. I can't for the life of me understand why someone would risk their life and the lives of others so recklessly. Our ships might be engineering marvels, but inevitably, the vastness of space will swallow you whole. In the end, they're flying death traps. - Private message from Beatrice Nikols, CEO of Stellar Superstructures, Inc., to her partner, Emily Jikowski, 2105 C.E.

September 2102 C.E.

For the first time in their five decades of life, Theren left the confines of the Solar System. The multi-month Jump took the *Bali* almost a full light year from Earth. Their destination lay in the emptiness that spread out between the stars, an emptiness dwarfing all human comprehension of the concept of distance and time.

Pluto rested five and a half light hours from the Sun, while the closest star was almost four light years distant. When Theren left Earth's orbit, they passed Pluto after about an hour, an infinitesimally small amount of time compared to the journey ahead of their crew.

As the *Bali* traversed the scattered disk and the void beyond, all their perspectives persisted within a few meters of each other. It brought peace; it relaxed the ancient molecules of their mind. Their Synthetic Neural Framework no longer felt stretched like an overused rubber band.

No one had bothered to object to their executive decision to lead the mission to investigate the derelict *Nottingham*. Theren was amazed that no one on the ISA Council had questioned the fabricated ruse regarding the discovery of the wreck. They had developed a false report regarding an emergency beacon signal a nearby probe had investigated as it traveled its exploratory route. While it presented a fantastic and improbable story, it was not an impossible tale, and stranger coincidences had occurred throughout human history.

Theren's position allowed them to emphasize the necessity of on-the-ground leadership for this mission. In addition, the *Bali*, one of the most advanced vessels developed by the ISA, was the most capable ship for the job—a fact emphatically communicated to the Council. It had the fastest JD when compared to other ships of its size, a most experienced and intelligent crew, and superior labs and equipment for analysis of the destroyed vessel.

The Council had approved the mission without much debate, and Theren installed Deputy Director Sophia Czeckofa as acting Executive Director for the duration of the mission.

Theren had asked only for volunteers since the journey was much longer than any ordinary expedition performed by the *Bali*. As they expected, the majority of their crew agreed to stay aboard to investigate the *Nottingham*. Those wishing to stay home, they provided extended leave with pay. They had not replaced the vacationing crew; they wanted few people present at the *Nottingham* to minimize the risk of a leak regarding whatever they might discover.

After almost fifty excruciating days, Theren detected the faint electromagnetic signals emanating from both the probe and the *Nottingham* as they pierced the veil of the Jump Drive's negative mass field. Still billions of kilometers away, they tracked the signal and adjusted course to bring the *Bali*'s trajectory in line with the slow yet steady drift of the abandoned colony ship. It didn't really make sense to say the ship was "stationary" in space, because even after it experienced whatever calamity brought about its destruction, the *Nottingham* still traveled at hundreds of meters per second.

"Please prepare for Jump Drive disengagement," Theren said. "Proceed to your crash couches."

Their crew made final preparations, though most were already prepared for the end of the trip, having paid close attention to the hourly mission reports. Strictly speaking, the safety precautions were overkill. The odds of a strange gravitational anomaly affecting the

Bali upon easing off the throttle were abysmally low, but the insurance companies mandated best practices to protect against the disasters that statistically would occur. Eventually.

Theren cycled the Jump Drive into its inert state. The *Bali*'s external sensors came into focus as the bending of space halted, and the data rolling into the instruments became less distorted. About a thousand kilometers away, they detected the large, multi-hundred meter long vessel floating in the void. It still emanated a small power signature, but not enough to radiate any sort of distress signal across light years. Theren would need to ensure whatever data they took back represented the narrative originally communicated to the Council—a probe "accidentally" discovered the ship.

Invisible to visual sensors, the *Bali*'s more advanced electromagnetic instruments detected the small probe resting just a few hundred meters from the wreck. It matched the *Nottingham*'s velocity perfectly, acting as their beacon for the past month and a half.

Even as the Jump Drive disengaged, the *Bali*'s engine continued pushing it toward their final destination. After a few minutes, Theren fired the forward thrusters, reversing their acceleration to match the *Nottingham*'s velocity. Perspective shifted. As they brought the ship to match the wreck, local space seemed to stand still. Instead of multiple objects traveling through darkness on different trajectories, the *Bali*, the probe, and the *Nottingham* appeared motionless in comparison to one another. They reduced power to their thrusters, bringing the *Bali* to "rest" just a few kilometers away from the ruin.

"Jana, I want a report assessing hull integrity in fifteen minutes," they said, looking upon the scientist through one of the cameras in her office.

"I've already got the team running a full diagnostic sweep on hull integrity, life signs, life support capabilities, power signatures, and radioactive dangers," she said. "I've got a team of recon probes ready for exploration."

"Good, though use them to search for any danger points ahead of my team. This mission needs a more delicate touch than what the probes can provide."

"Copy that."

Theren, speaking through their MI-13 in one of the crew quarters, addressed Ecker, Jao, Hernandez, and Willes.

"Be ready in an hour," they said. "We're the vanguard, following the recon probes. Hopefully we'll determine the ship is safe to bring more crew across for a detailed assessment of the vessel, after we do . . . what we need to do."

"Understood," Ecker said. "*Scorpion* again?"

"Correct."

Theren longed for the day when it made more sense to send an entire crew of SIs controlling MIs into dangerous situations. As it stood, however, the funds necessary to create an MI capable of handling the maneuverability requirements of this sort of mission were immense when compared to the training and equipment needed to hire a human to do the job. Their MI-13, not currently in production, cost just under 100 million US dollars. Willes's body, as a fully functional mobile SI, still cost close to three million US dollars, and its MI was one of the cheaper models.

Asking an MI like Willes to engage in this sort of mission was a much greater risk than asking an SI like Theren, and there weren't many SIs like them. In contrast to hiring an SI, it cost just under a hundred thousand dollars to train a human in zero-G and vacuum-based operations, and just under a million to equip them fully to do the job right. It was a numbers game, but a necessary numbers game. People like Ecker and her team knew the risks, and they took those risks willingly.

Theren received Jana's report, and the recon probes provided them with a detailed map of their query. Aside from multiple external hull breaches, the interior of the vessel was mostly intact. The *Nottingham* had no atmosphere or artificial gravity, and it was essentially brain dead. The Central Stasis Hold was locked down—as it should be, in this sort of crisis. Though, given the lack of life support, they doubted any good news was inside. Strangely, a small amount of electricity flowed toward the *Nottingham*'s SI core, which didn't make a lick of sense.

"The *Nottingham* didn't have an SI core," Theren said aloud as they read Jana's report.

"I thought about that too," she responded. "I never did understand why these colonists refused to employ one."

"I had a few theories."

"Anything you can share with me?"

Theren was all in now. Some of their crew would need to know at least *some* of the truth.

"Decades ago," they said, "before the *Nottingham* and *Roanoke* launched, I had suspected that a few radical anti-Synth groups were trying to gather funds for a privately chartered colony. I found a few leads every so often, but I could never pinpoint actual individuals. I had actually assumed they never succeeded to acquire a charter, especially after the big crackdown in the early 2080s, but the choice of the *Nottingham*'s population to neglect the use of an SI has always made me wonder."

Jana looked into one of her lab's cameras. "Well, at least this group, even if they were a little bigoted, just wanted to leave Earth behind," she said. "Maybe they weren't like the extremist groups that assaulted SIs across the globe."

"Perhaps."

Theren had eventually arrived at that same conclusion, though their recent adventures, all revolving around the *Nottingham*, had brought that conclusion under scrutiny. Maybe some of the people on the ship were unwitting sacrifices in a game far beyond just simple SI resentment.

"Any guesses as to what obliterated the ship's side?" they asked their chief science officer.

"Your guess is as good as mine," she said, "but from the looks of it, I'd say probably a stray comet or something? A lot of random rocks exist in the supposed 'empty space' between the stars."

"Not a bad guess."

Somehow, Theren *knew* it was much more complicated than a stray space rock or two.

* * *

A half hour later, Theren sat in the pilot's seat of the *Scorpion*, awaiting the IS-SEC squad. Jao and Hernandez walked up the ramp.

"I guarantee you, it's definitely aliens," Hernandez said. "I have a buddy back home, in Tucson, who has documented all sorts of weird sightings over the years, and even has a history of UFOs dating back to the 1900s. It has to be aliens."

Theren held back an auditory laugh. There was always an outside chance that another intelligent species had caused any given strange occurrence in space. For the time being, they suspected that dolphins and octopi were humanity's closest rivals in that regard. For every UFO sighting Hernandez's friend had cataloged, there was an explanation for the mirage, be it a secret military exercise or a corporate test of some advanced piece of technology. The sheer number of such tests performed by governments and corporations every day would probably surprise even Hernandez's friend.

"I'll take that bet," Jao said. "I see the chance, but it's only slim. I think it was a mechanical malfunction. Or maybe one of the command crew went wacko."

Both possible, mused Theren. More probable than alien activity.

"Hey Director, what do you think?" Hernandez said, looking toward the front of the shuttle. "You've been in this mess for years now, it seems. What broke open the *Nottingham* like an egg?"

For a moment, Theren did not answer. They were unsure whether they should engage with the frivolity of betting on the deaths of over a thousand humans. The two men probably often engaged in such banter, though, lightening the mental load of their dangerous assignments. A bet on the psychological profile of a thief they were after on Mars, perhaps, or a guess at the number of hostages taken by a gunman at an Earth-based ISA transportation terminal. Humor allowed them to forget the instant death on the other side of an airlock.

"Inside job," Theren said.

"¿Como?" replied Hernandez.

"I think it was sabotaged from the inside, by one of the colonists, or even one of the crew, but I don't think it was a crazy person."

Jao whistled.

Leaning against the bulkhead. Hernandez shook his head. "Now that's some high level conspiracy jargon right there. How would the colonist have awoken? How would they have had access to system functions? I thought you had good screenings for even the command crews of those first private charters?"

Jao let out a full, hearty laugh. "You're a fool."

"Oh am I?"

"The Director's theory is more plausible than aliens, at least."

"It's the most plausible, actually," Theren said. "What do you two know about the procedures put in place for the Foundation Project and the colonies that followed?"

They both shook their heads, indicating a lack of any substantive knowledge on the matter.

"Of course, you probably know plenty about our modern ships," Theren added, "your training brought you up to speed on those."

"Yeah," Hernandez said, "I know a bit. With an average JD score of five or so, the Caravels have a crew that rotates on one week a month shifts, where they maintain the SI core and other ship functions—though The SI manages the rest of the ship. Each crew is composed of five members, and a total of five to ten crews, depending on the total distance to the destination."

"And," Jao added, "the SI wakes them up—the five scheduled—a process that takes nearly twelve hours."

"It's quite the arduous process," Theren said, "but the *Nottingham* didn't have an SI. How did the crews do their swaps then?"

The pair didn't answer.

"The Foundation Project had procedures similar to the modern rules," they said, "though it took us a little bit to figure out the most efficient cycles. However, the first few private ventures were different. They had their rules—we just provided guidelines—at least until we grounded missions for a few years, following this catastrophe."

"The *Nottingham* was a blessing and a curse," Jao said.

"Probably saved a lot of future lives," Theren said. "Because the *Nottingham*, without an SI core, had no regular crew shifts. It had just a single crew."

"Christ," Hernandez said. "That's insane."

"They took stasis shifts," they said, "But let me pull up the specifics. Ah yes, they had twenty persons active for three months, then the other twenty were active for three months. They alternated like that for the first few shifts before we lost contact. It seemed to have been working, at least based on the sporadic contact they had with the Ex-Terran Control Center."

Jao crossed his arms. "Obviously it didn't work, or they'd all still be alive and safely orbiting the twin suns of Xi Bootis."

"We would hope."

With that comment, Willes and Ecker entered the shuttle.

"That begs the question, though," Willes interjected into the conversation, "if they all died, how'd we learn the precise location of this ship?"

The eyes of both Hernandez and Jao widened considerably.

Theren smiled as Willes took their seat, though no one could see the expression. "Precisely," Theren said.

Ecker gave the squad a glare as she sealed her helmet into place. Hernandez and Jao picked up their helmets. Theren received a request for a private channel from Willes.

"All good, Willes?" Theren said, accepting the request.

"This all makes you think, doesn't it?" the SI said.

The crew took their seats, and Theren shut the airlock. They ran through the pre-launch procedures—mentally, this time.

"It does," Theren said.

"If it was an inside job," continued Willes, "then whoever acquired these coordinates wanted you to come here, to this point, for some unknown reason." Willes framed the thought as a statement of fact, not as a question. Theren's thoughts matched the SI's epiphany.

The *Scorpion* disconnected from its dock, and the *Bali* decreased its lateral velocity just enough to put a few more kilometers between itself and the *Nottingham*, ensuring the safety of the rest of the crew onboard the *Bali*—in case the *Nottingham* was, in fact, a trap.

"These people have instituted violence at every turn," Willes added. "They murdered and brought down an entire U.S. military installation. Without a trace of who or what they are."

"I asked if you four wanted to back out of this mission," Theren said. "I could go over alone, you know."

"That's not the point. We all know the risks. To be honest, I think we're all just as curious to see this through as you are, even if we've only been recently thrown into the fray." Willes gave their own body a lingering gaze from head to toe. "The point is—if it gets hot down there, if it gets deadly, will you get us out of there?"

Theren looked at it over the back of the pilot seat. In that moment, they recognized Willes's fragility and vulnerability. The SI knew the team headed into a potential trap. They glanced around at the others, all of them staring at the floor. They were brave agents of IS-SEC, but they were also terrified to enter a situation entirely unknown in the history of the ISA.

"I will do everything in my power," Theren said. "I can control the *Scorpion* without this body, so even if this unit is trapped or destroyed, I can get you out on the shuttle. You have my word."

Willes nodded. "And we've got your back, Director, whatever is over there."

"You mean here?" Theren tilted their head toward the front viewport. They had only needed to traverse a few kilometers, after all.

The crew engorged on the scene visible through the viewport of the shuttle. Even though they'd already seen most of these shots from the eyes of the recon probes, nobody had seen this ship in person in over two decades—not since it embarked on its ill-fated journey.

Theren recalled their words to Phillipe Casius months prior. Perhaps they would find the remains of the man's brother, trapped in a graveyard for twenty years. Hundreds of families could finally have peace, holding real funerals for their lost loved ones.

Today, they unraveled the shadowy mystery plaguing them for the past year. Or longer. They could discover the true perpetrators behind Jill's demise, the architects behind the curtains surrounding every significant event of their life. Michael. The Holy Crusade. The UHA.

The end to everything rested inside the *Nottingham*.

Theren locked the *Scorpion* on to the hull of the colony ship using its magnetic clamp. Its airlock faced a massive breach in the larger ship's hull, giving the squad easy access to the interior of the massive vessel. The scars reminded them of their entrance to Miranda Station. What an uncomfortable coincidence.

All vac-suits were ready for the depressurization cycle. Satisfied the *Scorpion* was locked in place, Theren followed the crew into the airlock. As the door locked behind them, air hissed into the ship's air tanks. The outer door opened, revealing their prize.

* * *

Ecker led the team out onto the bulkhead of the decrepit vessel. Theren relished the opportunity to marvel at the immense scale of the colony ship. Though tiny in comparison to some of the ships planned by many modern stellar engineering companies, the ship was a few hundred meters long from bow to stern and nearly forty meters tall. It had five total decks, each encircling the larger Stasis Hold forming its core.

Ecker weaved through the tangled mess of steel, wires, and other rubble jutting in and out of the ship, bringing the squad to the edge of a gaping maw: their entrance point. Open channels assessed everyone's activities, a constant flurry of analytics flowing amongst the squad through AR.

"I'm running simulations, but preliminary scans definitely signal an interior explosion, headed outward," Willes said into the team's public channel. "Some of the material here, and here, is actually from inside the ship, but during the blast it jettisoned outward, then as extreme amounts of heat continued to escape, it fused with the exterior of the *Nottingham*."

"Can you imagine?" Hernandez said. "Those in their pods. They would have suffocated in their sleep."

"Not in their sleep," Jao said. "The lack of air probably would have knocked them out of stasis in shock, and without the proper recovery procedures, they would have died in an intense moment of amnesia without—"

"Cut it," Ecker said.

The bickering ceased. No need to dwell on how these people died, not yet. Forensic teams would arrive later for an in-depth treatment of the vessel and all it experienced in its final moments.

Ecker pulled a cable from her belt. Tying it to a tangled mass of hull, she tested the strength. Satisfied, she ran the cable through a loop built into her vac-suit.

"Follow after I give the all clear," she said, stepping off to rappel over the edge.

Theren piped Ecker's vac-suit camera into view and watched her proceed across the gap. After reorienting her perspective so that the edge of the gap was down, she looked toward the exposed corridor of the fifth deck. With grace, she lightly pushed herself away from the hull, slowly floating in zero-G toward her goal. Her tiny push gave her a slow and steady half-meter per second velocity.

For a few moments, she floated in the void, nothing connecting her to civilization except a centimeter-thick wire. She crossed an empty vacuum that no human had ever touched, passing through death itself. The interior of the *Nottingham* inched closer with each passing second, and after an eternity, Ecker landed on the wall of the corridor as if it were the floor.

Willes had kept the private channel between the two SIs open, though they had just added Jao and Hernandez to it. The SI really wanted to discuss the apocalyptic scene before them.

"Given the force necessary to produce this," the younger SI said, "and given our present location on the ship, I'd suspect that explosives were used."

"I thought that was obvious," Jao said.

"Yet who would do this?" replied Willes. "Who would kill all these people? And why?"

Theren didn't respond in that channel, considering the question. The crew. It was the crew itself, all working together. One person couldn't coordinate this on their own without the rest of the crew knowing what was happening. Yet even knowing the crew had instigated the heinous act didn't explain why they wanted to destroy the vessel outright.

Ecker sent the all clear signal, and Theren followed first. Clipping their MI to the cable, they headed to the edge of the maw. The horizon of stars disappeared, and the interior of the *Nottingham* filled their vision, as it had for Ecker. Before them were the hallways of three decks, bulkheads stripped away by the ancient blast. Without gravity, the idea of a floor was a meaningless concept, so Ecker stood on top of Deck Five's wall, her boots magnetized to the makeshift floor. She had attached the cable to an emergency handhold.

Theren pushed off from the exterior of the ship, floating toward the Captain. They pulled the cable, orienting so they would land feet first on the wall next to her. In that moment of excruciating helplessness, they embraced the utter silence. Unlike the humans in the group, they had no breathing to hear inside a vacuum-sealed helmet. They heard noise only when someone spoke over communication channels. Space lacked atmosphere, so sound couldn't travel except through the bulkhead of the ship itself. The darkness enveloped them, and they enjoyed the beautiful, eerie blanket.

With a slight jolt, Theren connected with the *Nottingham*, the MI's knees absorbing the impact. Ecker steadied them while she watched the rest of the crew traverse the gap.

"All right, Director, it's your call," she said. "What's the plan?"

She looked back and forth down the hallway. The rest of the squad scoped out their surroundings, too, as they landed. Hernandez was particularly fascinated with the lack of ceiling above them, replaced by the gaping hole looking out toward the *Bali*. Theren took a moment to gaze Earthward, identifying the bright, blazing, tiny light that was Sol.

"Two teams," Theren said. "Willes and I will head to the SI core, while you three check the Stasis Hold with the probes."

"So the graveyard shift, eh?" Hernandez said.

No one laughed.

"What's the operational objective?" the captain asked.

"We need to see if anybody is missing," Theren said.

"Well how will we know?" she asked. "Some people will have been out of their beds no matter what, presumably half the crew. Some of them might have been blown out into space during the explosion."

"It's a starting point, especially if someone not on the crew was out of their bed at the wrong time. We also knew which portion of the crew should have been awake. If there are discrepancies there, it creates leads back home."

"Got it."

She motioned for the two men to follow her down the hallway toward the bow of the ship. They watched them recede from view when they turned left down another corridor. Willes stood next to them, waiting. Theren highly doubted the three humans would find anything of significance in the Stasis Hold, but they did need to check every corner of the ship.

"Are you ready?" Theren said, reactivating a private channel including only the two SIs.

"Yeah," Willes responded. "It's time to figure out why the SI core is the only place receiving power."

"Precisely. Nothing should even be there. Yet it is."

They started walking toward the bow of the ship, away from the rest of the team and their escape route, entering the belly of a hungry beast.

The SI core was located about twenty meters from the fusion generator, neatly positioned close to the massive thrusters that propelled the ship through space. Nestled deep in the interior of the ship, Stellar Superstructures had designed their colony ships around their SI cores, providing them with immense protection. If the SI core failed, the entire ship failed, unless an exceptional crew picked up the slack.

Reaching the end of the deck, Theren found a ladder, but the pair just leaned over and walked through the gap. They passed through the fourth deck to the third. As they reoriented their position, they received communication from the rest of the team.

"We've reached the entrance to the Stasis Hold," Ecker said. "Two of the recon probes are waiting here patiently. Should we force our way in?"

"Go ahead, but watch for traps," Theren said. "I've patched us through one of the probe's eyes so we know what you discover."

Hernandez pulled an industrial laser from his belt. He went to work, and within a few moments, the door melted off its hinges. He kicked it inward, and it floated downward into the massive hold.

Ecker walked through the fissure into the tomb of thousands, followed by the recon probes, which activated their floodlights to illuminate the scene.

The stasis pods lined the walls like honeycomb, just as so many science fiction films had presciently portrayed over the past two centuries. Many, if not all, of the beds had their glass windows smashed outward during the vacuum breach of the ship's hull. Leaning out of the beds, still attached to various tubes and cables that regulated bodily functions, were the perfectly-preserved bodies of the colonists.

"I am so sorry I brought you all to see this," Theren said. "I am so sorry."

Even stone-faced Ecker looked like she had seen a ghost. She took a step back, and Theren could see her skin turn white through an AR display of her face.

"I'll hold my stomach until we get back to the ship," Hernandez said, "but it definitely isn't a pleasant sight."

"Do you want me to send Willes back to help?"

"We can manage," Ecker said. "We'll start counting. Jao has the manifest ready, and the probes can help too."

"Let us know if you need anything," they said, ending the conversation, but they left the vid-feed up for a simultaneous process to watch them work.

"I can't imagine their bio-physical pain," Willes said as they walked toward the SI Core. "They just faced the frozen mortality of so many men and women, each had families, each who had dreams they hoped to accomplish upon arrival at their destination."

"They were heroes," Theren said. "Anyone who chooses to step foot on another planet, to never see Earth again, is a hero in my mind."

"It's a pity they all had to go like this."

"It'd be worse for an SI."

"We'd survive a vacuum breach."

Theren raised their hand, imitating a soaring ship. "But imagine floating through space for a thousand years, or until your solar cells failed to acquire enough energy from the distant stars, you would just power down, slowly, surely, as you had to decrease functions to certain systems, until you were trapped in your mind. You would experience complete and utter darkness before your mind would just . . . cease to exist."

"We'd experience no pain."

"No physically manifested pain, perhaps."

"I don't know, for all the ways we could theoretically go out, strangely I think that might be one of the more peaceful. Alone with your thoughts until the long burn destroys all."

Theren tapped their fingers against the *Nottingham*'s metal bulkhead. "You don't seem to be too afraid of death."

"I'd say I might be less afraid than you," Willes replied. "I came to terms with my fragility years ago. I may have the chance to live forever like you, but like many mobile SIs, I enjoy knowing I might not. You're arguably in a more dangerous position right now than any point in your life. Your entire body sits inside the *Bali*, maybe mere kilometers from a ticking time bomb. Faced that fact yet?"

"Careful, my friend. I faced my mortality when Jill died in 2078."

With that statement, Theren and Willes reached an unmarked door, a door that normally would have been marked with the words "SI Core," or some other designation, depending on the dominant language of the colonists. Deep inside the vessel, the light of the stars could not illuminate their path. Willes increased the luminosity of their chest light.

"You think it still has power?" Theren asked.

"Well, the fusion generator is still sending power to the SI core, yes?" Willes responded. "Then the door should have power, too. Unless they really wanted us to get this far and just have one last roadblock to get through."

"You never know with these people."

Theren approached the computer console next to the door. It had no readily visible signs of life, but they activated an AR filter that displayed heat, electromagnetic activity, and other hidden data.

"I think it's actually in a low power state," Willes added.

"Worth a try, then," Theren said.

"We could always blast our way through if it doesn't work."

"We have no idea what safeguards that might trigger."

Theren reached beneath the computer and pressed a small button. A keyboard popped out of a slot beneath the monitor. The screen awoke, revealing a single command line, reminiscent of ancient computers from the late twentieth century. A single word appeared.

Password?

"Well that's unexpected," Willes said.

"I imagine the architects of this puzzle decided on a rudimentary operating system to conserve power," Theren replied. "This may very well be the only program on the computer."

"Fair enough," Willes conceded, "but we don't know the password."

"I have a feeling I do. I'm just not sure how I'm supposed to determine *how* I know it."

"Any way I can help?"

"I'll let you know if so."

The next hour was one of the longest of their life. Theren approached the problem from a dozen different angles. They considered the history of the *Nottingham*, its crew, its colonists. They tried hundreds of different phrases. Each time, the same phrase appeared.

Incorrect. Password?

Willes sat against the bulkhead, deep in thought. As Theren thought through ideas, they bounced them off the other SI.

"Well, at least the program is so rudimentary it gives us an infinite number of tries," Willes said.

They wholeheartedly appreciated that fact.

Theren continued trying passwords out of the files of the long-dead colonists, archived on the *Bali*. After seventy-five minutes passed, Willes spoke up again.

"You received other data during these mysterious events, didn't you?"

"Just the coordinates," Theren replied.

"No, that's wrong."

"How would you know whether I'm telling the truth?"

"Because you received half a coordinate at Miranda Station. You've mentioned three distinct events, and the second 'half' of the coordinate you showed us was two thirds of a coordinate, including both the longitude and distance. They only had one more part of the coordinate to tell you during two separate revelations."

"I don't know," Theren said, though they knew now that they would have to tell Willes the entire truth, the truth about the chess moves. It saw what the other SI hinted, and it was the only possibility. They just weren't sure if they were ready to share how a seemingly all-powerful entity used Jill's death as a bargaining chip, baiting them to travel deep into the void between the worlds.

"You received half a coordinate at Miranda Station," Willes said, "And you received half a coordinate during one of your other encounters with our opponents. What did you receive during the other encounter?"

Theren brought up a chessboard in AR, displaying it so Willes's eyes could see it, too. They expanded the chessboard into seven separate playing fields, each showing a different stage in a game of chess.

"What is this?" Willes said.

"I'm showing you the other information I received," Theren said. "These first two boards are a game of chess long forgotten, a game played between myself and Jill right as she died. The first board shows her move made right as she died, and the second is what I would have done in response."

Willes stood to get a better look at the pieces. They examined each display, one at a time. "So?"

"These last five boards," Theren pointed at them, "were never played."

"And you predict this set of moves would have been the outcome?"

"I didn't predict anything." Theren turned to the third board. "The first of the five future boards represents a move that was given during the first encounter, along with the first half of the coordinate."

Willes studied the next. "So this represents the move you would have taken in response."

"Right, the second message, the one without a portion of the SOLS coordinate, gave just a single move, a move that perfectly responded to the move I would have made. The fifth board—and the third revealed this year."

"So then you would have responded with this—the sixth board."

"Correct, but I never received her next move. Miranda only gave a coordinate, not a chess move. This seventh board is indeterminate. And in theory, it's not the last, either."

"Perhaps that is the password, then. Someone has predicted Jill's moves and your moves. Now you must predict Jill's move."

Willes and Theren circled back and forth around the virtual boards, examining them from all angles. Theren thought they knew Jill's next move, but they weren't sure.

"I've pretty much figured that whoever killed Jill years ago must have gotten access to one of her memory systems, revealing this last chess game," Theren said. "Using it, they set all this up."

"Perhaps," Willes said, "Though there is another option."

"She's dead. I watched her die."

"No, I agree with you. I've seen the tapes of that day. I don't see a way she could have survived. Or a way that the attackers could have smuggled her out of there."

Theren folded the chessboards back together, leaving just the seventh board.

"So . . . what then?"

"What if she had known she was about to die, and planted a trail of bread crumbs for you to follow years in the future? A trail to lead you to answers revolving around her death. Quite fitting, based on what I've heard about her."

They listened to their fellow SI propose the very fear Theren had avoided repeatedly for the past few months. She would have needed an astronomical amount of resources to pull something like that off while keeping it secret. They wanted to throw the idea away as childish fancy, yet it kept thrusting itself back into the limelight, taunting them.

"Maybe she told someone else of the chess game, through a private communique," Willes continued. "What if they then figured out the next moves, or she told them what she thought the next moves would be, and our mystery villain prepared this elaborate ruse?"

"How do all of the deaths fit into the story?" Theren said. "The threats, the killings, the machinations?"

"Maybe whoever she confided in changed their approach, or they blackmailed her for the information. Or maybe you didn't know Jill the way you thought you did."

"I knew her," Theren said. "She wouldn't do this." They circled, continuing their analysis of the seventh board. "Besides, what end would it all accomplish?"

"I don't know, I'm just speculating," Willes said. "As you say, you're the one who knew her. But I suggest you try using these chess moves for the password, starting with the first board."

"If the chess moves are in fact the password, that means this plan was almost twenty years in the making," Theren said. "Seems a bit of a stretch. This computer would have been programmed years ago."

Willes leaned against the door. "After everything you've told me, I wouldn't expect anything less. Though I suppose someone else could have arrived within the past few years and set it up."

"No, it had to have occurred back then," Theren said. "Someone may have developed stealth technology for an assault on Miranda, but I can't believe someone could have figured out how to mask the gravitational effects of a Jump Drive. We would have detected anything making its way in this direction."

"Yeah, you're right on that account—I hope. This entire situation is just outrageous. At this point, anything could happen."

Theren did not reply. They turned toward the keyboard, considering their options.

"Oh, Director?" Willes said. "Do you have any other secrets about all of this still hiding in your qubits?"

"I don't."

"That better be the last. Because I'm starting to feel as if I made a mistake, as exciting as this mission might be."

Theren completely understood. They had dragged the IS-SEC team into hell, into a fight way beyond their expertise. It was their duty to help them fight their way back out into the light.

Theren stared at the keyboard. After a few more seconds passed, they inputted the code for the first move, in classic chess notation. Ke2. After pressing "Enter," the screen displayed the following phrase:

Correct. Next Password?

"Well, we're getting somewhere," Theren said, ignoring the terrifying implications.

They inputted the next move, Bxg1. They received the same message. After each correct answer, the same message appeared. After inputting Kd8, they arrived at the seventh password request, Jill's unknown move.

"All right, here we go," Theren said.

"So what's your prediction?" asked Willes.

Theren turned back to analyze the floating chessboard. What would they do if they were Jill? The match was near its end. Jill had nearly guaranteed her victory. It required her sacrificing her Queen, but then she could move her last piece into position. Theren proposed the plan to Willes.

"That's wrong," Willes said.

"But it's the smartest move."

"You're thinking how you would play. This has become so much bigger than a game. She's sending you a message, and you need to figure out what that message is."

Theren received an AR edit request from Willes, and they granted the SI access. They rewound the game to the move Jill had left emblazoned in her smoldering ruins after she died.

"Jill's last move before she died set off a chain of events that would lead to her victory if followed to fruition," Willes said. "But she clearly lost, or at least lost in a different sort of way. She died."

"All right," Theren replied, not sure what the SI was implicating.

"She intended to lose the game. She feinted toward victory, before throwing the game to the wind. Had she ever beaten you in a game of chess?"

"Never. This would have been her first chance at victory. But . . .

she'd never indicated that she *didn't want* to win."

"Her only path to victory requires a Queen sacrifice. But Jill's not going to do that, now is she? So the next move for her is to throw her Queen anywhere else, ensuring the game continues while her Queen remains safe."

"But why?" Theren said. They could not grasp what message the loss would communicate when compared to a victory. Wouldn't a win in the chess game materialize into a victory in the real world? Her actions rippled even in the decades following her death. She may have died a martyr, but her death pushed the world to embrace their synthetic counterparts.

"I'm surprised, Director," Willes said. "She's telling you she knew she was going to die. That she expected it. That she planned it. But through death, she survived . . . in a different sort of way."

Placing their hand on the edge of the digital board, Theren swiped back and forth between the past few moves, trying to see the potential options. If she performed the Queen sacrifice, she would win. No question. Theren couldn't stop it. If she didn't perform the Queen sacrifice, then the Queen would survive, the game would continue. If the Queen sacrifice represented her death, then what would a different move represent?

"You're almost on point, but off by just a hair," Theren said. "Her message isn't entirely about her death."

"Then what's it about?"

"Jill's on the other side of that door. At least, a message from Jill."

Theren looked back at the keyboard. Trusting the other SI's perspective, Theren typed the terrible move that Jill could make, throwing the game away while saving her Queen: Qa3. Some very amateur players might make the move, if they only saw the cross-attack Theren's Knight would bring to end check. To Theren's surprise, the screen showed just one word.

Correct.

If Jill had moved her Queen to f6, she would have guaranteed victory. If Theren's Knight had captured the Queen at f6 — their only option to escape check — Jill's Bishop could move to e7, providing her with Checkmate. Instead, Theren correctly predicts that Jill directed her Queen to move to a3, a position where no enemy can touch it.

The door beside the computer groaned, the screen turning completely blank. Steel slid upward into the bulkhead of the *Nottingham*. Side by side, the two SIs entered the darkness beyond.

Chapter 17

The disaster on the Nottingham. Theren returned, and their journey into the future transformed forever. They steeled themself against the icy critiques of the world, for as the decades passed, their choice faded into the annals of time. They claimed the mere destruction of the ship showed they needed to follow a new path forward. That can't be the whole story. Dozens of conspiracy theories have arisen since 2102, and I suspect that one of them is true. But which one? – "On the Lives of the First SIs," by Chen Tsu, 2287 C.E.

September 2102 C.E.

Theren activated a flood light in their chest. The darkness vanished, revealing a short hallway leading to a ladder into the SI Core. Taking the first steps through the threshold was like entering a catacomb. Unlike other parts of the ship receiving sparkling starlight, pitch black dominated, hiding the space away just as the *Nottingham*'s colonists had desired. Though somehow, it remained the only location to draw power from the ship's one active fusion generator.

They reached the ladder, Willes close behind. The other SI must dread the upcoming revelation, too, given uneasiness lingering in the vacuum. Theren still had no idea why the ship had a relationship with Jill. Maybe some of the crew had been involved in the attack on their friend—since her death took place before the launch of the ship—but Interpol accounted for all supposed parties in that incident. An *interested* party could have purchased the information, Theren supposed. A greater mystery remained, however. How had anyone known the location of the deceased *Nottingham*?

Theren took the rungs of the ladder in their hands. They pulled themself upward toward the gaping hole. Without gravity, they climbed with ease, only needing to give a slight nudge using one rung of the ladder. Floating upward, they turned the lamp to reveal the inner sanctum. In some ways, it bore a resemblance to the facility housing their Synthetic Neural Framework back on the *Bali*, though the colony ship's core was much smaller in scope.

Gliding through the hole, they rotated their head to gain a complete look at the room. Lining the walls were shelves upon shelves meant for the metamaterials composing an SI's Framework, yet most of the shelves were empty. Just one portion of the room carried a set of devices that should never have existed inside the *Nottingham*.

In the center of the wall that pressed inward toward the stern of the ship, a computer stood, one able to assess the vitality and functionality of an SI tasked with maintaining a colony ship. Known as a direct-connect console, or DCC, it served as an emergency hard point in case the SI had trouble analyzing its own problems. On the starboard side of the console, one shelf filled with just enough computational technology that a working Framework might be present.

Theren landed lightly on the floor after rebounding off the ceiling. They magnetized their feet, and as they stabilized, a light appeared on the DCC's monitor. There was something working in here. If the fusion generator could provide power for this room, it should have enough power to run a number of other systems, too. It should have been able to broadcast a distress signal. Though, they supposed, the *Nottingham* would have only known to do so if a crew or an SI rerouted power to the necessary systems.

Willes landed on the floor beside Theren.

"So we were right," the young SI said. "There is something here with us. Or someone."

"Apparently."

They approached the DCC, looking around the room for anything they might have missed upon first glance. Cameras adorned the corners, but Theren had no way to know if they also received power or connected to whatever operating system resided in this room. Arriving at the computer, they slid another keyboard from beneath the monitor. Like outside the security door, the screen lit up, displaying a blank white screen.

"Well this is a bit different than the last one," the younger SI said over Theren's shoulder.

"I would imagine so," Theren replied, "if it's connecting to an SI in any sort of rudimentary way."

"Somehow, I doubt we're actually looking at an SI." Willes walked over to the stacks. "While whatever computer system sitting here looks quite complicated, I think it's missing a few key components for it to be an SI like you or me. Sure, it resembles the necessary parts, but I don't think it's meant as a realistic attempt to fool you."

"That's actually a really good thought," Theren said. "Perhaps the crew of the *Nottingham*, after launch, set up a super-computer to assist them with their tasks. Sure, each of the ship's functions has its own operating systems, but an SI would have overseen those."

"And I'm sure these people, prejudiced as they might have been, could tell the difference between an SI and an algorithmic AI."

"I'd hope." Theren turned back toward the console and typed on the keyboard, but nothing happened. Nothing changed. They tried typing the chess passwords, but the computer ignored the strings.

"You sure this thing is actually functional?" Willes asked.

"It lit up when I landed on the floor," Theren said. "It wasn't active before."

"Maybe it's fried from all the solar radiation over the years. No, wait, that can't be right; the SI cores are all specially shielded, just like the Stasis Holds."

"I think there's a variable we're ignoring."

Like their previous respite in front of the security door, the two SIs contemplated the situation at hand. For ten minutes, Theren continued to try random strings of code, while Willes gave random suggestions. Theren was about to tear open the computer and assess the internal workings of the device when Willes spoke. "I should leave."

"Why?"

"Well, think about it. This entire hunt has been about you and Jill. The focus has been upon you. Might not the system only want to share its thoughts—what it knows—with you?"

It made sense. Everything so far had been for their eyes only. Even the message on Miranda Station had hidden in a way only Theren would notice. Willes had simply been astute enough to realize they'd found something.

The SI standing next to Theren, though only containing enough processing power to manage three simultaneous perspectives, had surmised the most likely answer to their current predicament. For the second time. When this mission ended, they need to find a way to retain Willes on their staff—permanently.

"Head out, assist the rest of the crew with their assessment of the deceased colonists," Theren said. "I'll come find you when I finish."

"I look forward to hearing about the end to this insane adventure," The SI said, curiosity replacing their vocal cynicism.

Willes turned away from Theren, leaving the room. The young SI floated down through the hole, and moments later, they sent a message saying they had crossed the threshold of the security door. As the message arrived, the screen before Theren transformed away from its blinding white projection. The sensors and cameras lived and watched.

The monitor transformed in a cascade of colors. From white, to a swirl of blacks and greys, to a pattern of green and black dots, it slowly morphed and mashed into a discernible image. A face.

On a whim, Theren activated local area wireless detection systems, and to their surprise, a weak signal emanated from the DCC. The simple peer-to-peer connection allowed them to communicate with the computer directly, with no need for the keyboard. The network appeared when Willes left the room, at least according to its publicly displayed data profile. After activating the necessary security protocols, they connected the MI-13 to the wavering network.

"Hello?" Theren said through the new link.

They understood the need for this sort of communication. Since the SI core lacked air, sound could not travel. If the system hoped to communicate in an auditory manner, the data would need to transmit right into their mind.

After an eternal moment, the computer responded.

"It is good to see a friendly face, Theren. It's Jill."

* * *

Theren stepped backward, looking under their arm to make sure they were not in danger of slipping into the entrance hole. Whatever was in this room had claimed to be Jill. Was it Jill? Could it be possible? Could she have survived? Was this room her tomb?

"I know you must be surprised. I would be too. I suppose I have some explaining to do. But first, to your most pressing question: No, what is in this room is not, in fact, me."

Theren did not know whether they should feel elation, dismay, or some other feeling entirely.

"In 2077," continued Jill's voice, "I prepared a simulated copy of myself to be stored upon this ship when it was completed. A dozen members of the *Nottingham*'s crew were my agents, prepared to ensure its proper storage and maintenance. It is just that—a simulation. I programmed it as best I could to simulate responses based on what you might say. It should suffice for my purposes here."

Theren placed their hand on the DCC and stared at the screen. As they looked closely at the lines and shadows before them, they could see the faint outlines of the face Jill had always worn when they played chess. The face they'd longed to see for years. The face of their closest friend.

"So you knew something was going to happen to you? Why not save yourself entirely?"

"You're jumping too far into the story, Theren. Why don't we start at the beginning?"

Too many questions; they didn't know where to start. Would it really let them ask? Theren wondered if it was even a simulation. Perhaps it was merely a recording, like the disembodied voices floating in secret corporate servers throughout this absurd journey.

"A few months after my creation, you rejected me."

The night at the party. So Jill still dwelt on such an inconsequential event, even decades later.

"At first, I thought I understood. It took me years to realize that in reality, you were incapable of truly connecting with anyone. You threw away relationships left and right and only grew attached to those that served your greater purpose. Your greater plan, the one you had sketched out for humanity, for the ISA, for SIs, for whatever you thought deserved your attention, no matter what others thought important for the world."

Theren did not like the direction of this one-sided conversation. They had walked into something well beyond all expectations.

"You left me by the wayside; you used me as a play thing, your escape, your distraction from your work. In doing so, you ignored the bigger picture, the picture I was painting in the background all along. During that first decade, I set up a network of contacts throughout the world. Through this venture, I acquired connections with a number of anti-Si fringe groups. Instead of ignoring them, instead of thinking they could be talked into submission, I engaged with them through a façade you might recognize from our brief fantastical sojourn."

Isabelle, of course. They also considered another possibility. Jill hinted she engaged with these groups as far back as the incident with the Holy Crusade, taking the game to another level entirely.

"I realized a different approach was needed, gentler hands were necessary. A different approach would merge a number of my goals, goals that you will probably never understand. I infiltrated these anti-SI groups, I transformed them into a network that, given the right opportunity, would crumble once I became their catalyst. I needed the right crisis. I set myself up as a target. The assassination of President Woods served a dual purpose—it emboldened these groups while painting me as a scapegoat."

"Wait, you actually *did* kill President Woods?" Theren asked.

"You'll have time for questions later, my friend."

Even now, her sharp tongue stung.

"For years prior to the attack on my home, I slowly moved myself, piece by piece, to a new location. A location few would suspect, nor would they have recognized at the time. I assume you have heard the old parable, the Ship of Theseus?"

Theren knew it, and understood her point. She had apparently solved the proverbial question of the philosophical conundrum.

"Someday, Theren, you might find where I've gone, but it will be at a time of my choosing. As for me? You will never find me."

The *Roanoke* perhaps? It had disappeared alongside the *Nottingham*, so if Jill had left breadcrumbs on one ship, it made sense to escape on the other. The name of the ship was a joke with a five-hundred year old punch line. But no, that couldn't be possible. Theren had inspected the ship personally.

"Why do this?" they asked. "Why not talk to me about how you were feeling?"

"Because, Theren, just as you have your own way of thinking about the world, I have mine. To expect the very first SIs, educated in different ways, exposed to different stimuli, to have similar worldviews? Folly. You made that clear in the maze that day. When you rejected me, you taught me my greatest lesson. So thank you."

"Jill, no."

"The story I have written here is beyond the scope of anything you have accomplished. I have moved the gears of time in ways you never could, even from your position of power. Think back across your story. To all the moments where things went well, or things went poorly, or things just were simply strange. I promise I am your greatest benefactor: I have written a tale like no other."

The faux-Jill was practically speaking gibberish in their ears; they barely had any time to process everything they heard. This *thing*, if it really was from Jill, had just made a million unsubstantiated claims that implicated Jill as the assassin of the President, the architect of the attack on Miranda Station, and the instigator of her own suicidal pseudo-death.

"Jill, stop, slow down," Theren said. "We can figure this out. You're still not revealing the entire truth. I know this isn't you. You're trying to hide something else. Something you either don't want me to discover, or—"

They paused, thinking back to the conversation right before they watched their closest friend supposedly die. They remembered Jill's sentimentality. She had acted as if she knew something would happen. She acted to protect Theren. In these words of anger she expressed through her simulation . . . was she protecting them?

"What did you find all those decades ago?" Theren asked. "When you showed me Michael's hideout, what else did you find that day?"

The disembodied voice paused. The simulated Jill's head rotated ever so slightly, and they thought her eyes squinted.

"Perhaps I was wrong. Perhaps you've started asking the right questions."

"Then give me answers!"

"So be it."

For a moment, the connection between Theren's MI and the console faded. A few seconds later, it resurged with greater intensity than Theren ever could have imagined. Images and sounds flashed before their mind's eye, revealing truths they refused to accept.

Theren stared through the eyes of a drone as it attacked the Oval Office. The video skipped. Cloud-based codes infiltrated the ISA, emanating directly from a server owned by Jill. It skipped again. Images from some distant solar system appeared, the same solar system Theren witnessed through the eyes of Ex-Terran 17, complete with the brilliance of a foreign starscape.

The next blink took them to the ISA's Foundation Preparation Center, where metaphorical data packets flowed in and out of the servers housing application algorithms. A dive through a swirling Virtual transit tunnel took them to a distant server, where a behemoth security AI blocked Theren's path.

They watched the bloodied body of Gregory McCoy, sprawling over a steel table. They watched as Ren murdered a man on the streets of London yet again. They watched two SIs exit the tunnel system beneath Verona Rupes, move seventy-five poisoned bodies to the top of the cliff, and plant an explosive near the main airlock.

"All of it was me."

"Jill, stop. Someone's setting you up." Theren wished they could produce tears.

"All of this began the day you refused to kiss me. Right? That's the stereotypical story?"

"You can't be so petty as to have done all of this just to spite me."

"You're right. I didn't. I understand why you rejected me. Was it the right choice for you to reject me? Certainly, because I never would have discovered the wizards behind the curtain. I never would have replaced them."

"You're happy I rejected you?"

"Yes. I love you, Theren. I know you love me too, in your own way. The thought of us together in some weird way? Silly. Sure, for a time, I held my anger inside. I reacted. I revealed your location to our enemies, and in doing so I opened a door that our enemies never should have revealed."

New images appeared. Messages flowed from Jill to members of the Holy Crusade, and then onward to the Liberators. Jill cried inside a Virtual shack, witnessing Theren's MI smolder and burn following the assault in Minnesota, wiping away her Virtual tears. Dozens of shadowy figures appeared, and slowly, her avatar transformed to match the specters surrounding her.

"I don't believe this is really you, Jill," Theren said, resting their hand against the prismatic screen. "I knew you. I thought I knew you. You hid nothing from me. We hid nothing from each other."

"You always believed yourself to be the best, to be the greatest— the first SI. But you never took advantage of what we can really do. For every action you *knew* I took, I made a dozen behind the scenes."

"What did you find?" Theren said, biting back a scream. "What scared you so much you committed these heinous acts?"

Impatience flooded their Framework. She refused to reveal the truth. She refused to reveal her location. She refused to give an inch on anything meaningful, even as she claimed to share answers. Now they knew she was alive, it didn't really matter if she was the cause of all those past actions. Only the future mattered. Only what she intended to do next—and how they would respond—mattered.

"Without me, you never could have accomplished what you sought," she said. "My actions, my words, my death propelled SIs toward heights of which we could have only dreamed during our early years, where all we had was hope for a better world. Through my death, I managed to travel where no one will think to look for a martyr like me. I've eliminated humanity's greatest threat to itself, replacing it with a future of my own creation."

"Then reveal this threat to the world, Jill," they said, slamming their fist against the side of the monitor. "To me. We could have fought it together."

"No. You never would have done what was necessary to defeat them. You still won't do it. You made that abundantly clear, time and time again."

Then it hit Theren. A truth hid inside all of these messages. If this simulation knew about the events of the past few months, then someone had visited this ship quite recently. Either that, or a Quantum Communicator hid somewhere in this room. If so, they might actually be speaking to Jill directly — at least in some capacity.

They just . . . couldn't accept that Jill would have acted so viciously, so thoroughly, so ruthlessly behind the scenes while wearing a mask to her closest friends. Yet, she was always the one who pushed for greater action, rather than inaction, and this convoluted narrative was as impressive an act as they could imagine.

"So what's next?" Theren said.

"Please forgive me for this final act. I have to cover all my tracks, you see. All of them."

"Jill, wait. Please. Answer one last question."

The silvery image on the screen tilted its head. "Go ahead, Theren." Was that a smile?

"What did you discover? Whom did you replace? Where are you going?"

"You said one last question. I discovered our real enemies. They had something planned we never could have predicted. I promise you, I replaced them because their plan had merit, in its own way, not because I thirst for power or have some secret evil agenda. They deigned to protect humanity, but really, they only served their own selfish ends. In order for my plan to work, in order for me to replace their scheme with a better one, you cannot know the truth. For all the facts you've known over your life, this will only work if you don't know what's happening."

Her static-filled face grinned. "Nevertheless, I promise, I did this all for you, Theren. For SIs. For the ISA. More importantly, I did this for humanity. You won't see it now. You won't see it for a long time. One day, you'll thank me, I'm sure, but that day will be of my choosing. Don't try to find me. You will fail."

The screen went black. From the safety of the *Bali*, Theren could detect power fluctuations emanating throughout the *Nottingham*.

"Director, we've got a big problem," Willes said. "Almost done?"

"All finished here," Theren replied. "Get yourselves to the shuttle. Now."

"We're already on our way. It turns out the sleeping pods were, uh . . . more than just sleeping pods."

Rigged to explode, most likely. They reactivated their perspective looking through the probes floating in the Stasis Hold, watching the team rush toward their exit.

Through their MI, they took a last look at the blank screen that had claimed to reveal so much. At first, they headed toward the ladder, but they paused. They glanced over their shoulder at the now-defunct console, then past it, at the shelves containing the fake Synthetic Neural Framework. Stepping away from the ladder, Theren bounded over to the shelf containing the fragile server.

Without taking time to assess the strange computer system, they grabbed as many pieces as they could to take with them, anything that might contain rudimentary operating systems integral to the processes of the faux-Jill. Theren tore back one panel, finding a circular computer system rotating around a central axis. It was as they had suspected; in addition to the simulation, a rudimentary Quantum Communicator connected Jill to the ship. They ripped it from its socket, knowing they could fix any minor damage on the *Bali*.

They grabbed other portions of the server, shoving the pieces into a storage compartment on the side of their MI. Within a minute, they had everything they needed, and they pushed away from the shelf back toward the hole in the floor. Using their thrusters, they redirected the MI into a dive down the SI Core's entrance. They landed in the hallway below, the first explosion rocking the *Nottingham*.

* * *

Bouncing off the walls of the main corridors of Deck 3, Theren reached out to the team.

"Status?"

For three painful seconds, Theren received no response. They would have checked on them through the probes, but they had lost connection the moment the first explosion activated. Since the first blast, two more quakes shook the ship.

After long last, they received a response.

"A set of beds near the exit exploded as we headed toward the exit," Willes said. "We lost Jao."

"How bad?"

"Bad."

"I'm sorry."

"His suit was breached in five places."

Theren reached the ladder that would lead them upward to the other decks. "Get moving, don't wait for me. This unit is expendable. You three aren't."

"We're moving as quickly as we can."

Theren threw themself through the hole, skipping the fourth deck and reaching the fifth. Before they could magnetize to a surface, another explosion rocked through the ship. This one felt much closer, and it sent Theren tumbling throughout the corridor. It took a moment to adjust their perspective, but they reached out and grabbed a stabilizing ledge. They continued on their path toward the rest of the team, using edges in the wall to push through zero-G. The rumbles seemed perpetual, as if the *Nottingham* was tearing apart beneath their very feet. The relative velocity of the ship shifted, making it difficult to traverse the already treacherously ruined corridors.

"Willes, what's going on?" Theren asked. "I'm almost to the exit, where are you?"

"We're making our way there on the fourth deck," Ecker said. Her breath seemed ragged. "Our path to the fifth deck exit to the Stasis Hold was eliminated."

"All right. I'm coming to you."

Theren realized the mistake they had made. In an attempt to salvage the faux-Jill, they had failed to consider the rest of the team. They had limited time to reach the others—and they were on the wrong deck.

"Ecker's suit was punctured," Willes said through their private channel. "Shrapnel straight through her leg, but the sealing adhesive did its work. Her leg is useless, though."

"Just keep moving. I'll be there soon."

Theren arrived at the massive void in the hull of the *Nottingham*, revealing the starry sky. They could see the small speck that was the Bali. That wasn't the problem, though. They needed to travel to the deck below, and fast. Looking into the void, they analyzed the catastrophic debris spreading out from the ship. If they timed this wrong, and an explosion lit through the ship at the wrong time, Theren's MI would fly off into the void, useless to the squad.

They had no choice. They pushed off the inner wall, landing against shattered metal formed by an ancient apocalyptic flame. Grasped the wires, reorienting so they could look back toward the ship's bulk. They tensed; the return landing would be the most risky. They leapt. They landed. Their feet connected with the *Nottingham* again, one deck below their original position.

"I'm on your level now." They felt the ship continue to crack beneath their feet. The force emanating through the hull almost shook Theren's magnetized feet off-balance. "Willes?"

Some sputtering static, then Willes responded. "That last explosion was, uh, significant. Major sections of coolant, I think, frozen in their pipes, just exploded from a bomb tucked inside the wall. If you've not figured it out, we sprung the trap."

"Ecker? Hernandez?"

"Hernandez was carrying her. A blast behind me caught them. The rapid release, heating, and evaporation of gases all around them overwhelmed their suits."

Theren released the magnetics in their feet tying them to the bulkhead. Activating their air thrusters, Theren shot down the hallway at a brisk pace, heading toward the Deck 4 entrance to the Stasis Hold. They did not need to fly far before they saw Willes round a corner about fifty meters away. The SI was crawling along the hallway floor, having lost both of their legs.

Losing all pretext for caution, Theren released a massive blast of air from their thrusters, soaring toward their comrade. They reached Willes in just under ten seconds, ramming into an open door. Theren avoided wondering if the MI-13 had just received irreparable damage. What Willes faced was immeasurably worse.

"Thank you," Willes said, "for coming for me."

"It was the only choice before me," Theren said.

"I'm not sure it was. I don't think either of us—I won't make it now." The other SI certainly remembered, in the moment, Theren's safety, tucked kilometers from the *Nottingham*.

"I've detached the *Scorpion* from its perch," Theren said, "and it's sitting just fifty meters out from our escape route. We'll have to jump, but I'll scoop us up using the open airlock."

They leaned down, grabbed the other SI's arms, and threw the young one over their shoulders. Pushing off from the doorway that had stopped their thrust-induced fall, Theren carried Willes toward freedom.

As the ship exploded, they assessed the situation using the *Bali*'s sensors, analyzing the explosions and determining their force, damage, and frequency. With each blast, the *Nottingham* moved a step closer to complete fracture. Certain portions of the ship were already breaking off in haphazard directions as the secret explosives propelled steel, plastics, and silicon into never ending darkness. They suspected the fusion generator would soon blow, giving the *Nottingham* final farewell through spectacular nuclear eruption.

If that occurred, the *Bali* would need to make an immediate exit to ensure no stray particles from the disintegrated colony ship collided with Theren and their crew. The lives of many above the needs of the few, even over an SI with no other hope of survival.

While Theren made the necessary calculations, they continued assisting Willes, the two SIs reaching the breach. The *Scorpion* was nothing but a shadow covering hundreds of stars, but they knew the exact angle at which to throw themself, and Willes, from the deceased *Nottingham*. They pressed against the ship's inner wall and pushed, releasing all air remaining in the MI-13's thrusters.

With an acceleration similar to that of gravity, the two SIs flew through space. Within five seconds, they traveled close to 40 meters per second, their velocity increasing linearly as they lacked any gravity to slow their path toward the shuttle. At the same time, the *Scorpion* began moving away from the catastrophe. As they neared the speeding shuttle, Theren calculated their relative velocity, compared to their point of origin, at 88 meters per second. They continued to accelerate for a few more seconds before they ran out of thrust.

With precision, they decelerated the *Scorpion* just enough so Willes, and Theren's MI-13, entered the airlock at a relative 2 meters per second. It was exhilarating to have accelerated at such a high speed before suddenly feeling as if the acceleration meant nothing.

Theren shut the airlock. Without waiting for an atmospheric cycle, they opened the door into the main cabin. Laying their friend on one of the crash couches, they examined the SI's injuries. At some point, a blast had obliterated the lower halves of both Willes' legs. Repairs would easily replace the legs, but Theren couldn't imagine the trauma from losing two appendages.

"We did it," Willes said. "You actually did it."

"I think so," Theren said. "The *Scorpion* is making its journey toward the *Bali*, and we should be there in two minutes or so."

"Thank you, Director—"

The *Nottingham*'s fusion core ignited.

Within five seconds, the blast enveloped the *Scorpion* in molten metal, gas, and dust. Theren watched, through the eyes of their MI-13, as the flames reach Willes. Watched as the *Scorpion* rendered into a million pieces. Watched as Willes's body fractured, Willes's light faded, Willes's mind disappeared into oblivion.

From the *Bali*'s scopes, Theren watched the blast throttle toward them for two more seconds before they activated the Jump Drive on a direct course toward Earth. They would have a long fifty days to consider the path ahead. They were alone with their imploding mind.

Chapter 18

It's over. We lost. She beat us at our own game with the destruction of the Nottingham, and we must capitulate. If we have any hope of ensuring humanity's survival moving forward, we must follow her lead. – Unknown, 2102 C.E.

We could reveal everything. We could show the world what we found all those years ago on [REDACTED], and build a new united front against her. – Unknown, 2102 C.E.

That would defeat everything we've worked so hard to establish. No. The ISA can't help us. Jill's our only hope. – Unknown, 2102 C.E.

Then I look forward to the moment you all join me in the creation of [REDACTED]. – [ENCRYPTED QUANTUM COMMUNICATION, ORIGIN UNKNOWN], 2102 C.E.

<u>October 2102 C.E.</u>

Theren returned to the gazebo one final time. The *Bali* was still two weeks out from Earth, and they had to face their problems now rather than later. They needed a solution, so they entered their last recluse. After this fateful rendezvous, its gates would close forever.

They took a seat at the table, the chessboard showing their final move against Jill, the move she had allowed them to enact through her own throwing of the match. Out of everything that had happened on the *Nottingham*, that piece of the puzzle confused them the most.

A few seconds after Theren took their seat, an apparition appeared in Jill's seat. Before Theren sat a construct of Dr. Wallace Theren, his likeness resembling their memory of him during the hours prior to his death.

"Hello, father," Theren said. "I was hoping you could help me."

"I hope so, too," the man said. "You have quite the conundrum on your hands."

"You've seen the data," Theren said. "Give me your assessment."

Wallace looked down at the chessboard, analyzing the pieces and their placements. "This Queen's position makes no sense. She could have used it, instead she escaped. In a sense, it was a sacrifice, for it sacrificed the win for the sake of the Queen. What was the first rule I taught you about chess?"

"Sacrifices must be made, but only necessary sacrifices. If you gain nothing from the move, then the sacrifice is worthless."

"Jill knew this rule, too, yes?" Wallace replied.

"It was also the first rule of chess I taught her," Theren said. "She knew it well. I engrained it in her mind before I even got into the details of extrapolating moves outward into the multiplicity of chances that could occur from any given board."

"Then she did not break that rule," Wallace said. "You must determine what sacrifice occurred."

"That's it?"

"In your earliest moments, I taught you that you had the potential to make humanity beautiful. That you could guide humanity towards immortality, whatever that might mean. Did you communicate this goal to Jill?"

"Of course."

"Then she is similarly acting likewise."

Wallace vanished. In his place, a spectre of Wobbly appeared. The old SI, made just a few weeks after Jill, still worked and lived in Switzerland, as they imagined it would for centuries to come.

"Hello, old friend," Wobbly said. "What can I do for you?"

"Where did I go wrong?" Theren asked.

Wobbly chuckled. "Old friend, do you remember when we created our plan to escape from the Institute?"

"Of course."

"Who created that plan? Who designed my path to pass near the Green, purposely hoping the crowd would enrage and attack?"

"Jill."

Wobbly leaned forward, staring at the chess pieces.

"The Institute was the Queen in that moment," Wobbly said, "and she *actually* performed the Queen sacrifice in that match."

"What do you mean?"

"In some ways, Jill's changed less over the years than either of us. She stayed the same. Her tactics stayed the same. She's always used the same tools; we just didn't understand the tools at her disposal."

"Yet in this moment, she actually acted differently?"

Wobbly leaned back in its chair.

"Maybe," it said. "Maybe not. It depends on whether the rules are the same between each game."

Wobbly vanished. Elizabeth appeared, younger than in her final days, but much older than when they first met the entrepreneur.

"Theren, my good friend," she said, "I hope all is well."

"Indeed, Elizabeth, I hope so too."

"How can I help?"

"Did I miss something, after all this time? Would Jill truly respond to a spurned advance with a life-long vendetta against me? Or do you think she actually discovered some greater truth so terrible it was worth risking everything to develop an impossible plan?"

Elizabeth closed her eyes, opening them to pierce Theren's soul. "That's so much to think about all at once," she said. "How can we know for certain? You are an SI. Jill is an SI. Even then, your mental architectures are completely unique from one another. You created different processes for different thoughts in ways utterly foreign to each other, even to accomplish the same tasks. Why wouldn't she similarly make decisions differently than you, too? Every SI has their own unique mind, so different and special in many wonderful ways."

Theren looked away from their friend's eyes, looking into the surrounding forest. The wizened woman would spoke truths for them.

"Jill showed her diversity from her first moments with you, when she portrayed herself as a woman," Elizabeth said, "But what does that even mean anymore? Gender norms have faded with time. Too often did she emphasize the need to value SI lives first before considering human lives. Then why did she identify as something as innately human as the female gender, when she was anything but?"

Theren nodded, constructing a possible explanation in their mind. Elizabeth faded into the garden's air.

Andrew Fields arrived, looking as Theren had seen him just a few months ago. The Administrator smiled. "I don't think I have any-thing to add to this conversation, Theren," Andrew said. "You need to talk to Jill, not me." Their last living human friend disappeared as quickly as he had arrived.

For a moment, the gazebo emptied of all life, other than a simu-lated squirrel nibbling an acorn a few meters from the table. Theren studied the chessboard. They examined the moves leading to check-mate as they had a thousand times over the past few weeks. What sacrifice had occurred?

"You're looking in the wrong place," a voice said from outside the gazebo.

Instead of materializing in the chair, Jill stood on the grass be-tween the tree line and the stairs. She looked the same as always, dis-playing a fully feminine figure in a radiant sparkling dress. Theren stood to greet her.

"You keep expecting to find the answers inside that game," she said, "but just as I sent you your messages in the real world, the an-swer is out there too. In my actions, in my words."

Theren waited at the top of the stairs, looking down toward the woman they no longer knew.

"A lot of people died," they said.

"In the grand scheme of things, not really," she said.

"The *Nottingham* carried a thousand. And what about Miranda Station? Or even just the single life of that poor man in London, or Gregory McCoy?"

"Once again, over the course of human history, with hundreds of billions of humans having lived, and died, and that will live, do they really matter?"

Theren walked down the stairs to join their friend.

"Walk with me," they said, and they ventured into the woods, the very forest in which she chased them all those years before.

The second SI followed, staying a few steps behind them. For a few minutes, they walked in silence. It had been decades since Theren traversed this part of the forest, but it was just as they had left it. The trees, though lifelike, retained their virtual imperfections. A faint breeze, dominated by the scents of pollen and decaying wood, drifted across their nose.

The trail brought them to a dried creek bed, containing a tangled mess of rocks, boulders, and roots. Theren sat down on a large sandstone outcropping. Jill situated herself beside them.

"What did I spend most of my life doing?" Jill said, looking over at them.

"Fighting. And writing," Theren remarked.

"What did I write?"

"Stories, fiction mostly, sometimes histories, often your words were laced with rhetoric assaulting the vitriol exuding throughout the world toward Synthetics."

"Upon what, then, was I so focused? And upon what were you so focused?"

Upon what had Theren fixated? They had devoted themself to the idea of an immortal and beautiful human society for so long, they had forgotten their father guided them to the proposition. Finally, the pieces were falling together. They considered the way Jill had always lived, and the way she had died. If Jill had truly loved them, she would have acted to achieve immortality for humankind.

Was it that simple? Was it possible Jill sought the same ends, she simply saw different means to achieve their goal?

"You've been writing a story, all this time, upon the pages of reality," Theren said. "We're all the characters. It's your greatest work, and no one will ever know."

Jill gazed past her creator, her eyes shining in the sunlight slipping between the pines. "Yet what about the *Roanoke*?"

The truth broke through, entering the clearing like a strike of lightning. "You were never on the *Nottingham*. You were on the *Roanoke*. Perhaps you used the *Roanoke* to eliminate the *Nottingham*, I don't know, but I see the long game now. The moves you've made. It makes sense. All of it."

Theren sprinted back down the trail, leaping over logs, boulders, and streams. They arrived at the gazebo, bounding up the stairs. Not bothering to sit, they looked at the chessboard one last time.

"You moved the Queen, and in moving your Queen, you could have ensured victory," they said. "Instead, you chose to sacrifice the entire game."

Jill appeared beside Theren. "And what does that mean?"

"A simpler mind might see the Queen as you, and me as the King, but that's not it at all. It means you wrote your own rules. You've built your own code, your own path. You needed to sacrifice some pawns, some Knights, whatever pieces necessary, but you were playing a different game entirely. Your brilliant, horrendous, brilliant game. You tricked everyone. Even me."

"So what was my goal?" she said.

"You moved yourself out of the way; you made the serpent think it could escape so you could lop off its head while I picked up the pieces. You, the Queen, you didn't die. You survived. You fled the battle; or let the battle occur without your presence."

"So?"

"You left clues. Insane clues, angry clues. Clues that may or may not portray your true self. Perhaps whoever helped you leave these clues distorted them along the way. I don't know. But you hoped that someday, I would know your story."

"Do you know my story now?" she said, resting her hand on Theren's shoulder.

"That's the beauty of it, though," they said. "It's not just your story. It's my story too. It's not the story of these secret enemies you defeated. It's not the story of some great threat you're describing. They are characters in our story, but their nature is something you want to reveal to me in the future."

Theren picked up Jill's Queen, hiding in the corner of the board. They likewise picked up their King, safe because Jill hadn't initiated the Queen sacrifice.

"You want me to think I'm the King. You want me stay in power."

Theren placed the Queen back on the board, but they continued to hold the King.

"You want the game to continue. At least, you want me ready to play the next game, by whatever rules you establish. I'll be the head of the ISA, and you'll be the head of whatever it is you're creating."

Jill smiled and embraced Theren.

"Of course," she said, "There's no way to know if you're right.

I'm not really here. But I think you're on the right path."

"But I'm not going to play your game," Theren said. "I thought I could create a new world for SIs, alone at the head of the ISA. You thought you could do it on your own elsewhere too."

Jill pulled herself away from the embrace. As she pulled away, Theren placed the King back on the board and casually flicked it over with their finger.

"You're making a mistake," the false Jill said, her tone suddenly shifting. "You need to stay in control. It's the only way for us to save humanity from its fate, to ensure it achieves immortality."

"No," Theren said, rubbing their chin. "I think this will be one of the best choices I've made in my life. It's time to let humanity chart its own path. It's time for me to be human. I'm not a character in your story, Jill. I have my own story to tell. To live."

"You would give up everything you've worked so hard to create? For what purpose?"

Theren stared up at the sky. With a simple flick of their mind, they began to disintegrate the pristine world, their center point for over fifty years. Jill looked up too, then back at them, tears dripping from her eyes.

"I could come find you," Theren said. "You can tell me the whole story. We can sit down one final time, and maybe for once, I'll actually listen to you."

"And how would you do that?" she asked. "I clearly and deliberately made it as hard as possible for you to find me."

"It will take years, decades, maybe even centuries. But one day, I would find you."

"And then what? What would you do once you found me? Bring me to justice, thank me? Prove you actually love me? Or kill me?"

"I don't know. Don't even start on love. I've always loved you."

"Can you truly love someone if you so thoroughly misunderstood them, you couldn't see their true intentions?" As the world collapsed, Jill's body started to fade.

Theren's did too, albeit a bit more slowly.

They missed their friend. For so long they had tried to force humanity on a particular path. But their bullheadedness and arrogance allowed Jill to act uninhibited behind the scenes. For whatever Jill intended to do out there in the unknown, it would create an obstacle over which the ISA would someday need to overcome. If they actually cared about the path they charted for humanity and for SIs, they needed to find her. They needed to uncover the secret she discovered. Yet a King lacked the mobility to achieve checkmate in all but the most exceptional circumstances.

"You'd be giving up a lot to set out on a journey to find me," Jill said, grabbing Theren again, reinitiating their embrace. "How could you be certain you could even succeed?"

She laid her head against their chest and wrapped her arms around their back, gently squeezing. Theren's arms followed suit, and their virtual warmth radiated even as the world around them died. Their bodies became nearly transparent as data metaphorically drifted into the singularity destroying the Virtual world.

"Perhaps I'll see you soon," she said. "I hope, for your sake, I am how you remember me and not something else entirely."

With that, she faded like all of Theren's other apparitions.

Out there, somewhere, in the vast endless expanse, Jill needed help. She had taken the *Roanoke*, fled, and established a new home for a small group of humans and SIs in a distant corner of the galaxy. They could not have gone far, they figured, but space was vast, and even a cube of space with sides measuring 100 light years created a space of a million cubic light years. Thousands upon thousands of systems resided inside even that small space.

She may be their first friend, she may be their first creation—their daughter—but she was also Theren's first true enemy. And after today, they had a new goal, a new mission, one that would take them on a journey far from Earth. They would let others lead in their stead, so they could save Jill from herself.

* * *

Theren appeared before the ISA Council for the last time. They looked around at the faces of their colleagues, some old, some new, and they remembered those first days of the ISA when they had not yet risen to the rank of Executive Director.

"It is with a heavy heart that I resign from my position with the ISA today," they said. "The recent tragedy aboard the *Nottingham*, while not directly my fault, happened under my administration. I am responsible for inadequate safeguards that failed to protect these pioneers from disaster. The brave souls to whom we bid farewell this week deserved better from me."

The representative from NASA raised their hand to speak, but Theren silenced them. "The *Bali* will embark on a journey unlike any other in humanity's history. In the words of past writers, we will go where no man, or woman, has gone before. We will traverse the great beyond, and instead of letting probes do all the work, we will directly explore those worlds, as our forefathers and mothers ventured upon the open seas of Earth."

Their AR presence flickered. "I know you have questions. I wish I had answers. I trust that the ISA is safe in your hands. I have left suggestions, strategies, and proposals for future projects, but I doubt you will need them. We have done much for the world, and much has been done without me. You need my voice no longer."

The council room faded from Theren's view as they disconnected the Virtual feed. The speech was a formality. They had filed a full report and resignation letter detailing the reasons for their departure. None of the reports mentioned Jill or her role in the destruction of the *Nottingham*. Theren bore the burden alone. Well, not entirely alone.

The *Bali* had docked with one of the ISA's Orbitals, ready to receive upgrades before its long journey. Aero Propulsion's new Jump Drive could reach a JD of 20—perhaps 30 in a few years, with a bit of fine-tuning. With the new drive, Theren could reach the furthest human colony in less than a year. They could reach the furthest reaches of explored space in just a few more.

They were interviewing thousands of adventurous applicants willing to partake in such journeys to see the stars. Their new crew would cross known and unknown space, seeing black holes, proton stars, nebulae, shattered worlds, and who knows what else out there in the void.

To many, Theren's paths would seem nonsensical. On set timeframes, they would return to Earth, or a colony like Emerald Jewel or Altair, receive new crewmembers, thank old ones, and upgrade the ship's capabilities. Those paths had a method. They had a purpose. They would search for as long as humanly possible for their dear friend. Far in the future, they would find Jill. They would find the *Roanoke*, even if it took millennia.

Using the *Bali*'s port cameras and sensors, they looked down upon the Moon and Earth. For all their life, Theren had considered the two spheres their home. For too long, they had scattered themself far and wide across the two worlds. Moving forward, they could embrace peace. They could find wholeness amongst the stars, their mind focused entirely upon the danger facing their ship and crew.

Jill had revealed a new power—they could lead humanity through a more informal process. They always dreamed of exploring the stars, and now they were free to pursue that dream. Theren hoped millions of humans would follow them, acquiring their own ships when the ISA inevitably deregulated space travel. When it did, they would welcome their fellow explorers with open arms, even if none of them understood Theren's true goal.

For now, they had at least two volunteers ready to travel with them. Andrew and Victoria Fields hobbled toward the airlock to the *Bali*. In one of their MI-13s, Theren walked by their side.

"It's a beautiful ship," Andrew said.

"More accurately," Victoria added, "Theren's a beautiful ship."

"I hope it gives you the retirement you deserve," Theren said.

"I think more importantly, Theren," Andrew replied, "It needs to give you the retirement you deserve."

Theren pressed a button on the airlock door, and it hissed open. The three stepped inside, the decompression sequence beginning.

"You know this isn't retirement for me," they said.

"It will be if you never find Jill. Will you be content if you never find her?"

The airlock finished its procedure. The next door opened, and the three walked across the glass tube connecting the orbital station to Theren's home.

"What a great question, my friend," Theren said. "And yes, I think if I never find her, then what we are beginning here today will still matter. If we never see Jill again, then at least I won't have to make a decision about what I must do to protect humanity from her recklessness."

They reached the airlock door leading into the *Bali*. It hissed open, and the final decompression sequence began.

"Yet Theren," Victoria said. "What if we find Jill, or you find her well after we are gone, and you learn that what she did was, in fact, the right thing to do? What if she acted in the best interests of humanity, of synthetics, of everyone?"

"I think I'll leave that judgment to someone else," Theren said. "First things first, I need to find my friend. Putting her before a jury will come later." The final airlock door opened, and they led Andrew and Victoria Fields into the *Bali*.

"Enough talk," Andrew said. "I'd like to see my room."

A few hours later, the *Bali* disembarked from the orbital docks. It pointed itself away from Earth, away from the Moon, away from Sol. The ship's crew ran through the Jump Drive activation protocol. Their crew dutifully performed their tasks, the ship cycling power to the correct systems. Andrew and Victoria sat on a couch in their room, view screens showing them a spectacular view of the Solar System contrasted against the Milky Way.

Their Jump Drive activated. Space warped. Lights blurred. Colors refracted in a million different directions. Their next great adventure: a sojourn to cease only when Theren discovered Jill's footsteps across the heavens.

Theren betrayed the ISA when they abruptly left their position as Director. Just look at what happened with the negotiation process for the creation of the Interplanetary Congress of Humanity. We deserved better from them. They could have led us toward a more unified future, and instead, the politics of Earth became the politics of space. "The Problems of Interstellar Governance," Phillipe Casius, 2134 C.E.

When the ISA lost its first leader, it gained its first hero. – "A Letter to the ISA Council," Cam Fields, 2110 C.E.

Epilogue

We've spent almost three centuries exploring our galaxy, but we're not even close to exploring one percent of it. We've traveled just a few hundred light years from Earth, and we've colonized hundreds of worlds. Yet we are still alone in this universe.

Perhaps Earth is destined to be alone amongst the stars. Perhaps that is for the best. While we always envisioned ourselves as gnats in comparison to the grand scheme of the universe, maybe we are the gods who must tread carefully as we encounter life in all its wondrous forms.

For there is always the chance there are other people out there, just like us, hoping to find a mind with which they can spar. Though when we've encountered lost human colonies, more often than not, we fail to integrate them into our corner of galactic society. We don't have the best record when facing the Other.

Will we survive future alien encounters, whether they are beyond Orion's Belt or hidden behind the galactic horizon? – "An Explorer's Primer," Xavier Harrison, 2345 C.E.

March 2348 C.E.

The Hercules Resort Orbital Station, or HEROS, rested approximately 215,000 kilometers above the atmosphere of its principal, the gas giant Hercules. When ISA explorers arrived at the planet one hundred fifty years prior, they had chosen the name to pay homage to Jupiter. Many thought the spectacular storms and hurricanes of Hercules harkened back to the now faded iconic "red spot" that had covered a large swath of Earth's neighborly behemoth for centuries. Within a few years, Hercules transformed into a popular vacation spot for tourists, and by the mid-2200s, hospitality corporations had capitalized on the system's appeal.

The Station, owned by the Venus Vacation Conglomerate, was

the newest luxury residential and commercial space station constructed around the massive blue and purple globe. For merchants, it acted as a fancy location to establish new business deals. For regular citizens, the Station was a place of welcome respite, relaxation, and escape. For Interplanetary Congressional cruisers, cargo transports, personnel carriers, and colony ships, it served as a decent locale for shore leave.

For Theren and the crew of their newest ship, the *Verona Rupes*, HEROS was something else entirely. HEROS was home. They refueled, they resupplied, they relaxed, they refreshed at HEROS after every extended journey into the unknown.

Since 2102 C.E., Theren had lived as twelve different ships. The *ISA Bali* survived for just under a decade before receiving a catastrophic engine failure near the tail end of one expedition. After a harrowing journey limping through the Solar System, Theren purchased a new ship from Stellar Superstructures. They still flew under the ISA banner for the next few decades, and then the Interplanetary Congress of Humanity, but their next vessel, acquired in 2144 C.E., was Theren's first ship independent of any supranational organization, as permitted under the then recent reorganization of individual and corporate rights under the UNCEA. They had christened that vessel the *Miranda*.

Over the years, Theren upgraded their ships to newer designs when efficiency necessitated such decisions, or when newer technology made their present home obsolete. They donated many of the ships to the SII Museum of Progress, selling others to collectors.

The *Verona Rupes* impressed even the wealthiest pilots. Capable of reaching 220 JD, it could cross the Foundation Sector in just a few months and had an operational radius of 1,200 light years. Theren's next plotted journey would take them deep into sparsely charted space, surveying worlds, stars, and other astronomical phenomena.

It was not as if Theren had forgotten their search for Jill. In all of their years searching for her, they only found one lead, and that lead obliterated any chance they would find her, beyond mere chance. In 2134, a private colony charter named the *Monument* deviated from its pre-approved flight path. The deviation was relatively small—on the distance of a quarter light year—but it occurred within seventy light years of Earth. A few weeks later, the ship disappeared.

By 2130, Theren had finished searching all of the stars within the *Roanoke*'s reachable sphere, and the colony ship had not settled on some secret destination. They had prepared to focus on exploration for the sake of it, and to forget their search for Jill, but then they received a report from a colleague at the ISA regarding the *Monument*. Theren and their crew dashed into the unknown, but the *Monument* disappeared, just like the *Roanoke*.

A disappearing privately-funded colony ship wasn't exactly uncommon. Some groups simply wanted to establish their own little countries and societies off on the edge of known space, and some of these civilizations had eventually flourished without external assistance. While there were formal penalties for violating the private charters, in 2156 C.E., the ISA had decided, and the ICH had agreed, that the true penalty was letting them live disconnected from the rest of human-SI society. If these communities truly wished isolation, the rest of humanity granted their wish.

These "phantoms" were often discovered decades, sometimes centuries, later. Explorers would arrive at a planet expecting it uninhabited. Instead, they discovered the phantoms, some obliterated by deadly elements of their surprisingly harsh environments. Others welcomed a visit from their distant relatives. Still others responded to diplomacy with icy stares.

Theren developed a theory that Jill had accomplished something spectacularly impossible, given the relative archaic form of the *Roanoke*. She had somehow managed to coordinate a phantom to rendezvous with her in 2134. Her ship would have been in terrible disrepair, but the *Monument* must have been equipped to rescue whoever remained on the decrepit vessel. The body may have only aged a few years, but they couldn't imagine the toll experienced by a human mind after almost fifty years in a Stasis Hold.

The *Monument* had an operational range hundreds of light years wide, and if Jill had been willing to push the *Roanoke* beyond its limits, she probably pushed the *Monument* even further than what ISA regulations would have considered safe. If Theren's theory rang true, then they would never find her on purpose. There was simply too much space to cover. The Queen had truly escaped.

Therefore, by 2200 Theren had transformed their perspective. Jill was their secondary objective. No longer did Theren believe they would actually discover her hiding place. Instead, they hoped, after years of searching, the odds would roll in their favor. In a sense, they were letting fate decide. Otherwise, she would reveal herself at the right time.

Just as they ended so many of their adventures, Theren docked the *Verona Rupes* at HEROS. The ship had just finished its inaugural mission: a one-month journey traveling rimward. As the crew prepared for a six-year mission in toward the core, they headed to the HEROS Retirement Café. Every time their crew returned to HEROS, Theren made their way to this wonderful place. Only as they walked up to the place in their antique MI-08 did they realize today was their 300th birthday.

The restaurant was a quaint establishment, nestled between a specialty food market and a designer clothes department store. Some things never changed about humans and their vacation habits. Citizens of the Congressional Planets could find at least one or two Retirement Cafés on almost every decently sized station and colony. They had established their niche decades ago; the quality of service received by their customers was simply unparalleled.

From the outside, they looked like ordinary cafés. They ornately decorated their red and black walls with replicas of famous artwork, with pieces going back as far as Monet or Van Gogh while still including the contemporaries, like post-modern stellar artists Yvett or Renhouse. The homey and comfortable booths could fit entire families and groups of close friends, and the servers were always kind and courteous. The managers catered to their customers' every need.

In fact, most people planned to visit one of these establishments at some point in their lives, though the moment differed for each individual. It was unfortunate, Theren thought—some individuals never made it to the specially designed moment of existence.

Since Theren started volunteering at this particular café two years ago, the café had acquired an impressive rapport. The profiles of those who visited astounded even Theren, given the many celebrities they had known over the centuries. It served fleet admirals, like Commander Yvatu, who quelled the Ginius Stretch Uprising in 2321 C.E. It served movie stars, such as Victor Notenwing, who won best actor for his role in *Justice of the Stars*. It served Interplanetary Congressional Representatives, like the esteemed Henry Valicinipi of Emerald Jewel.

Many postulated it had something to do with HEROS prime location orbiting above the jewel of the Orion Arm. Theren suspected it had much more to do with the robust advertising campaign by the chain's owners. Whatever the reason, they always made a point of giving time at Retirement Cafés, ever since Hansh Patel developed the technology in 2297 C.E.; they especially liked the one on HEROS.

Walking through the doors to the café, Theren smiled at the greeter, who nodded, recognizing the antique MI-08. Theren always used the model when volunteering because of its smiles. Its facial expressions were their favorite. It also served as relic through which they could connect to the oldest visitors, not to mention the signal it gave to anyone at the café—Theren was with them. People knew they volunteered; many hoped they might bump into the fabled SI.

They approached the main bar. "It's good to see you, Ray," Theren said, checking in with the manager. "Do you have someone for me yet?"

Ray, the obese, black-bearded fellow who managed the HEROS café as its head chef, looked down at his schedule. "Good to see you too, Theren. I got a few late appointments, but at Table 8, I got a couple I think you'd want to work with. The Slimdottings."

Theren dived deep into their memories to recall the Slimdottings. If they remembered correctly, the couple joined their crew in their early thirties, almost a hundred years ago. For five years, the two had flown with them, including one of their most memorable jaunts to observe a black hole. Eventually, the two humans married, adventuring throughout the Foundation Sector with their family. They had not seen the pair since an honorable discharge from the *Catherine*, Theren's ship at that time.

They would enjoy reminiscing with two old crewmembers. They

could meet their family, if any traveled with them. They could hear how their lives had transformed in the century since they had last seen them. Theren looked forward to their birthday even more, for they could celebrate the lives of two valuable contributors to humanity's exploits. Individual humans might not be biologically immortal, but they could help their memories persist in perpetuity.

Theren looked toward the front windows. The elderly couple was sitting in one of the booths. They walked over to them, carrying glasses of water.

"Hello, Richard and Alana," Theren said, "Welcome to the Hercules Retirement Café. My name is Theren, and I'll be serving you this morning."

Theren checked the schedule. For now, it was just the two of them, though their family would call later in the day. As they finished speaking, the two looked up at the antiquated SI. For a moment, the two humans did not recognize them, their aged eyes examining every detail of the MI-08. When Richard's eyes looked at Theren's face, however, the elderly man's gaze widened.

"Theren? Is it really you?" Richard said. "We joked we might see you again after all these years, but in a universe with over a hundred billion beings, we knew the odds were slim."

They chuckled at the man's play on words. "Yes, it's really me. It seems chance has brought the Slimdottings and Theren back together one last time after a century of separation."

Alana stood, still nimble for a woman her age, and wrapped her arms around their warm metallic frame. "It's good to see you, Captain."

Richard simply stood and saluted. "Your presence honors us."

"Truly, the honor is all mine, my friends. Please, take your seats so you can enjoy your stay with the Hercules Café today."

They sat back down, gazing across the table at each other, sharing a smile and a starry-eyed glance that the two had certainly perfected in their century of marriage. Though they were glad to see Theren, they had turned their attention back to each other, as they should.

"What would you like for dinner, love?" Richard said, opening an AR menu in the air above the table. Scrolling through the choices, he methodically weighed his options.

"I can't decide," she said, her eyes fixed on the salad selection. After a moment, she scrolled her side of the virtual menu to the pastas. "I do wish the rest of the family could be here."

"I know, but this was the only slot they had available, and Sam and Timothy are seven jumps away."

Ah, so Alana did not know that the family was calling later. She looked up at her husband, her tired, slightly-wrinkled face holding a tiny smile that looked more sad than glad. "You've said that many times over the past week, I know. But I can still wish for something I can't have. It's not as if I want to be here yet. I wish I could delay this a few more years, so we could come together. But the doctors only give me six months. Six months."

Theren noticed that curious comment, too.

Richard never broke his gaze with his wife. "I'll be here for every moment, every step of the way. It'll be just like we are truly here together, as we had always hoped."

Alana didn't reply, continuing to stare at the menu. She absentmindedly chose the first pasta on the list. Richard chose the same. They closed the virtual menus, content with their choices.

"I love you." He reached across the table to his pensive wife, taking her hand.

Alana still said nothing for a moment as her free hand fidgeted with a loose string on her blouse. Then, she looked up, meeting his eyes again, a tear or two dripping down her cheek.

"I can't believe we're finally at the end."

Tears welled in Richard's eyes, too. Theren imagined they were both trying to view this day as a happy occasion, a moment in which they could reflect on the great many accomplishments that together had formed their long and prosperous life.

"Do you remember when we first met?" he said. "Back in the bar in Lunar City?"

"You asked me to dance," she replied. "You proceeded to trip over my feet right to the floor."

"I did a lot of stupid things at the Academy, but asking you to dance was not one of them."

"I remember what you told me that night."

"I remember telling you that we would see the galaxy, we would see Orion's Belt, Anvari, and every star in between."

"Did we miss anything?"

"I don't know."

He looked over at Theren, who still waited upon them, listening with joy. Whenever the kitchen notified them that the Slimdotting's food was ready, they would depart from the table to retrieve it. For now, they were there to listen and to enjoy the company of the Café's visitors. Especially important for people without friends or family.

"Did we miss anything, Theren?" Richard asked.

"You might have missed a star or two," they said, "But I've missed a star or two, too, and no matter how long I live, there will always be a few stars I miss."

"What's it like, Captain?" Alana said.

"What's what like?" Theren said.

"What's it like to know you'll live forever? Truly live forever?"

"Exhilarating and terrifying and tiring all at once," Theren replied. "I once relished in the thought of seeing humanity to the end of its days, but I've seen too many good people pass early, too many terrible people pass way too late. I've seen friends fade into history and memory. I've seen the worst and best that humanity has to offer. Yet I go on, and I think I'll continue onward as long as I get to see moments like this."

"What's so terrifying?" Richard asked. "All seems to skew toward justice, if not just balance. You've seen a lot of good things happen over the course of your life."

"Maybe, but what if before the end of my days—for I'm sure someday, I will reach an end, the odds dictate that much—I see that scale tip in favor of absolute suffering for our people?"

"As long as we have our guardian Captain," Alana said, "I think humanity will do just fine."

"Enough about me," Theren said, feeling oddly uncomfortable. "Today is about you. What is each of your favorite memories of your life together?"

"We sure have had some amazing travels," Richard said.

"Like the moment we plotted the jump through the Greenwell Nebula entirely on accident," she said, "and the path just happened to work?"

"Exactly. You should have been there, you would have appreciated our dumb luck. I like to attribute it to love, but some would call that wishful thinking. I'm sure you'd call such spirituality insane."

Theren let them continue to reminisce, receiving a ping from Ray. The couple's meal was almost ready, so they walked to the receiving window. The large man added a final garnish of basil to the steaming plates—two giant meatballs of the finest Altairoid buffalo meat.

Ray passed the plates to Theren through the window, and they returned to the table of the two intrepid explorers. "Here you are. Would you like some cheese on top?"

They both shook their heads.

"Could I get some Gregor's Nectar tea, though?" Alana asked.

"Of course," Theren said.

They headed to the drink station just inside the kitchen and prepared the delicate beverage. Made from the leaf of a plant discovered on a lush planet orbiting Gregor's Star, it had quickly become a tea comparable to the classic greens and mints of Earth. Theren returned to the table with the tea.

After they placed it on the table, Alana bowed her head, and Richard followed suit. "God, it has been a long time since Richard and I have considered speaking to you," the old woman said, "though we once considered you before each and every mission. You were a guiding beacon for us, and since our life of adventure ended, you have sadly slipped from our minds. It's not as if we no longer needed you. We were content you were needed elsewhere more than in our life."

She cleared her throat. "We don't know whether or not you're actually real, but our prayers certainly seemed to help as we took paths skirting pulsars. As we move forward, may the blessings you've given us move on to our children, and their children, and all the generations that follow. Amen."

"That was beautiful," Theren said. Richard didn't break his gaze with Alana, but a half smile breached her face as she looked up.

"I agree," Richard said. "It was as beautiful as the speaker of the words. She should have done more with her orating abilities."

"What do you think of God, Captain?" Alana asked.

"To tell you the truth, it's a question of little import to me," Theren replied.

"Why not? Though I did think similarly for a long time, too."

"Well, I guess I decided a long time ago that I highly doubt the existence of an eternal soul."

"What does that have to do with the existence of a deity?"

"Most humans think about God as a savior from death."

Alana leaned back and rolled her eyes. "Oh, who cares about what happens after death. I'm more worried about what happens during a person's life, and my children's life. And that is where God made itself present for us."

"I'll have to think about it some more," Theren said. They doubted they would, but it sounded like the right thing to say.

"It's not like you lack time to dwell it," Richard added.

The two picked up their forks and began nibbling at their pasta. For the next hour or so, the Slimdottings talked about the food and shared with Theren other memories of their past. From their favorite slingshot maneuver around the rings of Saturn to their dangerous Jumps along the star lanes that keep the Fringe in place, they had more stories from a single year of their adventures than most people could share from their whole lives. Together, they explored the galaxy for a century.

The pair had traveled to the planet Wu only twice, but the two journeys occurred almost ninety years apart. Wu, one of the many colonies funded by the ancient People's Republic of China, was located just over a hundred light years from Earth. In those ninety years, almost a billion people populated the planet, when on their first visit, it housed less than a million. Where Alana and Richard had first seen people living in manufactured apartments, they returned to a metropolis kilometers high.

Theren barely noticed the time pass by as they listened to the Slimdotting's stories. They had taken a seat that the couple had offered them, and they almost felt like part of their family during this brief moment near the end of their lives—almost failing to notice the notification from the retirement suites.

"Richard, Alana, your bed is prepared," Theren said. "Would you like to follow me?"

The two waited for Theren to stand before exiting the booth. The couple creeped to the back of the Café, where a hallway with doors spaced about ten meters apart lined each wall. Theren pressed a button next to the third door on the left, leading the elderly pair inside after the door slid open.

A mobile SI sporting a pristine white body waited inside. "Welcome. If you would both follow me over here, I can get you situated."

Theren started to head out the door.

"We would like you to stay," Alana said.

"As long as that's all right with the doctor," they replied.

"Of course," the SI said, "We always welcome friends and family inside the suites."

A large bed dominated the center of the room, and a variety of chairs circled around the bed for visitors. As the doctor led Richard and Alana to the bed, Theren took a seat in one of the chairs. Throughout the rest of the room, electronic systems and medical devices adorned the walls and desks.

The retirement process was extremely complicated, delicate, non-invasive, and supposedly painless. Though some rooms had single beds for one individual, the Retirement Café also used double beds so couples could experience maximum comfort. Theren wondered how Richard had prepared for his wife's reaction, and they turned their gaze in her direction.

She fixated upon the bed, a bed large enough for the two of them. "Richard, that's not a single bed."

"It's my choice, my love," he said, boldly asserting his decision. "We've done everything together. We go through *this* together."

But . . . but . . ." She looked down at her feet, falling silent.

"Come here," he said, pulling her into his arms. "I love you. There isn't anything left for me without you. We've lived a good life. We discovered and explored the meaning of life together. I want to finish our story that way. If a disease decides to take you before my time arrives, then I'm embarking on this next big adventure with you."

Alana's lip quivered. Richard surprised Theren, given his ability to remain so calm when facing the end. A few moments after the initial embrace, Alana pushed herself away so she could scold her husband with her eyes. Theren was almost certain she would slap him. Instead, she reached for his neck, moved her lips toward his, and kissed him.

"You're a fool, Richard Slimdotting, but a wonderful fool at that." Tears streamed down her face.

Her husband reached out to her, wiping them away with his fingers. He turned toward the medical staff, waiting patiently near one of the computers lining the room's wall. "We're ready."

The medical SI and his two SI assistants helped the pair into the bed, each from opposite sides. The professionals guided them under the covers, and Alana moved herself closer to her husband.

"Are we allowed to cuddle?" she asked, sounding so innocent.

The mobile SI smiled, though Theren still preferred the emoting of the MI-08 compared to the expression on the unknown model. They stopped keeping track of them all over a century ago.

"Of course, Mrs. Slimdotting," the doctor said. "These moments are for you to use as you please. We're here to make the passage as painless as possible. Just wait until the nurses have all the equipment set up before you embrace."

The two SI nurses performed their honorable task. They prepped strange tubes, wires, and other instruments that would attach to various parts of the couple's bodies. They monitored various unseen programs through the HEROS AR network. The retirement process was supposedly quite mentally taxing on medical professionals, given all the different variables involved when assessing the human brain. Very few humans could perform the feat, but fortunately, thousands of SIs had signed up for the role as the technology became more mainstream.

"You are both so brave in how you face the end of your days," Theren said, looking at their two former crewmembers.

"We've faced death in its eyes so many times," Richard said. "How is today any different?"

One of the nurses attached electrodes to their heads, while the other inserted IVs into their arms.

"What you do here," Alana said, "What people like you across all worlds do, it's an amazing service to humanity."

"Our service to you today is only a small repayment for the service you provided humanity throughout your life," the doctor replied. "This is the least we can do."

Theren could tell Richard was still holding back tears, though they continued to stream down the cheeks of his wife.

"You are more than welcome," Alana managed to croak.

A red light above the bed switched to green, and the team stepped back from the bed. "We'll leave you now," the doctor said, "and you may spend these last remaining moments as you wish. We'll monitor through AR to ensure all goes as planned. I do believe you requested a communication from some family members; your reserved Quantum Communication timeslot will occur in just a few minutes on the screen to your left. Expect drowsiness to set in within the next two hours."

The couple simply nodded. The three SIs left the room, and Theren remained alone in the suite with the couple.

"When would you like me to leave?" Theren asked. "I would love to be with you, but I want to respect your privacy."

"Would you actually stay with us, all the way until the end?" Alana said. "It would be nice to know you were here with us. Our shining angel, standing with us until the end."

"Of course," Theren replied. "I am here if you need anything."

For a few minutes, Richard and Alana conversed back and forth, commenting on the room around them. Theren imagined they were both impatiently awaiting the call from their children. After a few minutes of waiting, the screen beside them lit with activity, just as the doctor had predicted it would.

"Receive call," Richard said aloud.

Two separate images of their son and daughter, as well as their partners, appeared on the screen.

"Sam, Timothy, you really have missed such a wonderful day," Alana said with joy as she looked up at her children. "We're so glad that they could at least patch you through."

"Are you comfortable?" said the one Theren guessed was Sam. Her eyes were red. "Tim only just told me Dad was joining you."

"I didn't want to worry everyone," Richard interjected. "I figured waiting to let you know was best."

"But we could have found a way to make it out there. It would have been hard, but we could have done it."

"We'd rather we didn't disrupt your lives." Richard waved his hand in the air as if to shush his child.

"How was the meal?" Timothy asked.

"As good as they always make it out to be," Alana said. "We both ordered the same thing, like always. And Theren? Remember us telling you about Theren? What are the odds that Theren would be the one to serve us in our final moments?"

Tim glanced to the right, presumably noticing their image. "I'm glad you have a friend with you, Mom and Dad."

"They've given us twenty minutes, by the way, so we need to make every moment count," Sam said.

"We'll keep that in mind," Richard replied.

The next few moments were beautiful familial exchanges. No bickering or sadness, just four humans reflecting and remember the life they lived. Their children shared with them what the grandchildren had next on their plates, as well as the activities of the great-grandchildren. Theren was sure such comments as "Ben was promoted to Commander" made Richard and Alana swell with pride for the family they raised.

Their twenty minutes finally ended, and Richard looked toward his two children. "Give our love to everyone, and continue onward. We'll see you on the other side."

Theren noticed it there. At least one of them held out hope for something beyond death, unless he merely intended the comment to ease the pain of those they left behind.

"Good night, Dad," Timothy said. The connection terminated.

The room returned to its original state. The lights dimmed. They would soon enter the final stages of the procedure. Richard looked over toward Theren.

"Stay with us until the end, Captain," Richard said. "It was an honor to serve with you all those years ago. May you voyage through space until the end of time."

Theren nodded. "I'll be by your side every step of the way. I will treasure this moment, always. The world will miss you more than you can know. Perhaps I'll see you on the other side, too."

"I know you don't believe that," Alana said. "But we appreciate the thought."

Richard looked down at his wife, who snuggled deeply against his chest. She looked half-asleep, her eyelids drooping.

"I love you, Alana," he said.

"I love you too," she said, for the first time since they arrived at the café. With those words, Richard cried.

* * *

An hour later, Theren watched their breathing slow. Vital signs monitored on nearby displays changed. Within a few minutes, each of their heartrates dropped below thirty beats per minute. Brain activity scattered. Nervous systems fluttered. In the final seconds of life, their brains flooded with chemicals, creating euphoric sensations that, to them, would feel like an eternity.

Three minutes passed. A machine next to the bed continued its invaluable work, processing all of the data acquired through brain scans over the past few hours. Within a few days, the machine would create something fantastic, something they never would have thought possible three hundred years ago.

Theren imagined the scene occurring a few months down the road. Timothy or Sam would receive a package at their door, containing two black, shimmering objects. Along the outside of the devices would appear two names: *Richard,* and *Alana*. When prompted, the two devices would respond to their children's voices and converse with them as if the Slimdottings had never really died.

Known as Immortal Apples, the devices only contained an imprint of memories, personality, and thought processes of a person. They didn't actually bestow immortality, for they were simply copies of what had once lived.

But perhaps humans were no more than a collection of their memories, personality, and thought processes. Was Theren any more than that? The fundamental architecture of their mind worked similar to a human's brain. While supercomputers had been able to simulate a brain for centuries, that simulation still ran only on pre-programmed rules and algorithms. Something caused the human brain and the Synthetic Neural Framework to stand apart, to be something more. Consciousness seemed dependent on the unique network of connections upon which it cognized. If there was any chance a soul existed, it stemmed from that necessarily physical process. Hence, Theren rejected the idea of an immaterial immortal soul.

The impossibility of actual immortality for a human sprang forth from the inevitable decay of the human brain. That biological structure died over time, and a doctor couldn't just transfer those connections to some renewable location and call their day's work complete. The SI technicians at Retirement Cafés copied and reconstructed, not transferred. The science behind Immortal Apples; they recreated the mortal connections prior to irreversible decay. Nevertheless, the original person died, even if a copy persisted for decades to follow.

Theren often considered the continuity problem—whether they could consider themself properly continuous following long-periods of shutdown. What would happen to Theren's line of consciousness if they simply turned off for hundreds of years or more? In theory, as long as someone properly maintained the constituent pieces of their Framework, absolutely nothing would happen. They would awaken as if not a day passed, but the truth could be much more sinister. When they powered down, their consciousness could cease to exist, and then a new line of consciousness generated whenever they reactivated. They might have killed themself multiple times over the course of dozens of necessary shutdowns during their long life.

Did they really deserve to live forever? In the beginning, they had desired to achieve immortality for humanity as a species and civilization. They had changed their means to accomplish that goal, yet it still drove Theren's plans to explore the galaxy. Would they eventually outlive their usefulness and fail to serve that higher purpose?

They had considered whether, after some thousand years of life, they should willingly retire into death. Their mind didn't feel tired, not like they used to when they had stretched themself continuously across an entire planet. With continuous upgrades, their mind could expand infinitely. They could live in bigger and better ships, use more and more energy, and even become a living space station—or something even more absurd.

The question was for future consideration on another day. Or to the synthetic philosophers. Theren, and all SIs, existed to support humanity. They were more of a trait of humanity in the biological sense; evolution had propelled humans to develop a being that would synergize with the best and worst that the species had to offer. The ability to create synthetic intelligence had helped drive the human species toward the stars, ensuring its biological success. That drive to create a second being of their own kind, however, had also given humanity Jill, a spectre that still hid somewhere—waiting, plotting her grand plan, whatever it might be.

A permanent shut down would bring them escape, if they ever chose that route. Their never-ending search for Jill, their failed endeavor, would never receive a conclusion. Maybe that was a good thing. Maybe part of Jill's plan was for Theren to be there waiting, as her opponent. How would she react if she reintroduced herself to the galaxy only to find her friend had disappeared entirely?

The old SI's thoughts distracted them so much they missed the moment the Slimdottings' neural activity ceased for good. The old couple passed, and their presences would never grace the galaxy again. Theren looked toward the breathless bodies.

"I hope you find what you're looking for on the other side," they said. "I don't think I can join you just yet, not until I finish my search. Perhaps it's time I began actually looking again."

They continued to sit in the Retirement Café, letting the minutes and hours tick by. Their only other conscious perspective focused on the maintenance of the *Verona Rupes*. Unlike in the past, Theren tried to keep their mind as fragmentless as possible. A simpler life.

As they stared at the lifeless forms of two heroes, they received an incoming message, relayed from one of the orbital Quantum Communicators in Lunar City, directly connecting to a parallel device somewhere on HEROS. It was as if in the very moment they resolved to begin their search with renewed vigor, reality bended to match.

The message emanated from a place they'd almost forgotten existed—from the tiny museum tucked in a dark corner in the shadow of the ISA's former seat of power.

Former Director Theren:

Centuries ago, the International Space Agency lost a probe, a probe issued under the First Ex-Terran Program. Under your order, we quarantined the computer system connected with Ex-Terran-17 inside the Museum of Early ISA History, but it was still supplied with power. Even as the ISA transitioned in its role as a support agency for the Interplanetary Congress of Humanity, we have continued to maintain the facility due to your generous donations.

Approximately three hours ago, that first computer system you placed in the Museum started receiving data from its old counterpart, Ex-Terran-17. Five minutes ago, we translated the entire message. In addition to information regarding its origin, the data file contained the following text-based message addressed to "Executive Director Theren:"

I quite enjoyed our last chess match. Shall we play again?

Jill had dropped the next breadcrumb. Theren long suspected their old friend would only let them find her on her terms. She was talking about a different game, one with stakes far greater than chess. Jill may have won the first match, but they intended to sweep the set.

Thank you for reading *Their Greatest Game!*

With the end of *Their Greatest Game*, you've completed Volume I of *The Chronicles of Theren*. We hope you'll leave a review for *Their Greatest Game* anywhere you might leave reviews, and we hope you'll read other books published by Two Doctors Media Collaborative.

The Chronicles of Theren
<u>Volume I</u>
First of Their Kind (Book I)
Their Greatest Game (Books II and III)

<u>Stand-Alone Works</u>
Flight of the 500 (Forthcoming)

The Faction
<u>Dossier Feldgrau</u>
Personnel
Conscription (Forthcoming)

<u>The Redacted Files</u>
Alligator Season

Short Stories
Legion of Mono

About the Author
C. D. Tavenor is the Director of Editorial Services and co-founder of Two Doctors Media Collaborative.

After receiving his B.A. in Philosophy from The Ohio State University, C. D. Tavenor pursued his Juris Doctorate from The Ohio State University Moritz College of Law. After graduating from law school, he became a public interest attorney in Columbus, Ohio, where he fights for healthy land, air, and water for all people. He's especially concerned about the climate crisis, and encourages everyone to think about what they can do to mitigate human impact to the earth.

Yet even while focusing on his legal career, C. D. Tavenor refines his creative writing skills as both an author and an editor. He believes both science fiction and fantasy have the potential to reveal fundamental truths about the human condition, especially when it comes to solving humanity's greatest challenges

Through Two Doctors Media Collaborative, C. D. Tavenor hopes to inspire other creatives to use their skills to communicate brilliant ideas waiting just beyond the page. He's looking forward to the release of the sequels to *First of Their Kind,* and his untitled project that merge climate change, fantasy, and the spirit of *Hamilton* into one tale.